VOL. 2, NO. 3

ISSUE #7

FEATURES

NEW STORIES

CLASSIC REPRINT

FROM THE CAT'S PERCH

When John Betancourt suggested that *Black Cat Mystery Magazine* publish special themed issues, much like our sister magazine *Weirdbook,* the first words out of my mouth were "private eyes!"

Private eye fiction has played an important role in my writing career. My first PI story was published in 1988 and my first PI novel in 2001. I edited my first anthology of PI stories in 2001 and the most recent in 2019. I served as vice-president of the Private Eye Writers of America 2006-2008, have served several times on Shamus Awards committees, and was a featured speaker at the 2019 Shamus Awards banquet in Dallas.

After all these years hanging out—literally and figuratively—with private eye writers, my most memorable experience is the 2016 Shamus Awards Banquet in New Orleans where I sat with O'Neil De Noux (a contributor to this special edition), our wives, and several other writers. My tablemates created some of the most hardboiled private eye tales you'll ever read, and yet one of the primary topics of conversation was our cats. We told tales of how they helped—and mostly didn't help—us write, all while passing around photos of our furry friends.

And so, it only seems appropriate that, with the clear connection between cats and private eye writers, a publication named *Black Cat Mystery Magazine* should devote an entire issue to private eye stories.

Enjoy!

—Michael Bracken
Editor, *Black Cat Mystery Magazine*

Staff

PUBLISHER & EXECUTIVE EDITOR
John Gregory Betancourt

EDITOR
Michael Bracken

WILDSIDE PRESS SUBSCRIPTION SERVICES
Karl Würf

PRODUCTION TEAM
Sam Hogan
Karl Würf

THE CHARITY CASE

ROBERT LOPRESTI

"I don't mind telling you," Mrs. Werland told me, "that I am shocked at what is permitted to go on in a civilized community."

My first thought was to ask who had told her Atlantic City was civilized. My second thought was to keep my mouth shut and nod gravely. In a rare moment of wisdom I went with Thought Number Two.

Mrs. Werland continued. "My husband was robbed in broad daylight, Mr. Crow. On a public street, no less."

"Shocking," I said.

"He was carrying eight hundred dollars!"

I raised my eyebrows. "In cash?"

Werland nodded. He was a tall, balding man, creeping up on sixty. Since they stepped into my office he had done little but look vague and earnest. Now he opened his mouth, but his wife spoke first. "To buy samples."

"Samples?" I repeated.

She glanced at her husband. "Speak up, dear."

He cleared his throat. "I own a hardware store back home. We're here for a convention."

"And you would be shocked, Mr. Crow, to know what some of these supposedly respectable businessmen get up to when they leave their families behind for a few days." Mrs. Werland sniffed righteously, if you know what I mean. "The money they waste in those casinos!"

I tried to look virtuous. I hadn't been in a casino in a week, having wasted my own money on food and rent.

"What exactly do you want from me?"

"You'll have to ask him." She nodded toward hubby. "*I* said we should report it to the police. It's our duty. But he insisted we talk to a private investigator first. If we don't report it to the police—"

Werland interrupted; a first. "I don't want to get stuck here for weeks at some blasted trial. My nephew Jimmy is running the store—"

"Running it into the ground, most likely," said Mrs. Werland. "But I'm sure they wouldn't make you stay here for weeks."

"Probably not," I agreed. "But I think you were wise to come here first." I gave them my allegedly winning smile. "I have contacts in the police department. I can smooth the way for you, if you like. Make sure they don't waste your valuable time."

The gray-haired lady looked mollified. Her husband seemed, if anything, more uncomfortable. No surprise there.

"Now, ma'am, were you a witness to the crime?"

"No." She frowned. "Mr. Werland went out for a walk after lunch. I went to a presentation on salesmanship. A most unethical presentation, I might add."

"I'm sure." I shifted in my chair. "You know, I just had a thought. There's really no need for both of you to kill the afternoon with the police."

Mrs. Werland didn't like where this was leading. "A woman's place is with her husband."

"Absolutely," I murmured. "But—may I be frank? A lady's place is *not* in a police station. The people who come through there..." I attempted a shudder.

"Oh." She thought that over.

"He's right, dear," said Werland, with more eagerness than I had heard from him so far. "And you know, we still haven't bought souvenirs for the grandchildren."

That turned the trick. After a few last-minute instructions to both of us the formidable lady left.

Werland sat down again and wiped his forehead with a clean, starched handkerchief. He looked a bit more relaxed now, but not what I'd call comfortable.

I gave him a smile, still in my most sincere mode. "I'm very sorry this happened to you in Atlantic City, Mr. Werland."

He nodded. "I guess you get used to it. I mean, there's a lot of crime here."

"There sure is. And the authorities are very concerned about it, especially when tourists get hurt. They don't want people going home and spreading stories about us. Giving the city a bad name."

Werland shifted as if his chair was pinching him. "I can understand that."

"Why, do you know they've even gone so far as to prosecute people who file false reports of crimes? Now you wouldn't think they would care, with all the real crime, but—"

"Blast. Oh, *blast.*"

I had never heard anyone use that word with so much expression. It was probably as close as he ever came to swearing.

Werland shook his head in disgust. "It's that obvious, is it?"

"Well." I shrugged. "You aren't the first person who tried a story out on me before selling it to the cops."

"Of course not. Blast." Werland's Adam's apple bobbed up and down twice. "You're looking at a fool, Mr. Crow. I'm so stupid I can't even come up with an original lie."

"It takes practice to lie well," I told him. "Why don't you tell me what really happened to the eight hundred dollars?"

He squinted at me as if we were standing a mile apart on the broad prairie, which I assume is what you would see around his home. "What happened? The *usual,* I suppose. What's the usual true story when people come in here with a lie like mine?"

I leaned back in my chair, feeling professorial. Marty Crow, scholar of Atlantic City fibs and follies. "Well, there are two typical cases. Either they gambled the money away, or they were rolled by a hooker."

A frown. "What by a what?"

"Robbed by a prostitute. What happened to you, Mr. Werland?"

He sighed. "I gave it to a beggar in the street."

He was joking.

No, he wasn't.

"Well," I said. "Your lies may be old hat, but your truths are brand new."

He looked grave. "The old truths are the best, Mr. Crow."

"No doubt. Tell me about the man you gave the money to."

"He was grubby-looking, around thirty, I'd say. Greasy, shoulder-length hair. A gray raincoat that looked like he'd been scrubbing floors with it—"

"And oversized white basketball sneakers," I finished.

He looked doubtful. "They may have been white once. You know this man?"

I nodded. "His name is Avery Scoat, believe it or not. He's fairly prominent, as local panhandlers go. Always hangs around offering the tourists a sad story or a threat, depending on his mood."

I checked my watch. "We better get going if we want to find him before he spends all your money."

Werland's eyebrows shot up. "You think we can get him to give it back? Appeal to his better nature?"

I gave him assurances and held back facts. If Avery Scoat ever had a better nature, it had been clear-cut and bulldozed years ago.

* * * *

"It's kind of complicated," said Werland. We were in my car, hot on the trail of the happiest panhandler in Atlantic County, and I had just asked him the reason for his generosity.

"My wife and I belong to the Final Days Punctionalist Church. Ever hear of it?"

"Afraid not," I admitted. "I don't read the religion page much."

"If you did hear about us, it would most likely be in a paragraph listing a bunch of small fundamentalist churches."

"Them I've heard of."

"Oh, yes." He sounded tired. "You've probably gotten a good laugh out of us. The media always make us out to be a bunch of bigots and clowns."

I saw nothing to disagree with. "So what's this have to do with giving away eight hundred bucks?"

"Punctionalists are good people, by and large, Mr. Crow. We believe in helping outsiders. My son, for instance, is part of a church group in South America now."

"Missionaries?"

He shook his head. "We don't do missionary work of the kind you mean. My son is a carpenter. He's doing repairs after that big earthquake. We send Punctionalists all over the world to help out after disasters. No preaching, you see, but sometimes our actions lead people to want to know about our beliefs."

"I get it."

"We're good to everyone but our own members. The things we do to each other..." He shuddered.

I was curious now. At a red light I turned to look at him. "What exactly do you do?"

"Schisms. In the last century, every twenty years or so the church has been racked by division. Broken into bitter feuding fragments over minor, *stupid* points of doctrine." He spoke with more passion than I thought he possessed. "It's a horrible thing, Mr. Crow. Families split up. Lifelong friends become enemies and never speak again."

"Give me a for instance."

"When I was a teenager there was a split and the issue was, if you can believe it, the solar system."

"That's a *religious* issue?"

"The Bible says Joshua made the sun stand still."

I don't read the Bible as often as the racing form, but that struck a bell. "So?"

"So some of our members felt that meant the sun goes around the Earth."

"Brother," I muttered.

"That was a relatively minor split," said Werland. "Perhaps ten percent of our brethren broke away. Then twenty years ago came the really vicious fight. About wine."

"Wine?"

"All Punctionalists are against drunkenness, of course. Most are abstainers. But the question was whether wine is inherently evil. Or just the *misuse* of it. If you recall the wedding at Cana—"

"I follow," I told him. "But how does any of that relate to giving eight hundred bucks to a clown like Avery Scoat?"

"I'm getting to that," said Werland. "The Punctionalists are headed for another schism. This time the subject is charity."

"Ah." I was beginning to see the light, so to speak.

"The issue, essentially, is whether we should give charity to *all* poor people or only the deserving poor. What about people who have brought their misery on themselves? Through their evil habits, I mean."

"Go on."

"My wife had strong opinions in the dispute and this visit has settled her mind. Margaret sees Atlantic City as a modern Sodom, Mr. Crow, and it has goaded her to action.

"Over lunch today she told me that when our group has its annual meeting next month she plans to demand a vote. She wants to force out those who disagree with her." Werland made a face. "I hate this. I *hate* it."

I could guess the rest of the story by now. "Mrs. Werland believes you should only give charity to the deserving poor."

"That's right. When I left the lunch table I was depressed and angry. Then, outside on the street, I saw this...this disgusting shred of a man."

"Avery Scoat."

"So you say. He was drunk, filthy, wretched. I have never seen anyone *less* deserving. He swore at me, demanding that I give him spare change. Before I knew what I was doing I handed him the whole eight hundred dollars."

I nodded, just as if that made sense. "Because?"

Werland shrugged. "I suppose it was an act of defiance. Against Margaret and what her obstinacy is doing to our church."

"But now you've changed your mind."

"Well." He looked down at the pavement. "It didn't help anything, did it? All I really managed to accomplish was to lose eight hundred dollars."

"Hey, don't despair yet," I told him. "Let's have a little faith and hope. But no more charity."

Two hours later I was ready to act out my frustration too, although giving money away was not what I had in mind. We had checked every place Avery Scoat could usually be found: the rundown joints where he slept when he had enough for a room, the cheap liquor store where he bought his booze, the casino parking lots where he panhandled.

"I'm stumped," I confessed as we stepped out of the last flophouse.

The hardware man frowned. "You can't find him."

"It's funny. Avery is usually hard to avoid, not hard to find. But we've tried every one of his usual spots."

"I guess this is not his usual day," said Werland.

I stared at him. "That's good thinking."

"Me?"

"You've spotted the problem. I'm trying to trace Avery through a normal day, but nobody hands him eight hundred bucks on a normal day. Hell, I bet even *he* couldn't have predicted in advance what he'd do with that kind of money."

Werland looked grim. "He's doing it now."

I leaned against a telephone pole and tried to think. "Avery is your classic loser. That means he'll be getting rid of the money as soon as possible."

"How?"

I smiled. Losing money fast was something I knew how to do.

It wasn't hard to find the panhandler once we started to look in the right places. Avery was at the Golden Alley Casino, the third one we tried.

I found Hillie Jefferson, the place's head of security, and convinced her that it was in her employer's best interest to help us separate Avery from the gambling floor.

He was standing at the roulette table, a pile of chips in front of him. He looked as happy as a clam in Barnegat Bay until he saw us coming.

When he spotted Jefferson, Werland, and me bearing down on him, Scoat knew what was about to happen. A feverish gleam showed in the little creep's eyes. He shoved all of his chips forward. "Everything on red!"

"Goddamn it, stop him!" I yelled to Jefferson.

She signaled the operator, who held onto the little silver ball.

"Take your chips back, Mr. Scoat," said Jefferson. "We need to talk."

"Well, hell," said Avery. "Don't stop me now! I'm doing great. I just broke even."

Werland frowned. "How can you be doing great if you're breaking even? That means you're back where you started."

Avery and I exchanged a sympathetic glance. People who never gamble don't understand anything.

Hillie Jefferson grabbed Avery by the arm and hustled him off. She was a former Army MP and when she hustled you, you went.

I held back long enough to see the silver ball land on red.

I was glad Avery didn't see it. It would have broken his heart.

* * * *

"This is *my* money," growled Avery Scoat. "I didn't steal it. He *gave* it to me."

We were seated in a small interrogation room next to Jefferson's office. Avery was glaring at the floor and pouting. "That clown just *gave* it to me."

"But I had no idea," said Werland, "that you were going to squander it on gambling."

"Hold the phone," said Jefferson, wide-eyed. "You mean you really did give the man this money?"

"That's right," said my client.

She turned to me. "You told me this was a police matter, Crow. You said it was a freaking criminal case."

"I'm sorry if I gave that impression," I lied. "Just give us a little space here, all right, Hillie?"

Avery turned to Jefferson, hoping he had found an ally. "This guy handed me the money. What am I supposed to do, turn it down? Do I look like a freaking change machine?"

"Mr. Werland made a mistake," I improvised. "He thought he was giving you eight dollars. I'm sure he would be happy to offer a reasonable reward—"

"Is that what happened?" snapped Jefferson. Her dreadlocks were swinging around like whips.

"No," said my client, flatly. He was staring at Avery Scoat the way you might look at a curious specimen that had crawled out of your kitchen sink. "I gave it to him in good faith, although I regret it now. Perhaps I should keep my regret and he should keep the money."

"Damn straight!" said the beggar man.

"Now, hold on," I said.

"But answer me one question," said Werland. "What set you on the road to ruin, young man?"

"Me?" Avery laughed. "I've got eight hundred bucks and you don't. Looks like you're the one who's ruined."

The casino chips were still sitting on the table. I pushed them around. "Nobody has the eight hundred dollars until these chips get changed. Mr. Werland, why don't you take them to the cashier?"

Werland and Scoat both began to protest.

I shook my head. "No offense, Avery, but the cashiers will call security if someone who looks like you shows up demanding money. Let Mr. Werland do the work. You know you can trust him."

"Whatever," grumbled Werland. "Let's get it over with. I have to go back to the hotel and explain this to my wife. God help me."

He picked up the chips and let Hillie Jefferson lead him out.

Avery grinned at me. "There goes an honest man. Pathetic, ain't it?"

I sighed.

* * * *

They were back in twenty minutes, Werland holding a neat white envelope stuffed with cash. Jefferson carried nothing but a grudge. She was mad at me for breaking the rules, and I couldn't much blame her. Casinos are not in business to *stop* people from gambling.

"There's your money, Mr. Scoat," said Werland. "I hope you use it wisely."

"Don't you worry about that." Avery fumbled awkwardly as he slipped the envelope into a jacket pocket. He showed no signs of preparing to stand up. Instead he cleared his throat. "But, I guess...well. Maybe I owe you an apology."

My client looked startled. "For what?"

"You asked how I wound up...the way I am." Avery looked down at the floor, seeming embarrassed. "And I made a smart-mouth remark. The truth is, I come from a broken home."

"Oh brother," muttered Jefferson.

"I should have guessed." Werland's eyes were wide. "Please, son. Tell me about it."

"Well, if you want to know, it was booze that broke up my family."

"Ah." My client nodded sagely. "Your parents drank."

"No," said Avery. He ran a hand through his greasy hair. "No, that's the damned—darned thing. They didn't. But they belonged to this church, see? And when I was a kid, the people in the church got into a big fight about booze, and whether it's *always* bad— What's wrong?"

Werland had backed up to the far wall, pop-eyed and staring, as if Avery Scoat had sprouted horns. "Your parents were Punctionalists?" he croaked.

"Yeah," Scoat said, nodding. "I think that's right. I haven't heard the word since I was a kid. See, my Mom took one side of the argument and my Dad—"

"You poor boy!" Werland rushed forward as suddenly as he had backed up. He grabbed Avery's shoulders and announced solemnly: "It was our wicked schism that set you on the downhill road. You are a judgment come upon us!"

"What the hell—" said Jefferson. I stepped on her foot hard. There was no point in getting in the way of fate.

My client turned to me. "This is a sign, Mr. Crow! The new schism must not be allowed to happen."

And back to Avery. "Will you come with me, son? Tell my wife what happened to you? Tell all of us?"

"I don't get it," said Avery. "What's going on?"

"The church is busting up again," I explained.

"No!" He leapt to his feet, almost as agitated as Werland. "They can't do that!"

"You and I will prevent it. Together!" said the older man, shaking Avery's hand vigorously.

They turned and marched toward the door, off on a sacred mission.

"Mr. Werland," I called. "Remember, whatever Avery used to be, he's a sinner now. You can't trust him."

The hardware man gave me a hard smile. "We are all sinners, Mr. Crow. I'm sure we can handle our prodigal son." He threw a strong arm around Avery's shoulders and I thought Avery suddenly looked a little doubtful about the whole thing. But he didn't struggle.

"About my bill..." I called.

Avery turned, a wild gleam in his eye.

"Here!" He took the casino envelope from his jacket and threw it. It spun through the air and bounced on the table in front of me.

"Yes," said Werland. "The laborer is worthy of his hire!"

The door slammed behind them.

Jefferson stared at it. Then she gave me the stink eye. "You gonna explain this, Marty?"

"I'm gonna try." I picked up the envelope and counted the money. Avery had slipped out about half, which was fair enough, I guess. "Let's go to the bar, Hillie. I'll buy you a drink."

By the time I had told her the whole story we were well into her third gin and my second soda. "But that's not the whole story," she said.

"What do you mean?"

"Avery Scoat wasn't any freaking punctuater, or whatever you call it. After you sent Werland and me to cash the chips you told Avery about the split in the church and told him what to say."

"I'm shocked you would think that," I murmured.

"Which is not a denial. You said he could tell that story and freeload off those poor suckers for— How long do you think Avery's going to last among those teetotalers? And what's to keep him from robbing them blind?"

"They know what he is. They'll keep an eye on him. Hey, maybe they'll convert him."

She snorted. "Fat chance. You lied to your client, Marty. How do you justify that?"

"I did no such thing. According to you, Avery lied to him. But in any case, Werland was a satisfied customer when he left. And we might have prevented a schism."

"We stopped a schism." Hillie shook her dreadlocks. "Well, I'll be damned."

"Maybe," I said. "Then again, maybe not."

Robert Lopresti's short stories have been published for forty years in *Alfred Hitchcock's Mystery Magazine, Ellery Queen's Mystery Magazine, The Strand,* and many other publications. He has won the Derringer Award (three times) and the Black Orchid Novella Award, as well as being nominated for the Anthony. He has been reprinted in *Best American Mystery Stories* and *Year's Best Dark Fantasy and Horror Stories.* His novel *Greenfellas* is a comic caper about the Mafia trying to save the environment. He is a retired librarian and lives in the Pacific Northwest.

THE WHOLE STORY

ANDREW WELSH-HUGGINS

The man didn't bother to hold it together, which told Hayes something right there. He couldn't imagine there was any shortage of crying in prison. But maybe not a lot in windowless interview rooms while talking to a private eye you've never met, with the only other sound the metallic scrape of wrist and belly and ankle chains as you shift in a chair to wipe the tears from your face.

"I'm sorry. I usually do better than this."

"Take your time," Hayes said.

"It's been hard."

"I won't insult your intelligence by saying I understand. But I can see what you're going through."

The man nodded. The chains clinked. His name was Bobby Putnam. Thirty-seven but you could add ten years and no one would call you a liar. Two days' stubble patching his pale face. Not exactly fat but not far from it, either, which told Hayes something else. The Bobby Putnam in the courtroom photos had been a relatively fit, handsome fellow. Now he was six months into a twelve-year stretch for aggravated vehicular homicide and drunken driving and looking like he'd struggled every day of it. Hayes knew the details of the charge but only a little bit about why he was here, talking to Putnam, in a prison on the far eastern edge of Ohio where jobs keeping inmates inside aboveground bunkers had long ago replaced jobs pulling coal out of belowground bunkers.

Putnam said, "I'm not saying I'm not guilty. That I'm not responsible for what happened. You got that?"

"I do."

"My daughter's dead because of me, and me alone."

"Right."

"I'm not trying to change any of this." Chains clinked as he gestured as far as his restraints allowed, looking at the interview room door. "I ain't making no innocence claim. Understood?"

"Yup."

"I'm just saying what happened wasn't everything going on that day. I just want the full picture—that's all I'm asking."

It was Hayes's turn to nod, not sure what to say.

"You've seen the video?" Putnam asked.

Hayes told him he had.

"You see what I'm talking about?"

"Not really."

"That mean you don't believe me?"

"That means I didn't see what you're talking about. If I didn't believe you I wouldn't be here."

Putnam brushed away a single tear rolling down his right cheek. Clink clink.

"OK. I appreciate that. It's about all I got right now, you taking the time. So I guess that's good enough."

"Good enough for what?"

"Good enough to keep me going at least one more day."

* * * *

Of course Hayes had seen the video. Who hadn't? A year ago it led the local news for two days, not to mention careening around social media like a yellow jacket caught in a washed-out mayonnaise jar. Putnam's car, a beater of a Chevy Cruze, speeding north on Cleveland Avenue. Crossing the center line, crossing back, jumping the curb, bouncing back onto the street, then T-boning a white SUV as it made a left onto a side street. Whole thing caught on a City of Columbus security camera bolted to a light pole. Impact so hard it knocked the SUV onto the side and ejected Putnam's seven-year-old daughter, who wasn't wearing a seatbelt, partway through the front windshield. The news stations all blurred that part out, but it was there for the world to see on Facebook and Twitter and Reddit. The girl pronounced at the scene; she hadn't had a chance.

Hayes had watched it again, a week ago, on Karen Feinberg's laptop. The two of them sitting on a bench on the second floor of the Franklin County courthouse during a ten-minute break between two of Feinberg's hearings.

"What am I looking for?"

"Here." Feinberg pointed.

"What?" Hayes stared at the image frozen where Feinberg stopped the video.

"Him."

"Who?"

"That guy. On the sidewalk."

Hayes looked closer. In the picture, a man stood on the south side of the street, facing south, toward the direction of Putnam's car. White, youngish guy—younger than Hayes, anyway. In the tableau, Putnam was just about to plow into the turning SUV. For a moment Hayes felt intrusive, like a gawking time traveler examining a figure with no idea what the future held in a matter of microseconds. Feinberg restarted the video. Hayes saw the crash take place for the umpteenth time. But for the first time, he noticed that the man, whoever he was, jumped back at the sound of the collision, stood for a moment longer, hesitated, and then disappeared off screen.

"Who is he?"

"No idea," Feinberg said.

"What's he holding?"

"Grocery bag. There's a market across the street."

"Does Putnam know him?"

"No. But."

"But?"

"He thinks the driver of the SUV did. Know him, I mean."

"Why?"

"It's easier if he explains it. Short version, something about the expression on the driver's face right before the crash."

"He remembers that?"

"He says he does."

"What do you think?"

Feinberg's phone pinged. She picked it up, examined it, and answered a text. Hayes waited patiently. Feinberg was a busy defense attorney. Hayes also knew that she and her wife were always occupied with the activities of their young son and were now preparing for a second baby on the way. More importantly, he appreciated the work she found for him. He'd wait.

"Sorry," Feinberg said, returning the phone to her purse. "This is what I think. I have a lot of clients who didn't do it. They swear they're innocent. 'It was this other guy.' 'They got me mixed up with my cousin.' 'The cops have it out for me.' In a good month, six of ten like that. What I don't have very many of are clients like Bobby Putnam. Guys who admit they're guilty. Who aren't looking to get out of prison. Who aren't bugging me about the bad deal they got. He just wants someone to confirm his suspicions that the driver of the SUV knew the guy on the sidewalk. That's all."

"Cops make the connection?"

"Never came up."

"They know who the guy is?"

"Not as far as I know," Feinberg said. "Which isn't all that surprising. There were three other witnesses on the street that day, plus two other drivers, plus the video. He wasn't needed."

"Who was in the SUV?"

"Guy named Geoff Broomfield."

"Was he cited?"

"Are you kidding? The accident was entirely Putnam's fault. Broomfield was just trying to get out of the way."

"But Putnam still wants me to find that guy, the one on the sidewalk?"

"That's right."

Hayes said, "No offense, but the whole thing is one white coat short of looney bins, if I can be blunt. Why bother?"

"Normally, I'd agree. But like I told you, I don't get many ex-clients who contact me about *remaining* guilty. He's adamant on that point. Plus, he can pay. Or his family can, anyway. His brothers put up $2,500 for me to hire an investigator to make some inquiries."

"And knowing you, you told them it was a fool's errand and to save their money."

"I might have used stronger language, but yeah, that's the gist. They insisted on Bobby's behalf. I told them I'd see what I could do."

"And called me."

"I wanted the best."

"You're sweet. And also wily, since you're probably guessing I'm broke, and could use the money."

"Guessing?"

"Let's just say there might be room on my calendar. OK—I'll talk to the guy, see what I can do. But no promises—especially given the facts."

"That's all I can ask." Feinberg's phone pinged again and she retrieved it from her purse. "Sorry, next hearing's about to start. Thanks, Andy. I'll make the arrangements for you to visit Bobby. You'll let me know how it goes?"

"Yes. Just don't hold your breath."

"Roger that."

Hayes spent the next hour in the clerk's office, copying documents from Putnam's case. The details were grim. A blood sample taken when Putnam arrived at Grant Hospital showed a .17 blood-alcohol content, more than twice the legal limit. Prosecutors included a litany of traffic citations from Putnam's past in their arguments pushing for the harshest possible sentence, including a previous DUI, the fact Putnam was driving without insurance and on a suspended license, and worst of all: that he'd allowed his daughter to sit upfront without her seatbelt on. Feinberg had done her best to counter, noting Putnam was employed—he had a job cleaning office buildings downtown overnight—and had made good-faith efforts to attend substance abuse counseling sessions before the accident. The judge wasn't impressed and handed down the maximum sentence available.

Finished with the file, Hayes emailed a public records request for the investigation to the division of police. He hoped there was something in it. As it stood, he'd seen more helpful paperwork on lost puppy cases. And Putnam was going to need a lot more than that.

* * * *

"How can you be so sure Broomfield was looking at the guy?" Hayes said, knowing his time with Putnam was growing short and that it was a long drive back to Columbus from the prison.

"Because I saw him. His expression."

"Which was?"

"Like rage . . . pure rage."

"No offense, but you were drunk."

"I know."

"And you didn't say anything to the cops at the time."

Putnam nodded. Hayes knew all this because he'd read the police file he received a day earlier twice through. As he feared, it was all too thin. No mention of Broomfield looking at a man on the sidewalk as he made the turn onto Washington Street. No mention of the man, either. Police interviewed two women who'd been walking on the other side of the street, a guy a block down who saw Putnam jump the curb, and the other drivers Feinberg mentioned. Every story consistent with what was obvious on the video: a speeding drunk weaving back and forth nailed a driver making a legal left turn. Hayes momentarily wondered what Broomfield, a guy from the suburbs, was doing in that part of town, but his statement in the police file answered the question quickly. A contractor, he was on the way to a job site at the time, just happening to cut down a side street off Cleveland Avenue on his unlucky day.

"I didn't say anything to the cops because I didn't remember it right afterward. Took me weeks, drying out in a cell, clearing my head, before it came to me. By then it was too late."

"Too late?"

"Who's gonna believe me, huh? Barely employed shithead whose drinking gets his innocent daughter killed?" Putnam's eyes grew bright. "I ain't stupid. And I'm not naive. I know what I did."

"Chances aren't good I'll turn anything up."

"I know. But if anybody can find something, probably gonna be you."

"What do you mean?"

"Ain't you the guy played for the Browns?"

"Allegedly played, according to some. What's that got to do with anything?"

"Anybody play for the Browns the last thirty years knows about lost causes."

* * * *

The accident's investigating officer was a Central Casting Columbus sergeant named Pete Packer: straight arrow, bullshit detector set to high, an FOP picnic or two away from a dad bod but still in chase-'em-down-an-alley shape for now. A Bengals fan to boot, so not interested in Hayes's glory day up in Cleveland, however splendid that Sunday afternoon had been.

"Is this a joke?" Packer said. "That's the clearest-cut vehicular agg assault I've ever seen. Putnam got everything he deserved and more. How anybody could be that irresponsible with their own kid—"

"It's not about guilt," Hayes reminded him. "It's about the guy on the sidewalk."

"What about him?"

They were sitting in a coffee shop across the street from the substation Packer worked out of in Linden, the two cups of coffee Hayes had bought on the table between them.

"Any idea who he is?" Hayes said.

"Not a clue."

"Why not?"

Packer blew the steam off his coffee and took a sip. "He didn't matter. We had so many other witnesses we had to bring in extra guys just to take statements."

"Seem odd, he walks away after a crash like that?"

"Once upon a time, maybe. These days it's odd when people stick around. Maybe he had a warrant out on him—we see that all the time. Why do the right thing if it's going to end with a ride to jail? Maybe he hates cops. Maybe he's late for the dentist. Could be a million reasons. If the accident happened late at night with nobody else around but him, I'd maybe have a different opinion. But this one? Who cares?"

"Broomfield didn't mention him?"

"Who?"

"Geoff Broomfield. The guy Putnam hit. He didn't say anything about knowing the guy on the sidewalk?"

"Not to my knowledge. He had a few other things on his mind."

"Any idea why he turned left at that moment? He must have seen Putnam coming."

"He gambled, as I recall. Thought Putnam was going to his right. Turns out he called it wrong." Packer took another drink of coffee. "You read the file?"

Hayes tapped the folder before him and explained that he had.

"Nothing in there?"

"Nothing about Broomfield knowing the guy. I also tried a reverse image search on him."

"And?"

"And unless Rock Hudson is alive and walking the streets of Columbus, that's a dead-end too. No ID."

"Then that's it, I guess," Packer said.

"I guess so," Hayes said.

"Except you don't think it is."

Hayes's turn to drink coffee. "I think nothing in this case points to Broomfield knowing the guy on the sidewalk except for Putnam's word, which is worth about as much as a used Kleenex at this point. Which bugs me. I mean, why bother?"

"Easy. He's looking for grounds for an appeal."

"He says he's not."

"Oh really."

"He says he just wants to be proven right, that the two knew each other."

"And you believe that?"

"I believe that's what he wants."

"Good for you," Packer said, rising from his seat.

"You think it's a wild goose chase."

"I think it's your time to waste, Hayes. Do what you want."

* * * *

Once Packer had gone, Hayes pulled out his phone and dialed the number for Geoff Broomfield that he pulled off the police report. The contractor picked up on the third ring. Hayes gave him his name, dropped the word "investigator" and explained he was calling about Bobby Putnam.

"What about him?"

Carefully, Hayes said, "He's spinning a crazy story about the accident. Says there's more there than meets the eye. I was just meeting with the police about it. They're not happy, believe me."

"What kind of story?"

"Kind of thing could be grounds for an appeal, you know? Better if we nip it in the bud now."

"You're working for the police?"

"Maybe I could come by, clear things up. You still on that construction site on Mock?"

"What?"

Hayes repeated the question. After a moment, Broomfield said, "I'm working up north right now. Union County. It's not really convenient at the moment. Maybe another time."

"Only take a couple of minutes. If Putnam wins his appeal, he could be back on the streets in a month."

"You really think there's a chance of that?"

"You know how judges are these days."

"I'll think about it. I'll call you, OK?"

"Let me just check one thing. You turned to avoid hitting Putnam. Is that right?"

"Yeah."

"No other reason?"

"What other reason would there be? Hey—I've really got to go."

"Thanks for your time," Hayes said, cutting the connection. He opened the folder containing the police reports. Something was bothering him. He flipped backward through the pages of interviews and the police narrative, up to the initial incident report. He scanned it and found what he was looking for. *Victim said his view of the oncoming car was blocked by a van and SUV in front of him.*

Broomfield's view was blocked? That's not what he said later—his fuller statement to police included the story about turning left *to avoid* Putnam. So which was it? Hayes opened his notebook and found Broomfield's home address. But first, because he wasn't that far, he took a drive out to Mock Road to check on that construction site.

* * * *

Broomfield lived in a subdivision in Genoa Township on the northeast side in a butter-yellow two-story with a Japanese maple in the front yard. The house sat on a curving suburban street of other two-story houses, most of which also had trees in their front yards, along with kids' bikes in driveways, Ohio State flags on porches, and lawns mostly devoid of dandelions. The kind of neighborhood Hayes couldn't see himself living in but wouldn't mind visiting more often, especially if a cook-out was involved.

"Yes?"

A woman standing on the threshold, opening the door a minute after he rang the bell late that afternoon. Pleasant face, short brown hair, professional blouse, and slacks as if she hadn't been home from work all that long. He produced a business card and handed it to her, asking at the same time if Geoff was home.

"Not yet," she said, studying the card. "He usually works late. What's this about?"

Hayes gave her the book-jacket blurb for the reason for his visit. In line with what he told her husband over the phone that afternoon.

"I thought that was all wrapped up," she said. "The trial and everything. What that awful man did."

"Hopefully it is. But you never know. Any idea when he might be home?"

"Geoff works pretty long hours."

Behind them, a girl's voice yelling for mom. The woman sighed, hesitated, and beckoned Hayes inside. She gestured at a couch in the living room and disappeared down a hall. She returned a few moments later. She said her name was Jeannette. She was very sorry to hear that something might be happening to provide Putnam the right to an appeal.

"My husband could have been killed."

"I know. I've seen the video."

"So you know there's no question about what happened."

"Yes."

"Then what's left for Putnam to argue?"

Hayes reached into the pocket of his blue sports coat and retrieved an envelope. He opened it and pulled out a photo. A screen shot of the man on the sidewalk that he'd printed out at Walgreen's that morning.

"I know it sounds wacky. But Putnam"—he said the name dismissively, the way you say the names of serial killers or hedge fund traders—"has this idea that your husband knew this guy."

He handed her the photo and studied her face carefully. She showed no more emotion than had he confessed to preferring banana splits to hot fudge sundaes.

"Recognize him?"

She studied the photo a moment longer, shook her head, and handed the picture back to Hayes. "I'm sorry I can't help you."

"Keep it," Hayes said. "Maybe Geoff knows him."

"I doubt it."

"Worth a shot, though, don't you think? Anything to keep Putnam from a successful appeal?"

Before she could respond, another call for assistance from the kitchen. Jeannette excused herself again. Hayes said he understood. When she was gone, he walked over to the bookshelf beside the TV and examined some of the framed photos. Geoff and Jeannette and two kids, boy and girl, on the beach and in the woods and in a family portrait. One of Geoff by himself, hard hat on, shovel in his hands, at a construction site.

"Mom?"

The girl's voice again. Hayes felt himself sympathizing with Jeannette Broomfield. He knew from experience with his own boys the toll that the needs of teenagers could take, from summoning a parent for help with homework to disdain for that self-same help. Realizing time was short, he pulled out his phone and took a few pictures, including the one of Geoff with the shovel and one of Jeannette by herself, straddling a road touring bike, decked out in not unattractive Lycra riding gear, a smile on her face. The happiest she seemed in any of the photos.

"Mom?"

Hayes turned his head. That didn't sound right. Wasn't Jeannette—mom—already in the kitchen?

He stepped into the passageway separating the rooms and peered around the corner. Sitting at a table in an attached dining room was a girl, fourteen or fifteen, mouth full of braces, hair pulled back in a ponytail, her profile leaving little doubt she was Jeannette's daughter. She was staring at her mother. Hayes looked closer. Jeannette Broomfield was taking deep, gulping breaths, with her left hand on the kitchen island as if to keep herself from collapsing. In her right hand the picture of the man on the sidewalk, crumpled up like a grotesque attempt at origami.

"Mrs. Broomfield?" Hayes said. "Is everything all right?"

"Please get out of my house," she said, without turning around.

* * * *

Hayes thought about returning the next morning to tail Jeannette but just as quickly nixed the idea. That approach looked good on TV and in the movies, with the instigator's casual adjustment of sunglasses and the confident turn of the steering wheel as he swept into traffic. In reality, rainbow sherbet had a longer shelf life than the amount of time it would take someone in the Broomfields' neighborhood to bust a strange guy sitting in an unfamiliar Honda Odyssey parked on a street full of kids. Hayes had no interest in making the acquaintanceship of the Genoa Township cops, and he hoped the feeling was mutual.

Instead, he started his day at Walgreen's, printing out several more copies of the video screengrab of Sidewalk Guy, along with the photo of Jeannette on her bike. Done, he drove across downtown, turned north on Cleveland, and ten minutes later turned right onto Washington Street. He parked and walked back up to the intersection. Traffic flowed in both directions. A handful of people waited for a bus half a block up. A kid in a hoodie who probably should have been in school sauntered down the street on the opposite side. Naturally, a year later, no evidence remained of the accident. But as Hayes watched a small red car stop, wait for oncoming traffic, and then turn left onto Washington—just as Geoff Broomfield had tried to do in his much bigger vehicle—it was easy to imagine how the disaster unfolded.

But why? Because Broomfield didn't see Putnam? Or because he did and was trying to avoid him?

Hayes started at the corner market, where a young woman wearing a head-scarf manned the checkout counter. The store was the only one within a few blocks; if the guy on the sidewalk had just purchased something, as the bag in his hand suggested, and he were on foot, it had to be here. Hayes's hopes rose when the woman said the man looked familiar, though she didn't know who he was, then fell when she said she'd never seen Jeannette Broomfield before.

Deflated, Hayes moved down to the first house on the south side of the street closest to Cleveland Ave, a green bungalow with a hand-painted "Nora's Nails" sign in the yard, and knocked. And knocked again.

"Yeah?"

The face of the woman who answered the door was puffy and splotched with red as if she'd just woken up after a restless sleep or given herself a facial with witch hazel. She was wearing a purple bathrobe and authentic fuzzy slippers and smelled of cigarettes and nail polish remover. She was Hayes's age give or take a decennial census count.

"Sorry to bother you." He handed her the photos. "I'm looking for either of these people. Wondered if you know them?"

The opposite reaction this time. She recognized Jeanette Broomfield, had seen her on her bike on the street, but not for a while. She didn't know the man. She looked at Hayes closely as she handed the pictures back.

"Why are you looking for them?"

"They won the lottery. They need to claim their winnings."

"How much?"

"Enough to make it worth my while to find them."

"Why ask me?"

"You're the first house I started at."

"That's the only reason?"

Hayes told her it was.

"Lotteries don't work that way, sailor," she said. "But if you want to come inside and tell me more, I make a mean cup of coffee." As she spoke she brushed wisps of hair out of her eyes. Below her waist, Hayes detected the hint of an emergent knee at the parting of the robe.

"Trying to cut down on caffeine. But thanks."

"Suit yourself," she said, shutting the door louder than he really thought necessary.

And so it went, all the way down the street and up the other side. No one home at half the places. The rest, a mix of retirees, second-shifters just starting their day, a couple young moms, and more than one guy in a hoodie who probably should have been at school, or at work, or in a detention facility. He took a break at lunchtime, sitting in his van and eating a peanut-butter-and-jelly sandwich and reading *Dispatch* headlines on his phone. He texted Karen Feinberg and told her what he was up to, just to feel useful.

I know Bobby appreciates it, she replied.

It was almost three o'clock when he knocked on a neatly kept brick cottage two thirds of the way up the other side of Washington. He waited, gave it a second try, waited a bit more, crossed it off his list and headed down the steps. A moment later the sound of a deadbolt being thrown turned him around. Hayes introduced himself to the young man who opened the door and repeated his spiel.

"You know, I think that's Randy," the man said, studying the photo. A brown and white mutt materialized by his side a moment later.

"Randy?"

"Pretty sure, yeah. He has a beard now, so he looks different. I told him it made him look older, but not in a good way. Just joshing around, you know? But he said he was keeping it."

"How long has he had it?"

"The beard? Hard to say. Six months? No—maybe a year?"

"Which house is his?"

"It's the red one. But the thing is, you're on the wrong street."

"I'm sorry?"

"This is Washington. He lives one street south, on Carrington. I usually end up over there walking Louie." He reached down and scratched the top of his dog's head.

Hayes pushed him for a fuller description of the house. The man said it was hard to miss because Randy had made a lot of improvements. He thought he worked in construction. Hayes thanked him and asked if the man recognized Jeannette Broomfield.

"Yeah, I've seen her over there, once or twice. Maybe his girlfriend?" He dropped his voice. "She's not so friendly, if you know what I mean."

"Oh?"

"Doesn't say hi much. What's this about, if I can ask?"

"Silly civil deposition thing," Hayes said for the fiftieth time that morning, having dropped the lottery ruse after Nora's Nails. "No big deal."

"Well, tell him Shaquan said hi. And to lose the beard."

"Will do."

Hayes walked up to Cleveland, turned south, and turned left on Carrington Avenue. He found the house easily, because Shaquan was right about the work Randy had done. New siding, new gutters, new walkway. Climbing the steps to a renovated porch, Hayes found himself admiring its freshly painted railing spindles, poured concrete floor and glazed planter pots filled with begonias on either side of the top step. Hayes approached the door. No question here about someone home; he could hear voices through an open window. He knocked. The voices stopped as suddenly as a radio dropped into an Ohio farm pond. He knocked again. Silence. He knocked a third time and hit the bell as well.

After a full minute, the door cracked open. A man with a beard stared at Hayes through the narrow space.

"Randy?"

"Who are you?"

"I'm someone who needs to talk to you. And to Jeannette Broomfield."

"I don't know anyone named—"

"A regression analysis suggests otherwise. I'm not here to make trouble. I just have a couple of questions."

"About what?"

"About what happened up the street a year ago."

"You need to leave, right now. Get off my property."

"You can talk to me, or you can talk to the police. Trust me. I'm your better option."

"I told you—"

"It's OK. He knows."

A woman's voice. One Hayes recognized. A moment later the door swung all the way open. Jeannette Broomfield stood just behind Randy. She rested her left hand on his right shoulder.

"He's got no right," Randy said.

"Of course he doesn't," she said. "Because we haven't done anything wrong. None of this changes what Bobby Putnam did—to himself or to Geoff," she said, looking at Hayes, her eyes as hard as the newly installed siding on Randy's house.

"That's true—" Hayes said, but made it no further, interrupted by the sound of a vehicle screeching to a stop on the street behind him. A large vehicle. He turned to see a black Ford F-350 stopped in the middle of Carrington Avenue directly in front of Randy's house, blocking traffic in both directions. A magnetic vehicle sign on the driver's side door sported a pair of crossed shovels and said, "Broomfield Contracting—Home and Commercial." The driver's side door opened and a man climbed out, his back to the crowd on the porch as he reached into the truck. A moment later he turned, a real shovel in his right hand.

"You said this was over." Headed up the walk fast, shovel held in both hands. Geoff Bromfield.

"It is over," Jeannette said, voice tinged with fear. "I told you—"

"Then what are you doing here—"

"Get lost," Randy said, emerging onto the porch.

"You!" Broomfield said, picking up speed.

As Broomfield mounted the steps Hayes pivoted to face him, placing himself between him and Randy.

"Now just hold on."

"Who the hell are you?"

"A guy who should know better," Hayes said, grabbing the shovel with both hands. Broomfield's grip was firm and he didn't let go.

"Get out of my way."

"First put the shovel down."

"Mind your own business, asshole."

Broomfield was a big guy, and strong; an easy match for all the push-ups Hayes prided himself on. They stood there, gasping and grunting for what felt like a full minute, grappling like Greco-Roman wrestlers aiming for a comeback. Hayes was starting to lose his hold and fearing he might not be able to prevent Broomfield and the shovel from wreaking havoc on the couple behind him, when

Broomfield stepped back, missed the top step and nearly stumbled. As he did the edge of the shovel accidently flew up and struck him in the face. Broomfield staggered down the steps, letting go of the shovel as red bloomed from his nose. Hayes turned and presented the shovel to a pair of hands behind him, then pulled a handkerchief from his pocket and handed it to Broomfield to stem the blood flow. Which is why, back turned, he didn't see the blow coming. *Crack,* went the shovel head against the back of Hayes's head. The last thing he remembered was how pretty the begonias looked as he fell to his knees.

* * * *

Packer, from the Linden substation, arrived five minutes after the responding patrol officers. Hayes was already in cuffs, sitting in the back of a CPD cruiser. Packer heard Hayes out, from the beginning of the day's canvass of Washington Street to the encounter at Randy's house one street south.

"So Mrs. Broomfield was having an affair with this guy?"

"Looks that way."

"But what's that got to do with the accident?"

"With the crash itself? Nothing. Bobby Putnam was drunk and out of control and hit Mr. Broomfield. End of story. It's what Broomfield was doing here that matters."

"I thought he was cutting over to a construction site."

Hayes shook his head. "I checked. That project ended six months before the accident."

"So what, then?"

"Oldest story in the world after cheating on your taxes. Geoff found out his wife was having an affair, and with who, and drove over here to have it out with Randy. And he found him, just not where he expected."

"Meaning?"

"Meaning he saw him on the sidewalk up there"—Hayes nodded up the street—"and turned onto Washington instead."

"Instead of what?"

"Instead of onto Carrington, which is where Randy lives."

"What was Randy doing up there?"

Hayes related his conversation with the woman with the head scarf at the market. "Buying milk or something, is my guess. He'd just crossed the street when Broomfield saw him."

"And Broomfield planned to do what, turning like that?"

"Who knows? Run him down? Challenge him to mahjong? You'll have to ask him. Either way, he lied."

"Lied?"

"He wasn't turning to avoid Putnam. He was turning to go after Randy. His first story was probably half true—his view was blocked, but he was also focusing on the sidewalk, not the street."

Packer sighed and said he'd check it out. Eventually, it turned out Hayes was right. Randy was a subcontractor on a couple of Geoff's projects and met Jeannette at a Christmas party two years earlier. Things then transpired the way they often do between women and men who aren't entirely happy with the hand life has dealt them. Geoff found out and set out to do something about it but found himself at the wrong place at the wrong time, directly in the cross hairs of drunken Bobby Putnam.

It took a few days to straighten everything out. Broomfield spent the afternoon of the confrontation in the hospital having his broken nose reset. He sat in an emergency room bay three down from where Hayes sat, receiving seven staples to close the gash in his head. Broomfield withdrew his threat of assault charges against Hayes after Hayes informed him he had no intention of carrying out a similar threat against the person who struck him with the shovel—Jeannette Broomfield. Meanwhile, Randy lost the beard.

Hayes spoke briefly to Karen Feinberg the day everything went down. She assured him she'd let Bobby know.

He called her three days later to check in.

"Andy—I was just about to call you."

"Don't worry. It's not about the money. I just wanted to see how Bobby was. I was thinking I might go back and see him. A freebie."

A long pause. "You can't."

"Why not? It's no charge, for reals. I was hoping to—"

"He's dead, Andy. He was found unresponsive in his cell at three this morning. He hanged himself with his bedsheet."

Hayes couldn't speak for a moment. "Did he know? I mean, did you tell him?"

Feinberg told him that Putnam knew, that she'd explained what Hayes found out. That his suspicions had been confirmed.

"He left a note, just so you know. It won't be made public."

"What did it say?"

"It was to you."

"To me?"

"I can show you a copy, if you want. It just said to thank you."

"To thank me?"

"To tell you that was all he wanted. Just the truth."

"The truth?" Hayes said bitterly.

"The whole story," she said.

✗

Andrew Welsh-Huggins is a reporter for the Associated Press in Columbus and the author of six mysteries featuring Andy Hayes, a former Ohio State and Cleveland Browns quarterback turned private eye. Welsh-Huggins is also the editor of *Columbus Noir* from Akashic Books, and his short fiction has appeared in publications including *Ellery Queen's Mystery Magazine*, *Mystery Weekly*, and *Mystery Tribune*. His nonfiction book, *No Winners Here Tonight*, is the definitive history of the death penalty in Ohio.

THE STOPWATCH OF DEATH

JOSH PACHTER

Assemblies at Hearne High School were usually deadly boring. Some local doctor cautioning the boys to wear a rubber if they couldn't keep their dicks in their pants, stupid shit like that. But this one promised to be more interesting.

Students filed into the auditorium under the watchful eyes of their teachers and took their seats, buzzing with anticipation.

Exactly at 9 a.m., Principal Tito Rodriguez stepped up to the podium and tapped the microphone. "Is this on?" he said, and his amplified voice echoed through the huge room.

"Can I get all y'all to settle down, please, ladies and gentlemen?" The whispered conversations tapered off, and the principal cleared his throat and looked over his shoulder as a white screen descended from the flies.

On the screen, a slide clicked into view. In gigantic black capital letters against a stark white background, it read "THE STOPWATCH OF DEATH."

"No one who pays any attention at all to the news is unaware," Rodriguez said, "of the plague of school shootings that have terrified this country in recent decades. Fifteen dead at Columbine High School in Colorado. Seventeen dead at Stoneman Douglas High in Florida. Twenty-eight dead at Sandy Hook Elementary in Connecticut. Thirty-three dead at Virginia Tech. And we're not immune here in Texas. Shots fired at Prairie View A&M last January, though thank God no fatalities or injuries reported. Ten *dead* at Santa Fe High, though, in May of 2018. Eighteen dead at UT-Austin in 1966, the third-worst school shooting in American history."

Doom and gloom were exciting when they were built into a video game, but there was nothing exciting about this. The students were absolutely silent, hanging on every word.

"Helmut Erhard," Mr. Rodriguez went on, "is a private investigator here in Hearne, and I've asked him to talk with all y'all today about what to do in the event of an active-shooter incident on *our* campus." He paused for a moment, considering, then swallowed his hesitation and added, "Normally, I would have invited Chief Barnes to do this talk, but, as I'm sure all y'all know, he's locked up right now, awaiting trial for the murder of our poor Ms. Jordan the other month, and he ain't—he hasn't been replaced yet, so Mr. Erhard has kindly agreed to stand in for him. Helmut?"

Erhard got up from his seat in the front row and climbed the six carpeted steps to the stage. He was wearing a brown corduroy sports jacket over a chambray shirt and jeans, and he had a pair of scuffed red-stitched Justin work boots on his feet. He was five inches taller than Tito Rodriguez and had to adjust the metal stem of the mike so he could talk into it.

Looking out across the sea of expectant faces, he reached into the inside breast pocket of his jacket and fished out a sheaf of notes, unfolded them and smoothed them out on the podium and studied them for a few seconds before he spoke.

"Most of you kids," he began, and then stopped himself and shook his head. "No," he said, "you're not kids. You're young adults, and I hope to God you have long lives ahead of you." He snuffed in a breath and washed his hand across his mouth and jaw.

"U.S. Department of Justice statistics," he said, "are pretty darn clear: nationwide, the average response time to a report of an active shooter is fifteen minutes, and the average shooter fires one round every four or five seconds. That means that, by the time the cops show up, a shooter has had enough time to fire *hundreds* of rounds. They don't all hit their targets, thank the Lord, but we know shooters go for a high body count—they want to take down as many victims as possible as quick as possible. So that fifteen minutes it takes the police to respond is what law enforcement calls the Stopwatch of Death…."

* * * *

"That went well," Rodriguez said, walking the PI out to his K5 Blazer in the visitors' parking lot. The sun hung halfway up the pale-blue sky and burned with a heat that was still tolerable but would hit a hundred by noon. "I wish my faculty could get them to pay that much attention in class."

Erhard seemed embarrassed by the compliment. "It's not a happy subject," he said. "I just hope I did some good."

Rodriguez put out a hand, and they shook. "I think you did, Helmut. Thanks for coming out."

He hesitated briefly and then came to a decision. "Thanks for figuring out what happened to Elsie, too. She was a sweet girl, had a lot of promise. I just—"

"Amazes me," Erhard said. "Mitch Barnes, running around behind Bonnie's back with a kid, what, less than half his age? And then he up and *kills* her? You never know, do you, Tito? You just never know."

Rodriguez held open the Blazer's door and slammed it shut when Erhard had settled in behind the wheel. As the PI pulled out of the parking lot, he checked his rear-view mirror and saw the principal throw him a salute. He tapped his horn to acknowledge he'd seen it and headed up West Brown to the Dixie Café for a late breakfast.

* * * *

Donuts were not on Erhard's diet, but he'd earned a treat, he figured, and rewarded himself with a Boston Crème and a second cup of coffee. He sat in a booth by the window looking out across South Market to the Union Pacific tracks. A long freight train rattled by, and with nothing else to occupy his mind he counted the cars. Sixty-four.

Sixty-four would be his age on his next birthday, less than a month away. That put him a year and change off from Medicare. Erhard worked for himself in a profession that was being eaten away by the easy access every Tom, Dick, and Harry had to an almost unlimited ocean of data via the internet, and his income had gone *down* in each of the last three years.

There was no *way* he was gone be able to retire. And there was no one to take care of him in his old age. He had never married, had no children. None that he knew of, anyway, he thought wistfully. *Will you still need me, will you still feed me, when I'm sixty-four?*

Only honest answer to that question was *nope,* there wasn't nobody to take on that responsibility. Maybe in a year or so, after they sent Mitch Barnes over to the Eastham Unit in Lovelady, a Texas Department of Criminal Justice prison for men a hundred miles east of Hearne as the crow flies—maybe then he'd pay a call on Bonnie. He'd always had a thing for Bonnie—two years his senior and a tad bit bulkier than she'd been as a young woman, when she was Bonnie Ulrich and the prettiest girl on the block, but she was still a fine woman, a *fine* woman. She deserved better than Mitch had done her for, and he reckoned she'd divorce him soon enough and move on with her life.

Realistically, though, a senior romance probably wasn't in the cards. He'd have to figure out his future on his own.

Yawning, he slid out of the booth, slipped a couple of singles under his saucer, paid his check and went out to his car. He hadn't wanted to take any money for his talk at the high school, but Tito Rodriguez had insisted on paying him fifty bucks for his time, assured him the high school had a budget for guest speakers and it was use it or lose it. Might as well get the check deposited. He turned right onto Market, went under the overpass, and drove four blocks to the SouthStar Bank.

* * * *

The lobby was sparsely populated. Lunchtime rush wouldn't hit for another hour. Three of the four tellers' windows were unstaffed, and there were only two people in line at John Weinstein's station, Ximena Vasquez from the Lavanderia in a pretty floral dress, who looked to be buying rolls of quarters to restock the change machines at her laundromat up on North Market, and a jittery guy Erhard didn't recognize in dirty chinos and a hoodie.

Hoodie, he thought, and the skin on the back of his neck prickled. He looked around, and saw that Zeke Beauchamp, the security guard—seventy-five, if he was a day—was leaning back in a chair beneath the wall clock, flipping the pages of the *Reader's Digest.*

"If you see something, say something," he'd cautioned the kids at the high school—and, dammit, they *were* kids, despite his catering to their precious little egos calling them young adults. When he was their age, he *was* a young adult, but children these days were so coddled by their parents some of them never stopped being kids until the first time they found themselves unable to make a mortgage payment within the grace period.

Standard Operating Procedure in an active-shooter situation used to be shelter in place, lock the door if it was lockable, cower in a corner and pray. Locks are the high priests of false security, though—there wasn't a door lock made that could keep out a lunatic with a loaded AR-15. Nowadays, the mantra was "Run, Hide, Fight," in that order. Running was the best option: your typical shooter was not a trained marksman, and, if you were running, there was a good chance shots fired in your direction would miss. Even if you *did* get hit, eighty percent of those who take a bullet survive, long as they receive medical attention within the first hour. It usually isn't the bullet itself that kills you. You die by bleeding out, and that takes a while.

Over at John Weinstein's window, Ximena was loading her handbag with rolls of coins. She blew John a kiss and threw Erhard a wink as she walked past him, the skirt of her flowered dress swishing with every step. She and Alejandro were two of the hardest working people he knew. Actually, *most* of the Mexican immigrants he knew were hard-working folks. Those nimrods in Washington who wanted to send them home and build a wall couldn't tell the difference between a burro and a burrow. They didn't know their ass from a hole in the ground.

Now the guy in the hoodie was at the teller's window. He had his hands stuffed in his jacket pockets, and if anything he seemed more on edge than before.

Erhard hung back to keep an eye on the situation. He shot a glance at Zeke Beauchamp, who was chuckling at something in his magazine. "Life in These United States"? "Humor in Uniform"?

Forty percent of the time, he'd told the kids at HHS, the victims overpower the shooter and put an end to the incident. But if Erhard's Spidey sense was right and something bad was about to go down, the old security guard would be completely useless. The bank might as well have stuck a scarecrow in a bucket of dirt.

Oh, shit, he thought, as the guy in the hoodie pulled what looked from this distance to be a Taurus 709 Series Slim from the right pocket of his jacket and held it out, stiff-armed, pointing straight at John Weinstein's head. "You touch the alarm, you're a dead man!" the guy shouted. John's hands went up, but Erhard was sure he'd already tapped the silent alarm connected to the cop shop with his foot. That meant the Stopwatch of Death was ticking.

Run, he told himself. *You have* done *your good deed for the day.*

But even if the PD rolled out straight off, it would take them two and a half minutes to get here with sirens screaming, three if they came quiet—which they would, so as not to throw the perp into even more of a panic than he was already in. Three minutes was enough time for the jitterbug with the Taurus to turn John Weinstein, Zeke Beauchamp, Helmut Erhard, and anyone in the back of the bank to ground beef.

Like it or not, this was gone be Erhard's rodeo, and he was gone have to rope this calf himself and tie it down.

At that moment, the old security guard looked up and realized what was happening. In what seemed like slow motion, he struggled to his feet and reached for his hip. Without a word, the guy in the hoodie swiveled and fired.

Christ, Erhard thought. *That tears it.*

Keeping one eye on the Taurus, he hit the deck and reached for his own hip—and then remembered he'd come out unstrapped this morning. After all, what was on his agenda for the day? A little talk at the high school, a little breakfast at the Dixie Café, maybe run a couple errands. Shee-it, what a time to be unarmed. He scrabbled across the polished linoleum floor to Zeke's side. "You hit?" he said.

"Cain't say for sure," the old man wheezed. "Don't think so. I'm scared as hell, though."

"Ayep," Erhard nodded. "I can see why you would be. Your gun loaded?"

The old man looked at him like he was two slices short of a loaf. "Wouldn't be much point packin' it if it wudn't, son, would there?"

"May I," Erhard said, the steadiness and politeness of his voice taking him by surprise, "borrow it for just a sec?"

"Yes, indeed," Zeke said, handing it over. "You be my guest."

Shoveling wads of cash into a plastic sack from the Dollar General, the guy in the hoodie was paying no attention to the two of them. One shot fired, and he seemed to reckon that made him King of the Hill.

The gun Erhard now held was an M1911, single-action, semi-automatic, recoil-operated, chambered for the .45 ACP cartridge. A lot of gun for a security guard in his seventies. "Full magazine?" he asked.

"Eight rounds," Zeke nodded. "Plus one in the chamber. Cleaned it last night. Clean it *every* night I'm comin' to work the next day."

Right hand wrapped around the grip, Erhard rolled away from the old man. If he was going to draw fire, better one body in the bullet's path than two.

"You need to rethink your morning, pal," he yelled across the lobby. "You been lucky, so far, ain't nobody hurt. Like to keep it that way, if we can."

"Makes no difference to me," the answer came back, high-pitched and full of rage. Erhard could see the guy's face, now, and he couldn't have been more than twenty years old, twenty-two, tops. "I got two strikes on me already. This here's a felony, anybody gets hurt or not, and one more felony I go away for fifteen to life. What I got to lose?"

A minute gone, Erhard thought. *Two more and all hell's fixin' to break loose.* He watched the guy scratch his left forearm with the 709's barrel. *Check.* A mouth full of rotten teeth. *Check.* Paranoid and pissed. *Check and check.*

Guy's a tweaker, he realized. And once the meth takes over, anything can happen.

Aim for an arm or a leg, the TV lawmen would do. Incapacitate, but don't execute. 'Course, television shows were basically fairy tales interrupted by commercials. A dirtbag with a bullet in his thigh can still pull a trigger. So Erhard aimed for center mass and gently squeezed off three rounds.

Zeke Beauchamp jerked back at the sound, covered his eyes with his hands as the guy in the hoodie was blown back against the partition that separated the tellers from the customers, the Taurus flying out of his hand and skidding across the linoleum. The guy bounced forward and landed face down on the floor, leaving a streak of bright red on the wall where he'd hit.

"It's over," Erhard shouted. "He's down. All clear."

Noise outside the bank told him the police had arrived. *Ahead of schedule*, he thought. *They made damn good time.* Inside his head, he clicked the button on the Stopwatch of Death.

Erhard laid the M1911 carefully down on the floor and put his hands up, fingers spread, to show he was unarmed. He walked slowly across the silent lobby, bumped the plate-glass door open with his butt and went outside into the bright yellow sun.

✗

Josh Pachter is a writer, editor and translator. Almost a hundred of his short crime stories have appeared in *Black Cat Mystery Magazine, Ellery Queen's Mystery Magazine, Alfred Hitchcock's Mystery Magazine,* and many other places; *The Tree of Life* (Wildside Press, 2015) collected all ten of his Mahboob Chaudri stories, and he collaborated with Belgian author Bavo Dhooge on the zombie-cop novel *Styx* (Simon & Schuster, 2015). His recent editorial projects include *The Beat of Black Wings: Crime Fiction Inspired by the Songs of Joni Mitchell* (Untreed Reads, 2020), *The Misadventures of Nero Wolfe* (Mysterious Press, 2020), and *Amsterdam Noir* (Akashic, 2019). His translations of stories by Dutch, Flemish, and other authors turn up regularly in *EQMM*'s "Passport to Crime" department. Visit him online at www.joshpachter.com.

THE FUGITIVE WITH THE DRAGON TATTOO

BEV VINCENT

Wendy always knew when Vic wasn't giving her his full attention. They were sitting at their assigned table in the cruise ship dining room, eating steak that had been seared to their individual specifications and sharing a bottle of Argentinian Malbec, but Vic kept looking—surreptitiously, or so he thought—at a table diagonally across from them.

Wendy put her knife on her plate with a clank and looked over her shoulder.

"Phssst," Vic said. "Don't do that."

Wendy rolled her eyes. "I can't ogle the blond babe in the red dress, too?"

"What?" Vic said. "Oh, her. That's not who I'm looking at."

"Really," Wendy said, turning it into a three-syllable word. She glanced at the other table again.

"Stop that," Vic said. "He'll notice."

"If you've got a crush on that hairy hunk of beef, maybe we should talk."

Vic frowned. "His name is Xavier Abbott." Then he cut off another morsel of steak and stuck it into his mouth.

"And we know him how?"

He finished chewing and swallowed before replying. "He's a fugitive. From Austin. His hair is longer and his beard is fuller, but that's definitely him."

"I don't believe this," Wendy said. "I finally get you to take a vacation and you're still working."

Vic shrugged.

"Is he gonna know you?"

"Our paths have never crossed."

"But you know him."

"I look over the wanted posters every now and then. Just in case."

"Right." More syllables than Vic could count. "Just in case a fugitive winds up on a cruise ship with us. I don't believe it," she repeated.

Vic had nothing to add, but Wendy was far from finished. "What happens now? You gonna call the Marshals Service so they can swoop in on helicopters like commandos and take him away?"

"We're in international waters. They have no jurisdiction out here."

"So…what? Someone'll be waiting for us when we get into Cozumel tomorrow?"

Vic returned to his steak. "There's a field office in Mexico City. I *could* make a call."

"Why do I get the feeling you're not gonna do that?"

"Big fish. Whoever reels him in…" He looked at her and raised his eyebrows.

"How much is the reward?" Wendy was suddenly interested.

"More than enough to pay for this cruise."

"So you wait until we get back to Galveston?"

"Something like that. For now, just don't look at him again. Don't want to spook the guy. He's not someone you want to make nervous."

* * * *

Vic signed up for a scuba-diving excursion in Cozumel, but Wendy decided to go shopping instead. "You'll find someone to buddy up with," she said. "Kiss an angelfish for me."

When Vic saw Abbott among the group being escorted to one side of the dock for the scuba outing, he casually took a spot near him. The dive master gave his pre-dive briefing and then reviewed the buddy situation. Vic waited for Abbott to make the overture.

"Got a partner?" Abbott muttered at last.

"Nope. All by my lonesome," Vic said. He offered a hand. "Vic."

"Fred," Abbott said, and that was the sum total of their dialog for the duration of the trip. On the boat, "Fred" kept to himself, checking his gear like he knew what he was doing. He went into the water first and stayed close to Vic without making more than occasional eye contact.

After the dive boat returned to the pier, Vic dried off, changed into shorts and a festive shirt, and wandered into the Three Amigos for a margarita. He was halfway through the drink, embracing the drifting, surreal sensation of a post-dive high, when he heard his wife's voice. "Knew I'd find you here." He turned to greet her, then froze. Wendy was accompanied by the woman who'd been sitting with Abbott at dinner the previous evening.

"I made a new friend," Wendy said. "We were in a shop and got to talking. How was the dive? See anything interesting?"

Vic put on his friendliest smile and said, "One big shark."

"Oh, my," Wendy's new acquaintance said. She put a hand to her throat. A very nice throat, Vic observed. "My Freddy went on that dive, too. I hope he's okay."

"I'm sure Vic's exaggerating," Wendy said, and Vic smiled again to show how copacetic everything was. "Sit. Sit," she continued. "We have plenty of time before we have to be back on board. I'm gonna go find the ladies' room."

Before Vic could say anything, his wife spun on her heel and disappeared into the crowd milling around in front of the bar.

A waitress appeared. "Can I get you something?" Vic asked. "The frozen margaritas are pretty good."

"That would be nice," the woman said. "Sorry—we haven't been introduced. I'm Ilona."

"Vic," he said, taking her proffered hand. He looked straight into her gray eyes, though the temptation was strong to glance at the semi-transparent garment she was wearing over the briefest of bikinis. "So you're on the same ship as us?" He realized he was still holding her hand and released it.

"Oh, yes. In fact, I saw you at dinner last night."

"I'm sure I would have remembered that."

She flashed a million dollar grin and a wink. Her skin was flawless and her teeth unnaturally even. She'd either been blessed with good genes or, more likely, high-priced cosmetic surgeons. "Don't worry. I won't tell."

"Huh?"

Her margarita arrived. Ilona paused to sip through the varicolored straw. "Yum," she said. "You're right. This *is* good. Where was I? Oh, yes. I saw you looking at me last night at dinner. Did you recognize me?"

Vic almost choked on his drink. "Why would you think that?"

She pouted for a second, then grinned again. "Oh. I just thought. I'm an actress."

"Aha," Vic said. "What have you been in?"

"I did a reality show a couple of years back. Now I'm on a cable series." She said the show's name. "It's on late at night—or, rather, early in the morning." She winked again. "You'd see a lot more of me if you watched. Most of the time, I don't have any clothes on. I thought maybe you were undressing me. You know, with your eyes."

Vic wasn't sure how to react, so he just smiled and drank more of his margarita.

"It was no accident that your wife bumped into me in the shop."

"Oh?"

"Like I said, I noticed you noticing me, so I sort of accidentally on purpose started a conversation with her. Figured it would give me a chance to meet you. You're cute, in a manly way, if you know what I mean."

Vic took another sip of his margarita, which was by now nearly finished. The tequila was giving him a warm glow. Women occasionally came onto him, but when it was the partner of a wanted felon, he had to wonder why. He looked around for Wendy.

"I'm making you nervous," she said. She patted his arm. "Don't worry. It'll be our little secret. But if you want to get a preview of my show, come up to the top deck tomorrow. The one where they allow topless sunbathing."

"And your husband?"

"Freddy's not my husband. He's just a guy who buys me things and takes me places. Don't worry. He doesn't go out on deck much. I was surprised when he signed up for the dive trip."

I'll bet, Vic thought. Abbott was taking a chance showing his face in public.

Just then, he saw Wendy approaching. He pinned a twenty to the table with the salt shaker and got up to greet her. "We should head back," he said. "There's probably a line waiting to board."

"I think I'll stay here a bit longer," Ilona said. "Finish my drink. Nice meeting you, Wendy and, uh…"

"Vic."

"Vic. Maybe we'll see each other on board." She looked at Vic while saying this, but she flashed a big smile that took in Wendy as well.

"*Hasta luego*," Wendy said.

As they strolled to the gangway, Wendy said, "She seems nice. What's her husband wanted for?"

"Not her husband, apparently. Money laundering, felony possession, and racketeering."

"So he's not a murderer."

"Not that anyone's ever proved."

"Did you know she's an actress?"

"She mentioned that."

"She was one of those single women who played the temptress to a bunch of married couples living on an island."

"You saw it?"

Wendy laughed. "The first few episodes. I didn't recognize her until she mentioned it. Do you find her tempting?"

"Not in the least," he said.

"We'll have to check out her new show when we get home. She says she's naked in it a lot. Maybe you'll change your mind."

"Maybe," Vic said. Which earned him a good-natured swat on the shoulder.

* * * *

Once they were back on board, Vic went to the business center, where he paid through the teeth for fifteen minutes on the internet. He pulled up Abbott's wanted poster and a press release from the Marshals Service website. Seeing the man's picture on the screen silenced any doubts he might have had.

Next, he accessed the cruise ship's layout and ascertained the location of the deck Ilona had mentioned, the little-advertised area where topless sunbathing was permitted. Then he cleared the browser's cache and history before signing off. He almost bumped into Abbott when he was exiting the business center. Abbott gave no sign that he saw him, but Vic had to wonder if the guy had been checking up on him.

In the dining room that evening, Vic made a wide circle around Abbot's table, but Ilona spotted them, got up and waved. "Over here!" Vic ignored her, but Wendy waved back. Vic clenched his teeth for a second before putting on his polite smile.

Ilona, dressed in a black dress that was even slinkier than the red one she'd worn the previous evening, insisted that they join them, despite the cruise line's assigned seating policy. "There's plenty of room," Ilona said in the offhand manner of someone used to getting her way.

Abbott gave a grunt of recognition when he saw Vic.

"Huh," Vic said. "Small world." He turned to Wendy. "Meet my dive partner," he said. "Fred, right?"

"Right." Abbott didn't look particularly pleased, but he put on a brave face, stood long enough to greet the new arrivals, and slumped back into his seat.

Ilona liked to talk about herself, so making conversation wasn't an issue. She lived in Austin, she said, but commuted to L.A. regularly for her TV show. "What do you do?" she asked Vic.

"I work for the Postal Service," he said, watching Abbott out of the corner of his eye to see what reaction that would bring.

"Neither rain nor sleet nor gloom of night," Ilona said.

Vic smiled. "I work inside, in an office. Management. What about you... Fred?"

"I own a few garages. Collision repairs, like that."

He didn't seem eager to talk, so Vic let the women carry on. Wendy and Ilona chatted about their excursion in Cozumel and the best places to shop in Houston and Austin. Ilona regaled them with Hollywood gossip, most of which seemed to be gleaned from the covers of magazines in grocery store checkout lines. Vic was concentrating on his rack of lamb when he felt something brush against his calf—Ilona's bare foot, as far as he could tell. He pretended not to notice, in case it was an accident.

Abbott ordered a second bottle of wine and consumed most of it himself, growing increasingly sullen as the meal progressed. While they were waiting for dessert, he excused himself to have a cigarette in one of the few smoking areas on the ship.

"Don't mind Freddy," Ilona said. "He's the strong, silent type." She caressed Vic's leg with her foot again as she said this.

Abbott didn't return to the table, so the trio split his crème brûlée and finished off the wine. Vic and Wendy had tickets to see a show in the amphitheater, so they excused themselves and made their way back to their cabin to get ready. "I wonder what deck they're on." Wendy mused. "Is there a fugitive wing?"

As long as it was far from theirs, Vic didn't care.

* * * *

The next day was their second last on board. The ship would arrive in Galveston the following morning. After breakfast, Vic relaxed on their balcony while Wendy got a bamboo massage, which didn't sound pleasant to Vic at all. He tried to read for a while but his mind was occupied by his dilemma. How could he bring Abbott in and get full credit for the arrest? If he waited until they docked, he might lose the fugitive in the chaos of disembarkation. Vic was unarmed, but he did have his PI license with him, at least.

His thoughts were distracted by images of Ilona. The way she had looked in that sheer bikini wrap in Cozumel, and the slinky dress she'd been wearing at dinner. Her surreptitious caresses. Did she expect him to respond to her flirtation? If so, how could he use that to his advantage? Or was she trying to use it to theirs?

He decided to explore the private deck, which was at the front of the ship where passengers were unlikely to stumble upon it by chance. NO CHILDREN BEYOND THIS POINT, a small sign read beside the narrow staircase that led up from the main deck.

It didn't occur to him until he was halfway up the stairs how it would look for a guy to be entering the topless sunbathing area by himself. Running into Abbott would be especially awkward. He could always say he was looking for his wife, a lame but plausible excuse. He needn't have worried, though. Ilona was the only person availing herself of the secluded area.

Lying face down, she didn't appear to notice him until his shadow fell across her. The top of her bikini was strung across a deck chair beside her, next to a bottle of tanning lotion, and her thong bottom might as well have been, too, for all it covered. Her strawberry blond hair was up in a bun. The long expanse of exposed flesh was already golden.

She opened one eye. "I was wondering when you'd show up."

When, not if. He perched on the edge of the deck chair.

"I have to say, you don't look like a postal worker," she said, rolling onto her side.

It was obvious she wanted him to take in her body, so he did. "Don't I?" He was wearing Bermuda shorts, a tank top, and an Indiana Jones-style hat to protect his face and neck from the sun. He'd tried wearing sunglasses but they made him look too much like a Fed.

"Too buff and too—I don't know—too much like you spend time outside. Not in an office."

"I'm outside now," he said.

She rolled onto her back and squinted into the sun. "Funny guy." If the rest of the passengers had known what was on display here, Vic thought the resulting stampede would have capsized the ship.

He noticed a colorful design entwined around her right breast—green, yellow, and orange. Since she didn't seem to mind him looking at her, he leaned in. "What's that?"

She glanced down. "This? It's Rhaegal." She traced the outline of the figure with her finger. "You know. One of the dragons from *Game of Thrones*. Freddy has one on his arm, too, except his is Drogon. He's bigger and meaner."

"Like Freddy, you mean?"

"You scared of him?"

"What would he do if he caught me up here with you?"

"He doesn't like the sun."

"Still."

"You look like you can handle yourself."

"You'd like that, wouldn't you? Couple of men fighting over you."

She reached out one long arm and plucked the tube of tanning lotion from the seat next to Vic's leg. He didn't allow himself to flinch when her hand brushed his thigh. She held the tube out. "Want to do my back?"

That wasn't all he wanted to do, and they both knew it. He got to his feet. "I need to get back."

"Austin's not very far from Houston."

Vic said nothing.

"Do postal workers have business cards?" she asked.

Vic shook his head.

"But you must have an email address, right? Slip yours to me at dinner to-night. We can stay in touch. See what happens."

Vic nodded and headed toward the stairs. He looked back at her one last time before he descended to the main deck. She was still on her side, staring at him.

* * * *

Wendy was lounging on their balcony when he got back, reading a novel on her iPad.

"How was the bamboo massage?"

"Heavenly. I'm ready for a drink. What have you been up to?"

"Reconnaissance," he said.

"Figured out what you're gonna do yet?"

"Sort of," he lied.

"You should call what's his name. That special agent buddy of yours. Rod?" She shrugged. "Have backup waiting in Galveston."

"I'm thinking about it. There's still time."

A little while later, an alert went out over the intercom system. "Frederick Yager, please report to your cabin."

"Wonder what that's all about?" Wendy asked. "Is that your guy?"

"Hmmm." Vic said.

The announcement was repeated several times. Then the ship slowed and came to a halt. Vic and Wendy went onto the deck, where people were looking over the railings into the deep, dark waters of the Gulf of Mexico.

Vic hailed a uniformed employee passing by. "What's going on?"

The man seemed reluctant to talk but he responded to the authority in Vic's voice. "Someone might have gone overboard, sir."

"In the middle of the day?"

The man shrugged. "We have a passenger unaccounted for, sir."

"Do you think he suspected something?" Wendy asked after the crewman was out of earshot.

"Maybe," Vic said.

"Jumping into the ocean. He must really not want to get caught."

After reconnoitering with a Coast Guard vessel, the cruise ship returned on her course toward Galveston. The crew tried to make light of the situation, but

Vic recognized the signs of stress in their faces. Losing passengers was bad for business.

Ilona and "Freddy" weren't at their assigned dinner table that evening. Later, in bed, Vic tossed and turned. Assuming the missing man was Xavier Abbott, aka Freddy Yager, he'd missed his chance at a huge and lucrative catch. Wendy was right. He should have called someone. That way, Abbott would have been confined to quarters instead of making good his escape.

Had Abbott arranged for a boat to pick him up? Another crew member told Vic they were reviewing video footage but so far none of their security cameras had captured him going overboard. "He may still turn up," the crewman said, but he didn't sound optimistic.

The ship was scheduled to arrive at the Port of Galveston at 8 a.m. but they were running late because of the previous afternoon's delay. Vic and Wendy packed their carry-on bags—the crew had picked up their suitcases from the hall outside the cabin during the night—settled their bill, and went to the restaurant for breakfast. As soon as Vic saw the entrance to the ship channel in the distance, he kissed Wendy and told her he'd see her later. "I've got my cell phone," he said.

"Don't worry about your shoulder bag," she said. "I've got it."

Vic headed down to departure level and talked to several crew members until he found one who could authorize his request. He showed the man his PI license and explained the situation.

"Our missing passenger is a wanted fugitive?"

"Yes."

"Dangerous?"

"Possibly."

"I need to alert port security."

"Okay, but do it discreetly," Vic said. "I don't want to tip him off."

"You think he's still on board?"

"We'll see."

After the cruise ship performed an impressive U-turn in the narrow channel and eased into its berth, the lower decks turned into a hub of activity. The ship was made fast and paperwork was handed back and forth through the still-closed gate to clear the vessel and its contents for arrival. Announcements blared over the intercom telling passengers when and how to disembark from the ship. Everything was color-coded and no one was allowed onto the departure level until their color was called, to avoid congestion on the gangways.

Vic found a quiet corner where he could watch passengers streaming down the staircases. He spotted Ilona, who was being escorted by two female crewmembers. When she saw Vic, she made a beeline for him. "Oh, Vic. It's so terrible. I can't tell you what I've been through. Why would he do this to me? Why? Oh, why?" Her eyes were red, as if she'd been crying, but Vic wasn't convinced. He doubted she was in the running to win any acting awards.

She flung herself into his arms and pressed her body against him. Despite her supposed stress, she hadn't neglected to anoint herself with perfume, he noticed. Vic kept a close eye over her shoulder in case she'd been sent to distract him. He pried her loose and allowed the crewmembers to guide her off the ship, where she would, no doubt, have to answer questions and file paperwork concerning her traveling companion's disappearance.

Wendy joined him when their color was called. Two sets of eyes were better than one, she said. Eventually, the crowd thinned out as the stragglers—those who didn't have a plane to catch or any other pressing engagements—finally disembarked.

Vic was about to give up when a man in a uniform, holding a clipboard and making notes as he shuffled toward the gangplank, caught his attention. Other than a mustache, he was clean-shaven, with a crisp, short haircut like most of the other crew, but his shirt seemed too small for him. His biceps bulged within the tight stricture of his sleeves. When he moved his arm to write on the clipboard, Vic spotted something else: a tattoo. He couldn't make out what it was, so he moved in for a closer look.

The man looked up when Vic was less than five feet away.

Vic used his most authoritative voice to say, "Xavier Abbott, I'm taking you in."

Abbott froze. "I knew it," he said with a snarl, and lunged at Vic.

Vic took a step back, his hand going instinctively to his hip. Even though Vic was clearly unarmed, the motion was enough to make Abbott pause. His eyes darted left and right. He leaned in the direction from which he'd just come, but changed his mind. He must have realized that if he ran back into the ship, it would only be a matter of time before security tracked him down. When Vic stepped forward, Abbott feinted to the right, toward the gauntlet of customs and immigration officials. He stopped again.

Just as Vic was about to seize the man, Abbott spun around and made for the railing. The gap between the moored cruise ship and the pier opened and closed, opened and closed with the motion of the channel waters. Vic grabbed his prey from the railing seconds before he was crushed to death by the 100,000-ton ship and flung him to the ground.

A few seconds later, a security officer arrived on the scene. "Do you have handcuffs?" Vic asked. "This man is a wanted fugitive."

"Just zip ties."

"That'll do," Vic said.

"Can I see your paperwork?"

"That's going to take a while," Vic said, showing him his license. "I have to call it in. I didn't take this cruise expecting to find a fugitive."

Abbott didn't resist when Vic told him to put his hands behind his back. Vic led him to a chair and made him sit. It took a few hours to get everything straightened out and to turn Abbott over to a Marshal for transportation. Vic still had paperwork to complete, but that could wait until Monday.

To celebrate, he and Wendy treated themselves to a nice dinner at Luigi's, near the cruise terminal, before picking up their car for the drive back to Houston. While they ate, Vic brought Wendy up to date.

"Turns out Abbott paid a crewman to make the man-overboard report. Then this morning, Ilona lured the guy into their cabin and talked him out of his uniform. Not to mention his ID and passport." Vic raised an eyebrow. "Guess her gig as a temptress paid off, for a little while at least."

"How'd you recognize him?" Wendy asked. "Even after you tackled him, I wasn't sure."

"I'm a trained observer," Vic said.

"No, really."

"I noticed that his shirt didn't fit."

"That's it?"

"That and the tattoo."

"Huh?"

"A dragon. I saw the tail peeking out from under his sleeve. Ilona has one, too."

"I didn't notice any tattoos on her. Where was it?"

"Um," Vic said. "How about another glass of wine?"

✗

Bev Vincent is the author of *The Dark Tower Companion; The Road to the Dark Tower,* nominated for a Bram Stoker Award; and *The Stephen King Illustrated Companion,* nominated for a 2010 Edgar Award and a 2009 Bram Stoker Award. In 2018, he co-edited the anthology *Flight or Fright* with Stephen King. He has published more than 90 short stories, which have appeared in publications like *Ellery Queen's Mystery Magazine, Alfred Hitchcock's Mystery Magazine, The Eyes of Texas,* and *The Blue Religion.* Four of his stories were collected in *When the Night Comes Down* and another four in a CD Select eBook. His 2010 story "The Bank Job" won the Al Blanchard Award. "The Honey Trap" from *Ice Cold* was nominated for an ITW Thriller Award in 2015. He has been a contributing editor with *Cemetery Dance* magazine since 2001 and writes book reviews for *Onyx Reviews* and *Dead Reckonings.* His work has been translated into more than fifteen languages. To learn more, visit bevvincent.com.

LOVE PIRATE
O'NEIL DE NOUX

"We need a man with moxie," said the short woman sitting in one of the chairs in front of my desk.

Moxie—I thought. *I'm in another B-movie.*

"I have moxie." I pointed across my wide office to the kitchen area. "I store it in my spiffy new 1949 model Frigidaire Cold Pantry fridge." I smiled. "Keeps everything fresh."

Cannot believe I said "spiffy." Too much coffee-and-chicory this morning.

The tall woman in the other chair gave her friend a wide-eyed look. Both women turned to me with narrowed eyes. So much for trying humor. I shook my head, lost the smile as I pulled out my Parker 51 fountain pen with new cobalt blue ink and my Moleskine notebook.

The short woman had introduced herself as Myra Hindley, attorney-at-law. She wore a dark blue tailored suit with a pencil skirt and fitted jacket, which she'd removed and folded in her lap. The tall woman, her client Donna Mullenger, wore a dress with a full skirt and fitted short-sleeved jacket, which was also removed and folded in her lap. Both were in their thirties, had their brown hair cut short and what appeared to be brown eyes.

Myra sat up straighter, said, "We have papers for you to serve on someone avoiding service. It's going to take moxie to serve these papers."

She explained Donna Mullenger was seeking divorce from husband Carl Mullenger for abandonment and adultery and Carl had been served papers and deposed and admitted everything, offered a settlement which they were considering.

"Carl Mullenger?" I asked. "As in the Mullenger Shipping?"

Donna nodded.

Myrna went on. "The papers we need served is on the love pirate for alienating Carl's affections and causing severe heart balm in my client."

"You're going too fast. What is heart balm?" Sounded like a salve or a cream.

"A civil wrong producing legal liability such as breaches of promise to marry, seduction, alienation of affection and the like."

The ceiling fans brought a whiff of perfume across my desk, the ever-popular Chanel No. 5. I'd splashed on Ice Blue Aqua Velva aftershave that morning to go with my navy-blue suit and ice-silver tie. My suit jacket hung on the coat rack next to the door.

"OK, what's a love pirate?"

"A female who allures married men into illicit affairs. Stealing them from their wives. Usually younger secretaries or stenographers using their feminine wiles to seduce unsuspecting men. In this case a demure long-legged typewriter girl in tailor-made outfits who calls herself Justine Lake, although her real name is Justine Puddinglake."

I could not write fast enough and raised my left hand to slow Myra down.

"Puddinglake?" I spelled it out.

"Yes. There's a town in England. I looked it up. Her father is the Right Reverend Adam Puddinglake, an Episcopal priest in Cornish, New Hampshire. The papers we need served are for two lawsuits. One against the love pirate. One against the employment agency that sent this seductress to Carl. Court process servers have been unable to serve Justine."

Myra stood and pulled a sheet of paper from the manila folder she'd brought and slid it across the desk to me. It was a page from a slick magazine, an ad for Remington typewriters with a pretty model sitting at a desk with a typewriter in front of her. The model was looking over her shoulder and smiling at the camera.

"What do you see?"

"Is this a trick question?"

"You see a young, attractive stenographer. A secretary. Correct?"

I nodded.

"She's not just a secretary. She's a love pirate."

The woman in the ad looked familiar. Not just your ordinary pretty model.

Myra patted her client's arm. "We're going to make a statement against love pirates and the people who promote them. These *steno-girls* are groomed and trained for seduction. Like soldiers trained for battle. We plan to warn all wives with husbands who employ women in their office."

Donna teared up. "I saw it coming but could do nothing. I saw that woman watch my husband lovingly, giving him sweet smiles, come-hither looks."

May have had something to do with the long legs—I thought.

"She stole his heart." Donna set her mouth, said, "This way is easier than shooting her with my Browning .25 caliber pistol." She patted her large purse.

Does she have a pistol in there?

Myra touched Donna's hand.

I asked for a description of Justine Lake and wrote down—blond, blue eyes, about five feet, eight inches tall, thin build, New England accent.

"OK, I follow Carl from work. Find out where she lives."

Myra huffed. "I am not finished. We know where she lives. He has her stashed in a penthouse apartment atop the Maison Blanche Building. And he's got the doormen and elevator operators bribed to keep strangers out."

Myra slid more papers across the desk. "It has to be personal service. A set for Justine. A set for the employment agency when you find which agency was used."

She signaled Donna, who pulled a checkbook from her purse. I told them I charged thirty dollars a day plus expenses and Donna wrote out a check, passed it to me. Check was for five hundred dollars. They stood up and I went around to shake their hands. Up close I saw their eyes were both brown. Wondered what they looked like if they smiled. The jilted wife Donna stood nearly six feet tall, her eyes level with mine, and she wore low heels.

Myra handed me her business card. "I anticipate your living up to your reputation, Mr. Caye."

"I have a reputation?"

"You caught that public enemy number one guy and that marriage swindler."

"And the gungirl," Donna added.

"Don't believe everything you read in the papers."

They crossed the room, opened the door to leave, and I remembered and called out, "Janet Leigh."

They turned.

"The secretary in the ad. She's a movie star. Saw her in *Act of Violence* with Van Heflin and Robert Ryan."

"Love Pirate," Myra corrected me.

They turned again and left. I went to the windows facing Barracks Street and Cabrini Park and watched them climb into a green 1948 Chrysler Imperial parked behind my gray, pre-war DeSoto. Myra Hindley, who stood maybe five feet tall, looked like a kid behind the steering wheel of her daddy's car.

I glanced at Myra's business card. Printed beneath Myra Ethel Hindley was 1948 NEW ORLEANS ATTORNEY OF THE YEAR. Beneath that in smaller print: Louisiana Bar Association.

Lawyer of the year? Like an MVP award?

I endorsed Donna's check, thumbed through the legal papers, signed as the process server and separated the return-of-service forms to put aside until I made service. I kicked my feet up on the desk and let the black revolving desk fan breeze over me and thought about how to handle this adventure.

At least I was familiar with the Maison Blanche Building. Handled a wandering daughter case there last year. Elevators blocked, right? Well, every building has stairs and Maison Blanche Department Store occupied the first three floors. If I could find a way through the store, I would avoid the doorman. Gotta be back stairs and fire escapes. I'd find a way up to the penthouses, wherein lay my next problem. There were six penthouses in each of the two towers. I couldn't just linger in the hall. Had to knock on doors. So long as I did not get tossed off the roof of a twelve-story building, I might succeed.

As the fan cooled me on this typical muggy New Orleans late autumn day, I thought about how they were putting all this on the stenographer, the female, the seductress, the love pirate. Not the wayward husband, not the poor innocent man who violated his marriage vow.

We were at the mid-point of the 20th Century and the woman was still the guilty party. Like Hester, whatever her last name was, who had to go around wearing a scarlet *A*. Stenographers as love pirates assumed they use their sexuality to lure honest husbands away from their wives, instead of skirt-chasing husbands trading wives in for younger models.

Oh, well. I had a job to do. Serve papers and let the court settle this. Better than shooting a spouse. How had Donna put it? "With a Browning .25 caliber pistol."

* * * *

After depositing the check at my bank and keeping out fifty dollars, it took about an hour to locate the back stairs of the Maison Blanche building. At the rear of the department store, I found the art department offices where other potential love pirates drew and painted ads on drawing tables, ads for dresses, men's suits, jewelry, perfume bottles. Spotted a few men artists, one wearing a beret, another in a red Basque shirt right out of the Spanish Civil War. Large department store like MB ran ads in every newspaper every day.

I pretended to write notes in my Moleskine notebook as I walked around until I spotted a rear door marked FIRE DOOR at the back of the building along Iberville Street.

"May I help you?" A matronly woman who'd come up behind me asked.

I extended my right hand to shake, said, "Alexander Bose. I'm one of the building's new architects."

I knew I looked spiffy in my blue suit and ice-silver tie, my dark hair freshly cut and cleft chin freshly shaved.

There's that word *spiffy* again. Damn.

She took my hand with her fingers and thumb, introduced herself as the art director.

I nodded to the fire door. "I need to check out the layout of your fire escape."

"Yes. It's right there. Is there a problem?"

"No, ma'am. No problem at all. We're drawing up plans for modernizing the building."

She smiled, said if I needed anything. She pointed to an office.

"Nice suit," she complimented me.

I thanked her. I'd bought the suit right here at MB a few months ago.

No lock on the fire door. I stepped into an enclosed stairwell running all the way down and all the way up to the roof. I went to the top floor and opened the door to a hallway. It had a tan carpet and six doors to the penthouses along the back wing of the building. I reached under my coat to the small of my back where my new Smith and Wesson .357 magnum revolver rested in its holster and pulled out a thin lady's pocketbook I'd tucked in my waistband.

My knock on the first door brought a gray-haired woman in a white blouse and red slacks, a coffee cup in hand.

I held up the pocketbook, asked, "Are you Justine Lake?"

"No, but I could be. Who are you?"

"Store detective from downstairs. Maison Blanche. Lady told the saleslady she lived in one of the penthouses up here and forgot this at a register."

"Don't know any Justine up here." The woman said she knew the people in all the penthouses on the rear tower. No Justine. I described Justine. No luck.

"Do all the store detectives look like you, like Cary Grant?"

"I thought I looked like Gregory Peck."

"Same thing. Tall, dark and handsome."

I started backing away. "No ma'am. The women detectives look like June Allyson and Ava Gardner."

She took a sip of coffee.

"You got a girl downstairs looks like Ava Gardner and you're up here?"

"I know. Life can be so cruel." I kept backing away. "She likes the short, goofy, Mickey Rooney-looking guys."

No answer to my knocking on the first two doors of the front penthouses that overlooked Canal Street. A chic blonde in a sleeveless pink blouse and flyaway white skirt answered the next door. She blinked her blues eyes at me. She was maybe twenty years old, had her hair up and her face made up for a fashion photo session.

I held up the pocketbook. "Are you Justine Lake?"

"Yes."

I pulled the legal papers from my inside coat pocket and pressed them against her right shoulder.

"This is for you."

The papers started to fall, and she caught them. I slipped the pocketbook into my coat pocket.

"What is this?" Yep. New England accent.

"Legal papers. You've just been served."

She opened the papers and I inched away.

"Too bad about the employment agency."

"Employment agency?" The blue eyes looked into my eyes again. She did not have to look up too high, I stood six feet even and she was only a few inches shorter.

"The one sent you to Mullenger Shipping. They had to evacuate the building."

"The entire building?"

She was hooked and kept biting at the bait.

"Roach infestation. Have to fumigate the entire building."

"The entire Baronne Building? It's nine stories."

I nodded. "Don't you hate roaches?"

She shivered. I thanked her and backed away. She looked at the papers and said, "Thank you. I suppose."

A nice young woman caught in a trap called love. Such is life. I took the fire stairs all the way down.

* * * *

I parked on Carondelet Street. Temperature had to be in the mid-nineties matched with ninety percent humidity. No breeze added perspiration to my temples. I walked to the corner. The hulking Baronne Building was not on Baronne

Street but at the corner of Carondelet and Common Street. Whoever painted its concrete walls tan should have used paint that did not fade in strong sunlight.

Found two employment agencies in the building. The Trance Employment Service on the first floor did not handle office workers. The Aileen Addison Agency on the second floor specialized in secretaries, stenographers and typists. Did not think the pocketbook ruse was going to work until the young receptionist blurted out, "I know Justine. How is she doing at the shipping company?"

I shrugged.

"She left that at Maison Blanche?"

"Yes. I'm a detective." I pulled out my notebook and pen. "I have to turn this over to a manager. Is your manager in?"

The receptionist whose named turned out to be Bonnie Blue, a blue-eyed blonde from Saint Tammany Parish across the lake, asked me to take a seat and picked up her phone. I sat at the far end of a sofa where another well-dressed woman sat reading *Life* magazine. Like Bonnie, this woman wore a smart skirt-suit and was also a blonde.

The woman who came into the reception area from the interior offices had her dark brown hair up and wore a chic light gray skirt-suit. I stood as she stepped up and introduced herself as Aileen Addison.

I held up the empty pocketbook and said, "I don't need a receipt. Your business card will suffice."

She smiled and took out a thin card case and gave me her card.

"How is Justine?"

I shrugged again, handed her the empty pocketbook and the legal papers.

"What's this?"

"You've been served, ma'am."

I left her with a perplexed look on her face. Bonnie waved at me and I waved back.

By three p.m. I was finished. I'd call Myra Hindley, attorney-at-law, with the good news in the morning.

* * * *

The phone woke me from a dreamless sleep and my electric clock read— 5:15. I answered after the third ring.

"Morning, Pretty Baby. On your way over, pick up three coffees from Morning Call, will ya?"

Only one person called me *Pretty Baby*, Lieutenant Frenchy Capdeville, NOPD Homicide. Only time he called this early was from a crime scene he somehow linked to me.

"Where you at?" I asked in New Orleans lingo as I sat up in bed.

"You know you ain't invisible."

I stood slowly and stretched.

"Man fitting your exact description down to the cleft chin went around these penthouses asking about tonight's victim."

"Victim?" My stomach bottomed out as a picture of Justine Lake's pretty face came to mind.

"One shot in the forehead. She's on her back in the open doorway of her penthouse. You got an alibi for tonight?"

I hear him suck on a cigarette, stomach acid rising in my throat. I force it back down.

"Man fitting my description exactly, right?"

"We also found some legal papers with your signature, Mr. Process Server."

Damn. She was dead. All that young life gone.

I heard a voice behind Frenchy who told the voice "yes" before Frenchy came back on.

"OK. Bring the coffees to the autopsy. We're finished here."

"When did this go down?"

"Little after one a.m. Lady next door heard what she thought was a fire-cracker."

Justine Puddinglake who called herself Justine Lake opened her door to murder.

"Cream and sugar, right?"

"All the way around. See you in a few." Frenchy hung up on me.

* * * *

A police homicide cliché came to mind as I stepped into the autopsy room of the New Orleans coroner's office where Justine's cadaver lay on a cold steel table. Her clothes removed, her body lay pasty white beneath the harsh lamps. The cliché—there was no dignity in death, no privacy in murder, the most important piece of evidence in any homicide case was the body of the victim.

The NOCO autopsy room, better known as the chamber of horrors, was large enough to spread the smells around—formaldehyde and other acidic odors, decaying flesh, the stench of old blood.

Pathologist Dr. Alois Ziegler adjusted his wire-rimmed glasses as he dictated a description of the body into a microphone suspended from white fluorescent lights above the autopsy table, "… well-nourished white female measuring five feet, nine inches in length and weighing one hundred twenty pounds with natural blond hair, no visible scars, marks, or tattoos on the front of the cadaver."

Two coroner assistants turned the body over, and the pathologist noted no scars, marks, or tattoos on the backside. No exit wound at the rear of Justine's head. Justine was turned back over, and the pathologist measured the wound and noted, "One penetrating gunshot wound in the forehead one and one-eighth inch above the crown of the left eye. Wound appears to be from a small caliber weapon. Wound measures three thirty-seconds of an inch in diameter."

He took a long steel rod and gingerly inserted it into the wound, showing us the angle of entry and made note, "Angle of entry forty-seven degrees upward."

Dr. Ziegler's scalpel laid her open. Frenchy and I backed away to let our nostrils grow accustomed to the inner stink of a dead human. Frenchy fired up a cigarette. His normally rumpled suit looked as if he hadn't changed clothes in a couple days. His black, curly hair needed cutting, and his pencil-thin moustache needed trimming. A dead-ringer for Tyrone Power's Zorro—except for a wide nose and no Tyrone's good looks—Frenchy Capdeville has been my mentor since I was a rookie cop before the war. More like an older brother at times.

After the electric saw buzzed through Justine's cranium, the doctor located the bullet near the center of her brain, took it to a sink where he rinsed it off. Then he used a diamond scriber to inscribe his initials on the base of the projectile, away from the grooves and striations left on the soft bullet as it had traveled through the barrel of the gun—grooves and striations unique enough to positively identify the gun used, if the police found it. He passed the bullet to Frenchy on his way back to finish his autopsy.

"Small caliber, all right," Frenchy said as he used his own diamond scriber to put his initials on the bullet before dropping it in a small paper envelope. "Looks like a .25 caliber." He slipped the envelope into his coat pocket. "Just like the gun and shell casing we found at the scene."

"Gun on the scene?"

"Yep," went Frenchy.

My heartbeat rose. "Was it a Browning?"

"How'd you know that?" Frenchy fired up another cigarette. "Lifted two good prints from it."

I let out a long breath. "Yesterday, Mrs. Donna Mullenger came to my office with her lawyer and those papers I served. Said your victim stole her husband's heart. Said suing Justine was easier than shooting her with a Browning .25 caliber pistol."

"You don't say."

"I do say."

I did not bother to mention another police cliché. Detectives don't believe in coincidences.

"You got her address?"

"And her lawyer's," I told him.

"Where are those coffees?"

"I left them in the hall."

* * * *

This time it wasn't the phone, but the doorbell and it wasn't midnight yet.

I stepped out on the landing to see who I buzzed into the building as Frenchy trailed smoke up the stairs. I left my apartment door open and went to my other Frigidaire and pulled out two icy Falstaffs.

"Hit me, Pretty Baby," Frenchy said as he closed the door on the way in.

I brought him a beer and took the other to the big easy chair. He plopped on the sofa, took a hit of Falstaff, and smiled at me.

"Do all private eyes wear baby blue pajamas?"

"Marlowe prefers green."

Frenchy raised his free hand, dropped it palm down on my coffee table.

"Open and shut," he said. "Just booked Mrs. Donna Mullenger with the murder of Miss Justine Lake. It was Donna's gun, and her fingerprints on it. She has no alibi and was awake when we arrived at her house."

"She cop out?"

"Nope. She didn't believe Justine was dead at first, refused to give us a statement, and asked for her lawyer."

I took a sip of Falstaff and he told me he needed a statement from me. He pointed a finger at my nose. "My office. Eight a.m. I need that quote. What she said about that .25 caliber Browning in your office."

I nodded, asked, "Did you figure out how your killer got up to the penthouses?"

He drank more beer.

"I had to go through the department store and up the rear stairs. The store's locked up at night, isn't it?"

Frenchy grinned, "Didn't happen to notice the back door to the rear stairs, the one that opens on to Iberville Street? The lock's busted."

"It wasn't busted yesterday."

"You sure?"

"Positive."

We both downed another swallow before Frenchy went, "The question of the evening for you is did you give the penthouse apartment number to Mrs. Mullenger or her lawyer?"

I shook my head, "Nope. She didn't call and I thought I'd let you run with this before I talked to her."

I had my own questions of the evening but didn't ask them. Not yet. When Frenchy left, I opened another Falstaff and leaned back in the easy chair.

First question—How did Donna find out the penthouse number? She didn't go knocking on doors at one a.m. Maybe she knew all along. Maybe Myra knew. For certain—Carl Mullenger knew.

Second question—How does a six-foot-tall tall woman shoot a five-foot-nine woman in the forehead at a forty-seven degree upward angle? Unless Donna was a quick-draw gunslinger. Shoot from the hip.

* * * *

A copy of the two-page statement I'd signed at the Detective Bureau went into my filing cabinet. I'd carefully described my meeting with Donna Mullenger and Myra Hindley, quoting Donna saying, "She stole his heart. This way is easier that shooting her with my Browning .25 caliber pistol." I put in how Donna patted her purse and Myra touched Donna's hand to calm her.

I crossed my office to my desk with a fresh cup of café-au-lait made with steamy coffee-and-chicory and heated Pet milk, plus two heaping spoons of sugar.

If Myra were any good, she'd probably get my statement thrown out claiming attorney-client privilege since Myra came to hire me so I was part of her legal team. Better for her if it was her law firm's check I took to the bank rather than Donna's. No such thing as private eye-client privilege in Louisiana. Well, that was all lawyer stuff. My statement's true and that's all that mattered.

I scooped up *The Eagle* as I sat behind my desk and caught the headline— "Author of *Gone With the Wind* dies."

My feet went back up on my desk as I began reading how forty-nine-year-old Margaret Mitchell succumbed to "injuries received when she was struck by a speeding car in Atlanta five days ago." The article went on to explain how Mitchell's 1,037-page book brought her over one million dollars in royalties and movie payments from "the greatest movie ever produced."

The article quoted Mitchell about why she had written nothing since *GWTW*, "I haven't had time to sit down at the typewriter since 1936."

The phone rang and I scooped up the receiver.

"Lucien. It's Myra Hindley. Did you get the employment agency served?"

"I got both served."

"Well we won't need the return-of-service for the love pirate, but I'm still filing against the employment agency. I'm going to get ahold of Justine's family. Get them to join in. That agency groomed Justine to be a love pirate. What a tragedy. We have real work cut out for us now."

"We?" I put the newspaper aside.

"You didn't use up your five-hundred dollar retainer in one day. You're on the defense team now. Donna is in big trouble."

"Did you say you're going to get a hold of Justine's family on the civil matter?"

"Yes. Our case would only get stronger."

"Wouldn't that be a conflict of interest? Donna Mullenger's defense lawyer partnering up with her murder victim's family to sue a third party?"

"You don't know much about the Louisiana Bar Association. The ethics committee are the biggest crooks in the state. We're not called America's Banana Republic for nothing."

I waited a second before telling her I couldn't be on the defense team.

"Why not?"

"I just gave a statement to the police. I'm a prosecution witness."

"What? What the hell are you talking about?"

"Can't say, counselor. I'm on the DA's team at the moment."

"I'll call him right away."

"Try Lieutenant Capdeville first. He's the one who knows about the statement."

"You pull this on me, Lucien Caye, and I'll see every lawyer in this city learns you're a backstabber."

"Take your best shot, lady. How many public enemies have you caught?"

She hung up. Go ahead, let them all know I shoot straight. Only the crooked lawyers might not use me and who needs them. Uh, wait a minute. Lotta crooked lawyers in New Orleans need private eyes. Oh, well.

Spiffy. Just freakin spiffy.

* * * *

I typed out my report to Myra Hindley, attorney-at-law, and took it and the returns-of-service to the address on her business card: Law Office of Battock, Brown, and Willy, Suite 802 of the Commerce Building near the corner of Carondelet and Gravier, a short block from the Baronne Building.

I followed the returning lunchtime crowd to the elevators and waited, picking up scents of perfume and cigarette smoke. The elevator girl wore a dark purple bell-hop uniform with a double row of brass buttons. She said good afternoons to the people she recognized as they stepped in. I ended up mid-way in the elevator, turned around to face the door when the girl said, "Afternoon, Miss Hindley."

I peeked around a big man in front of me as Myra Hindley stepped in with a man who stood about five feet nine. Myra wore a snug-fitting beige skirt-suit, the man a gray silk suit. They turned their backs to me. The elevator filled. Myra smiled up at the man with her, who leaned down to whisper in her ear. She giggled and I realized they were holding hands. The door shut and the elevator started up.

Something about a lawyer in love made me a little queasy. Slow elevator took a half minute before it stopped and the operator announced, "Second floor."

Myra and her man whispered back and forth as people jostled off. They let go their hands and his hand caressed her butt, rubbed it for a half minute before they rejoined hands. Two men followed them off on the eighth floor and I trailed behind. They let go hands as they approached the second suite on the right and went in.

A minute later I moved to the glass door, peeked in, spotted a young receptionist behind a long counter. No one else was in the foyer, so I rushed in, holding the envelope with my report and the returns-of-service. The receptionist looked up when I arrived at the counter.

"I just missed her," I said.

"Who?" She was maybe twenty, her dark brown hair cut in a short page boy and she had braces, which gave her pretty face a schoolgirl look.

"Miss Hindley. Saw her in the elevator. Was that Mr. Battock with her?"

She crinkled her brow, said, "Mr. Battock's retired. That was Mr. Mullenger with Miss Hindley. I can tell her you're here."

Mullenger.

"No."

She nodded at the envelope in my hand. "You can leave that if it's for her."

I looked around the wide foyer with its Audubon prints on light gray walls, lighter gray carpet and cushioned chairs covered in silver upholstery. Two long coffee tables stood dotted with magazine.

"I'll wait."

She leaned close. "You might be a while. Their meetings go on and on."

I stuck out my hand for her to shake.

"I'm Lucien."

"I'm Clara Bow Anderson. My mother is big movie fan."

"So am I."

"There's coffee in the first room on the left," she pointed that way.

I sat in a chair and ran it through my mind. No wonder Mullenger offered a settlement. Kill the wife and everyone looks at the husband. Kill the girlfriend everyone looks at the wife. Get a solid alibi and have your girlfriend killed and pin it on your wife. Which made Myra Hindley my new prime suspect. A lawyer in love.

It made sense, but I was talking about murder and murders rarely made sense. Except in movies and bad detective stories.

But if I was right, how do I prove my case? Put it to Myra face-to-face? Maybe she'll get shook. Maybe slip up, say something. I doubted that. Someone cold enough to shoot a woman in the face won't get easily rattled. Maybe I should just leave the envelope and work on this on the sly. Still, how do I prove it?

* * * *

An hour and a half later, Clara Bow Anderson, sporting her Clara Bow haircut, gave me an "harrumpf" as I dozed. Myra led Carl Mullenger into the foyer, both smiling and holding hands again until Myra spotted me rising from my chair.

Mullenger was saying something about Florida when I stepped up with the envelope in hand.

She raised a finger to me. "I'll be with you in a minute."

I extend my right hand to Mullenger.

"I'm Lucien Caye, Mr. Mullenger." I leaned close, spoke softly but with enough volume so they both could hear. "I saw that little butt rub in the elevator on the way up."

I reached over, picked up Myra's hand and put the envelope in it.

Both looked at me with wide eyes.

I told Myra, "So this is the man who offered that settlement which you and Donna were considering."

I turned to Mullenger, keeping my voice still low. "Did the settlement include pinning a murder rap on your wife?"

He grew pale, backed away from me.

I looked at Myra. "Was this your idea? Get rid of the girlfriend *and* the wife at the same time."

Myra grimaced, leaned close and snarled, "You better get out of here."

"Or what? You're gonna call the police on me. Go ahead. Save me a nickel. Justine was 5'9". Shot came from forty-seven-degree angle upward. From someone short. Like you. Not from someone taller than Justine, like Donna Mullenger. You stole her pistol and took care of business."

Myra's eyes turned narrow. I looked at a wide-eyed Carl Mullenger.

"I know what you did, you cold-hearted bastards. And I won't go away. You can't call my supervisor on me or put political pressure on me. I'm a private eye with a good press agent."

I gave Myra a cold smile. "You read about me in the papers all the time, don't you?" I tapped my temple. "I got moxie, remember?"

* * * *

The call came at three p.m., sharp.

"OK, Pretty Baby. I got Carl Mullenger in my office with his new attorney, James Long, who says he worked with you on the Gungirl Case. He's all impressed with you."

My old Holy Cross classmate, Jim Long.

"All right. What's their beef?"

"They're worried about that statement you gave me. I let them worry."

"That's it?"

"No. Carl came to tell me he had nothing to do with the murder of Justine Lake."

"So?"

"So." I heard Frenchy take a hit of cigarette. He did that when he wanted to add drama to a conversation. "He says Myra Hindley did it all on her own."

I jump out of my desk chair.

"What? He said that!"

"We're waiting for the stenographer to get it on paper, but he already gave me a verbal statement."

"I can't believe it." Wasn't easy controlling my voice. "He folded."

Then it hit me. "Wait. You're not gonna let him walk on this?"

"Hell, no. Got two men picking up Myra as we speak. We'll see what she has to say. I plan on booking them both."

"Yeah, you're right. Myra got Justine's penthouse number from someone, and Carl's the only one besides Justine who knew it. I had to knock on doors to figure it out. Anyone knock on doors before the murder at one a.m.?"

"Nope." He sucked on his cigarette again. "I'll keep you advised."

* * * *

I wanted to be there so badly, but I wasn't a real detective. I was just a private eye, and if Frenchy wanted me there, he would have asked. I meandered up to my apartment. Fixed a ham-and-cheese sandwich and downed it with iced tea. This wasn't the time for beer.

I lay on my sofa, a surprisingly cool breeze flowing in through the open French doors. The scenario kept running through my mind, and every time I changed it, it kept coming back to Myra pulling the trigger. Did Carl know? Or maybe Donna did it after all? A quick draw. No. It was Myra. Had to be.

Didn't realize I'd fallen asleep until the phone woke me at two a.m.

"Classic, Pretty Baby. Classic." Frenchy's voice sounded scratchy. "He gave her up. She gave him up. She copped out to the shooting, but it was a collaboration. He said she did it all by herself. He has a good alibi for the night of the shooting. He was at a legislative dinner in Baton Rouge. Rode back with two state senators. Got in after two in the morning."

Not that it mattered but the newspapers and the public loved to know *why* so I asked.

"He says Myra's a crazy, possessive lover. Myra says they planned it together. Get rid of the wife. No community property split, no alimony. Old story. Kill the wife, we go after the husband. Kill the girlfriend we go after the wife. Nobody goes after the lawyer."

Frenchy yawns. "You got any smiles left?"

"Six-pack of Schlitz. Six-pack of Falstaff. Six-pack of Pabst Blue Ribbon."

"I'll be right over."

"You released Donna Mullenger?"

"Yep." Before he got off the line, he went, "You did good. Almost like a real detective." He hung up laughing. Yeah, laughing. He had arrested an innocent woman.

I got up, went out on the balcony and looked up at the dark sky. No moon. Not a star in sight. Low clouds hung over the rooftops of the old French Quarter. A cat howled and hissed, and I spotted a white streak racing through the oaks of Cabrini Park across the street. A scent of bananas breezed over me from the wharves down by the river. Someone played a violin in the distance and Justine Puddinglake, who changed her name to Lake, lay in a coffin.

Love Pirate. The hell. Justine was no love pirate. She was a young woman starting a career, accomplishing something before she fell for an older, rich man with no use for his wife anymore. The lawsuit claimed it was Justine's fault. She was a vixen, a rapacious vamp. And look what they did to her.

I whispered into the breeze, "Sorry I didn't know you, Justine Puddinglake. Sorry I didn't see this coming. If only—"

I wanted to tell her we got them, but what's the use when you're dead.

My throat tightened.

There was no solace in this. How could there be?

✗

Born in New Orleans, **O'Neil De Noux** is the author of forty-two books, more than four-hundred short stories, and a screenplay. A retired police officer and former homicide detective, De Noux has garnered a number of awards including the United Kingdom Short Story Prize, the Shamus Award, the Derringer Award, and Police Book of the Year. Two of his stories have been featured in *The Best American Mystery Stories* (2003 and 2013). In 2012, De Noux received an Artist Services Career Advancement Award from the Louisiana Division of the Arts for *Battle Kiss*, a 320,000-word epic novel of the Battle of New Orleans. He received the *2015 Literary Artist of the Year President's Award* from the St. Tammany Parish Art's Council, St. Tammany Parish, La. He is a past Vice-President of the Private Eye Writers of America. Visit him online at oneildenoux.com.

PICTURES OF LILY

GRAHAM POWELL

"The traffic cop said, 'Is it true you rammed this woman's rear end?' I said, 'Ram her? I hardly know her!'"

We were still chuckling about that when Sheila came in. Everyone else suddenly remembered some work they had to take care of right away—story time was over. "Sheila," I said. "Always a nice to see you. What brings you down to the bullpen?"

She sighed. "You can't call it that anymore, it's offensive. Now it's an open-plan office. And the Old Man wants to see you."

I heaved my bulk up out of my chair. "Got a client for me?"

"I suppose."

"A woman?"

Sheila looked back at me and rolled her eyes. She'd been a lot of fun when she was just an admin, but since her promotion to office manager she'd gotten kind of stuffy. She still looked great, though; the whole way up to the boss's office I watched her hips bouncing around like two Sumo wrestlers going at it.

"Old Man" was more of a title than anything else. The original Old Man, Murray Henkhaus, who started Professional Private Investigations, had been retired for ten years when I joined the company. His son Jack was a crusty old codger who'd died at his desk a year ago, leaving the firm to a nephew. At twenty-nine, the current Old Man was a year younger than I was.

With his slight build, thinning blond hair, and little Lennon glasses, David Evans looked more like a bookkeeper than a detective. He took that image and ran with it, smoking a pipe and wearing argyle sweater vests around the office. People thought he was smart because he kept his mouth shut, but to me, the only reason to keep quiet is to keep something stupid from slipping out.

He was chatting with a tall, dark type—black hair, black eyes, and though he'd shaved today, heavy black stubble. For variety, his suit was gray. I pegged him as a banker or stockbroker, something like that. They both looked up as I came in. "This is the man I was telling you about," said Evans. "Oliver Brownstone, our top operative."

Which was crap. Our top operative was in Monterrey, California, looking for the twenty-two-year-old daughter of the local Buick dealer. Or maybe he'd found her and decided not to come back. I'd seen the pictures; it was a toss-up.

Anyway, I smiled and shook hands, saying, "It's a pleasure."

Darkman looked me over. "Peter Grant," he said. "Nice to meet you."

"Peter is my brother-in-law," said David. "He has a problem and he needs our help."

We moved to a conference table over by the windows and sat down. Grant said, "Let's have a prayer," and he and Evans bowed their heads. I prayed for Sheila to... Well, I prayed for Sheila. When that was done Grant was ready to get down to business.

"Mr. Brownstone, I'm a respectable businessman, with a wonderful wife and two beautiful kids, but before I found my way to the church a few years ago, well, I was a little on the wild side. I drank, took drugs, stole... There's no doubt that I was bound for Hell.

"Fortunately, I met my wife Rose, David's sister, and with her help I got my life in order. My first wife and I were separated at the time, and she was more than willing to give me a divorce, as well as custody of our children. We were headed in different directions, I'm afraid, and I haven't spoken to her since our marriage ended almost twelve years ago.

"But the twins are turning sixteen this year, and they're beginning to show an interest in their birth mother. They want her to come to their birthday party later this month, and I agreed to do my best to get in touch. But I don't know if she's still in town, or even what name she's using now. My wife suggested I use David's firm. So here I am."

"All right, I'll just need some basic information to get started. What's her name? What kind of work does she do?"

Grant reddened. "Well...when she worked—which was not often—she sometimes, well, prostituted herself."

"Prostituted herself? You mean walked the streets? Turned tricks? Peddled her—"

"Yes," he said. "That's what I mean. You have to understand, we were young, we had no money. We did what was necessary to survive."

I shrugged and brought out a notepad. "I'm not one to judge. So, what's her real name?"

"Lily, Lily Fish, although she used other names when she was working, of course."

Of course. I would have too if my name was Lily Fish. "Do you remember any of them?"

He couldn't.

"How about acquaintances? Do you ever see any of your old friends?"

"No. That part of my life is over."

"How about a forwarding address?" I said.

"I tried our old apartment building, but she moved out years ago. They didn't know where she'd gone."

I studied what information I had and said, "It's the first time I've ever been *paid* to find a hooker, but what the hell! If she's still in town I can probably wrap this up by the weekend."

We all stood and Grant shook my hand. "Thank you for your help," he said. "I can't tell you how much this means to me."

"Hey, no problem." I looked over at the Old Man, who was giving me the Hard Stare. "So, Dave, cocktails after work as usual?"

David didn't drink. "That'll be all, Brownstone."

I left with a little wave and headed back to my office.

* * * *

My computer was already on, so I logged in and fired up the municipal deeds database. I called up the addresses for all combinations of "L" and "Fish," plus all first names "Lily." It took a good hour to download the data and scrub all the garbage out of it. I pulled four pages from the printer and looked over the results.

The very first hit: Lily Fish, 4402 Alvin Place. I should have looked in the damn phone book.

Alvin Place was a little cul-de-sac in a townhouse community just south of the local community college. Number 4402 was second from the end, a clapboard unit painted pale yellow. As I drove up, a blonde in maroon scrubs was at the front door, fumbling in her purse.

I climbed out and walked up the drive. "Excuse me, are you Lily Fish?" I said.

She turned and looked at me with cool blue eyes. "Why yes, I am. Can I help you?"

Well, that was easy. I got out my wallet, pulled out a random business card, and passed it over with a smile. "A friend of yours told me that you might be interested in my company's services."

She looked at the card for a moment and passed it back. "I don't think so, Mr. Nolan. Sorry."

I glanced at the card surreptitiously as I put it away. It said I was Bill Nolan and sold industrial lubricants. "Er, if you'll just give me a few minutes… We're trying to break into the household market, you know, consumers. I'm sure someone in your line of work needs reliable lubrication…" I felt a giggle percolating at the back of my throat.

Fish crossed her arms. "And what line of work would that be?" she said.

I broke down and laughed. "Look, I'm sorry. I'm actually a private detective. Are you the Lily Fish who was married to Peter Grant?"

She shifted uncertainly. "Yes, we were married. Why? What's wrong?"

"Oh, nothing. Earlier today he hired me to help him get in touch with you."

"Peter's looking for me? I don't understand."

"It's your kids. Their birthday's coming up, and they'd like to meet their birth mother."

"The twins?" she said, lighting up. "They want to meet me? But what about their stepmom?"

I shrugged. "Apparently she's okay with it. Can we go inside and talk?"

* * * *

The house wasn't much, two bedrooms upstairs, a living room, and a kitchen, but it was well maintained and absolutely spotless. Maybe I could hire Lily to clean *my* apartment.

We climbed the stairs to the master bedroom. Lily sat at a small dressing table and picked up a hairbrush. "I hope you don't mind. I'm going out in a little while."

"Oh, please, be my guest," I said.

Where Sheila was stick-skinny, Lily was more substantial in every way. Broad shoulders that tapered smoothly to a slender waist. Flaring hips, and a slightly plump derriere. Her hair was long and honey-gold, a shade or two lighter than her deeply tanned skin.

And her breasts, my God. They stood to attention like good soldiers when she reached back to tie her hair in a ponytail. I swear, my little dinghy nearly slipped its moorings.

"So the twins are excited to see me?" she asked.

"Uh, so I've heard. I think they're more curious than anything."

"Yes," she said. "I wish I'd met them years ago, but Pete wanted me to stay away. I suppose it was for the best. He really hired a private detective?"

"I'm living proof." I stopped staring at her breasts long enough to take a look around the room. Pictures of the two boys covered much of the walls. In their baby pictures they were held by a younger Lily, sometimes with a bushy-haired Grant looking on. After the age of four the photos mostly showed the boys alone.

"What did that crack about 'my line of work' mean?" she asked suddenly.

"What? Oh yeah, the lubricant gag. I got that card from a client like five, maybe six years ago—"

"But what's it got to do with *me?*"

"Well, ah, Grant said that you used to, how best to put it…"

"Put out?" she said. "Sell my body?"

"Exchange sex for cash, yeah."

She shrugged. "I quit that a long time ago. I'm too old to sit around in bars or stand on street corners."

I looked at her scrubs. "So now you're a nurse?"

"Oh, I just wear these around town. These days I mostly I do porn."

My ears weren't the only things that perked up. "You *what?*"

"I'm a cam girl—you know, on the Internet. You may have heard of that? I stroll around the house *au natural*, put on a solo show every once in a while, that kind of thing. Sometimes if I meet a guy I like I'll bring him home and make him a star. Plenty of dorks online will pay twenty bucks a month to look at a naked woman."

I looked around again. "Are we on camera right now?"

She laughed. "I have another place I use for that, a kind of studio. Don't worry, no one's staring at your gut."

"What gut?" I said, sucking in a little. "So you still work in the buff, but now you're mostly on your own?"

"It's safer." She gave me a little smile. "But, if someone wants to take me to the Winchester Suites for the weekend, buy me a nice dinner, maybe an unexpected gift or two, of course I'd be grateful. Very, very grateful."

"Really? How much would all that run?"

"If you have to ask, you can't afford it." She glanced at my midsection. "Besides, dude, that thing might kill me."

I swelled with pride, among other things. Then she said, "No, not *that* thing—your belly! And there's no workman's comp for dirty movies."

"Just hop on top," I said. "My girlfriend says it's like bouncing on a beach ball."

"You have a girlfriend?" She rolled her eyes. "*Men!*"

I let out a guffaw. "All right, no weekend at the Winchester. What else you got?"

"You don't give up, do you?" Lily turned to me and smiled sweetly. "I'll tell you what. For twenty bucks I'll let you watch me get dressed."

My eyes got a little wider. "No kidding."

"Same deal as my website, or my name's not Ainsley Pierce."

"Your name's *not* Ainsley Pierce."

"It's the Internet—who's gonna know? Now pony up."

I had my wallet open before she'd finished speaking. She took my Andrew Jackson and tucked it into her hip pocket. Then, without further ado, she peeled off her top and shucked out of her pants.

In white cotton underwear she waltzed across the floor and into the bathroom. As she reached up to undo the clasp of her bra, she looked at me over her shoulder and winked. "Make yourself at home," she said, and shut the door.

I took her at her word gave the bedroom a good once-over. Tucked away in the dresser I found half an ounce of fine Columbian and some cigarette paper, so I rolled myself a nice fatty and was puffing away when Lily emerged from the bathroom, wrapped in a towel.

"Hey!" she said. "That's my stash!"

"It *was* your stash."

"Man, that's just rude. And what the hell were you doing in my underwear drawer?"

"Just poking around. Want a hit?"

She chuckled and shook her head. "You're really something," she said. Then she slipped off the towel and casually tossed it on the bed.

I nearly had a stroke. That golden brown tan covered every inch of her body. Her skin ran smooth, without a wrinkle or blemish, from her shoulders down to her ankles. She'd missed a few spots when she dried herself—beads of water clung to the undersides of those lovely golden globes. I wanted to dive in and splash around a bit.

"I see you're a natural blond," I said.

She glanced down and laughed. "Some girls bleach down there."

"No shit? The mind boggles."

She pulled out a pair of red satin underwear and stepped into them, then got out some sort of lace-up bustier. "Some help?" she said.

Lily held the thing in place while I struggled to pull it tight. It was at least two sizes too small. Strapped in, her chest looked like a bomb ready to explode. Over that she put on a demure long-waisted frock. Her hair she wound up into a bun. A large pair of glasses completed the ensemble.

"Schoolmarm?" I asked.

"Librarian. Some men long to awaken the passion of the prude."

"Not just some," I said. "What are you doing later on?"

"Working. Listen, I'm free tomorrow. Why don't you give Pete a call and set up a meeting?"

"Pete?"

"Peter Grant. Your client."

"Oh, uh, yeah, that sounds like a fine idea. I suppose it's best to meet on neutral ground. Why don't I come pick you up, say about seven?"

"Just like a date. What would your girlfriend say?"

"What she doesn't know can't hurt her," I said. "And, more important, it can't hurt *me*."

She smiled. "See you at tomorrow."

* * * *

I climbed in my Corolla and headed back downtown. I needed to put in some more billable hours on this job so I stopped off at the Noble Savage. Their pepperoni pizza really hit the spot, as did the beer I washed it down with.

After another beer I called the Old Man on my cell phone. "I found Lily. She wants to meet with Grant tomorrow night, somewhere quiet."

"You already—wait, are you at a bar?"

"It's really more of a restaurant. I'm just around the corner, I'll come up in a minute and submit my report."

A minute turned into another two beers. By the time I returned to the office it was around seven, and most everyone had gone home. There was still a light burning in the Old Man's office, so I stopped in.

I brought him up to speed on the events of the afternoon. When I'd finished, he said, "Nice work, Brownstone. How many hours do you have on this case?"

"Six," I said quickly.

His eyebrows went up a notch. "Really. Peter only hired us about six hours ago."

"And I've been working tirelessly ever since."

"All right." He took off his glasses and rubbed his eyes. "Just type up your report and email it to me. I'm going home."

"Will do. And don't forget," I said, leering. "If you want to check her out, just search for Ainsley Pierce."

He just stood there silently until I shuffled off to my cubicle.

The report I banged out in fifteen minutes, then I downloaded Sheila's picture from the company website and wasted an hour Photoshopping her face on the models from RedHotMammaJammas.edu.

* * * *

The next day I worked a few routine cases, but mostly I dodged the boss and surfed the web in my cube. Lily's site was pretty basic, but what it lacked in style, it made up for in content. In the cold light of day it was clear that my senses had not been impaired by her intoxicating nearness—she was a very attractive woman. Most of the fifty or so pics in the free gallery showed her alone in a spartan bedroom, usually naked, occasionally joined by one "friend" or another. At six thirty I logged off and headed to her place.

I reached Lily's house a few minutes before seven. She didn't answer when I rang her bell. I waited a few minutes and rang again, then rapped on the door with my knuckles.

It swung open halfway.

I pushed it open the rest of the way and went in, calling Lily's name. No reply. The ground floor was uninhabited, and I climbed the stairs to her bedroom.

A few of bottles of makeup lay on the floor beside her dressing table. The bed was mussed, the bedspread lying in a heap on the floor. Aside from that, nothing. If there had been a struggle it must have been between pygmies.

I resisted the urge to go through her underwear drawer again and gave the place one more look before calling in the cops, and that's when I saw it.

Poking out from under the bedspread was a bare foot.

I knelt down and steeled myself for what I would find, then carefully lifted the bedspread and looked beneath it.

I wasn't ready.

* * * *

I had never seen the Old Man's face so red. "You found a *what*?" he shouted.

"A severed leg."

"From a *what*?"

"An animatronic sex doll. She moans, moves around, does everything but fix breakfast."

Evans was out from behind his desk, pacing up and down the room. "But why severed? And what was it doing in her house?"

"Hell, I don't know. Maybe Lily needed a friend to talk to, someone who would understand her."

He stopped and glared at me. "This isn't funny, Brownstone."

"I never said it was. So where's Lily? Kidnapped? Hiding?"

"What are you asking me for? How would I know?"

"It was a rhetorical question, and here's another: is it a coincidence that I found her yesterday, and she's disappeared today?"

"You think Peter had something to do with it?"

I waited while Evans tugged at his lip. Finally he said, "If we screwed up, I want it kept in-house. She's not officially missing for seventy-two hours. If we haven't found her by then, we'll bring in the cops. Now I have to call Peter and tell him the meeting's off."

"Tell him it's been delayed an hour. I'll meet him then. Oh, and I'll need the company credit card."

He was in no mood to argue.

I went back to my office and within five minutes I had purchased a membership granting me full access to Lily's website. Quickly I looked through the members-only galleries for anything out of the ordinary. Within half an hour I had picked out five of the photos and sent them to the color laser printer. I stuffed the hardcopies in a briefcase and hurried out to meet Grant.

We'd reserved a small private dining room at the Old Orleans restaurant, situated on a small bluff overlooking the river. Grant was waiting for me.

"Well, it's about time," he said as I shut the door behind me and took a seat. "Where's Lily?"

"She's not coming. You and I need to talk. And I hope you checked your bullshit at the door."

He started to protest, and I tossed the pictures on the table.

Grant's eyes widened and his mouth worked silently as he stared down at the paper spread before him. The pictures from Lily's webcam showed the two of them engaged in the favorite sexual positions of missionaries, dogs, and the French. "It was a mistake, only one night. What do you want? Money? I'll pay, but for God's sake don't tell my wife."

"This isn't a prayer group, so let's leave God out of it. I'm more interested in your reasons for retaining the services of my employer. You obviously had Lily's address."

He ran a hand through his hair. "How long have you known?"

"That your story was crap? Since I first set foot in Lily's house. You said you hadn't talked to her in years, but she had pictures of the kids plastered on every surface, many of them recent."

"I had to keep it a secret. My wife would never understand. Yeah, we talked from time to time, and I sent her pictures of the kids. But this…" He waved at the photographs. "I was out with some friends after work. When they left I stayed to finish my beer. Lily turned up as I was leaving. She looked great and was happy to see me. Pretty soon we were doing it just like old times."

"You're a jerk and a hypocrite, Grant, but I believe you. These pictures have a timestamp in the top right corner. All taken the same day, all within half an hour of each other." I chuckled. "Half an hour. Is that the best you can do, Romeo?"

He turned bright red and I laughed loudly. "So, why did you actually hire us? Why not just say you did, and then produce Lily's address?"

"It was my wife, she suggested it. David's her brother. If I lied about bringing you in, she'd find out about it. I didn't have any choice, man, I was stuck!"

"When was the last time you spoke to Lily?"

"Not for a week or more. I have to be careful. My receptionist goes to our church. I think my wife has her spying on me." He took a sip of his water. "My wife's a hard woman, Brownstone. She cleaned me up, got me back on the right track, but she only knows one way. You do things the way she wants or you face the consequences. She has ways of punishing you."

I stood. "There're worse things than not getting any. You shouldn't let her lead you around by the dick." I handed him one of my cards. "If you hear from Lily, call me immediately. It's very important."

It was his turn to smile. "Miss her already?" he said.

"Go home, Grant," I replied. "And say hello to the Snow Queen for me."

* * * *

I slept fitfully and dragged in to work around seven. Lily was still gone, and I didn't have a clue where to start looking. I could have started on all the routine drudgery, running known associates, tracking her movements the day she disappeared, and so on, but while that works, it's boring as hell and better left to the police. I'd have more luck putting up flyers.

And that *did* give me an idea. I brought up her site and found a good picture of her kneeling on the bed, naked, staring straight into the camera. Her face was as clear as a bottle of vodka, but you had to look carefully to see the T&A. And that was the point. To make you look carefully.

I created a *Missing* flyer with my name and number across the top, ran off a dozen copies, then pulled on my coat and hustled over to the other side of downtown.

The Winchester was a boutique hotel, pricey and exclusive. They'd carved it out of the old Dixon building in the mid-80s—twenty-three luxury suites in the heart of the city and only a few blocks from the riverfront, a perfect love shack for lonely businessmen. All the comforts of home without the missus dragging you down. Lily mentioned she'd had an occasional tryst there. Maybe somebody knew something.

Of course, a place like that provided discretion along with the Perrier. They wouldn't talk without a little encouragement.

I walked past the desk without slowing and continued to the elevator. As soon as the doors closed, I taped a flyer below the row of buttons. At the second floor I got off and made my way to the ice machine and posted another flyer there. I spread those dirty pictures around like a venereal disease. After finishing up the fifth floor I caught the elevator back down to the lobby.

A big, burly man and a small, fussy one were waiting for me, dressed like twins in burgundy suit coats with the hotel's crest on the pocket. The muscleman had one of my flyers in his hand. "This is the guy," he said.

The little one looked me over, lip curling. "Throw the bum out."

"Good idea," I said. "On the sidewalk I can pass these out by hand, make sure all your guests see them."

The bruiser started forward but the other one laid a hand on his arm. "Wait a sec, Gene. Maybe I'd better find out what his game is."

Gene didn't like it, but the little guy finally convinced him. He led me to a door labeled *Concierge* in the corner of the lobby. The office was as artsy-fartsy as I'd expected, with prim little plaster statues and lots of cut glass and flowers. I made myself comfortable while he stood behind the desk, sulking.

"If it's money you want, you won't find it here," he said. "We don't deal with blackmailers."

"I already have a job. I'm just looking for a little information. As soon as I get it, I'm out of here and you can get back to concierging." I glanced at his nametag. "Sound like a deal, Richard?"

"I prefer Dick."

"Sorry, I'm taken." I passed over a flyer. "Have a look at this girl. When was the last time you saw her?"

He tossed the paper to his desk. "I've never seen her before…"

"Don't bullshit me, Dick. I know that she comes through here a couple times a month. Who have you seen her with?"

His mouth tightened until his lips disappeared. "I'm don't discuss the private business of our guests."

"If I was running a whorehouse, I wouldn't advertise it either, but you don't have that option." I waved the flyers. "Either tell me what I want or grease up for a reaming."

He looked at the photo. "I may have seen her before," he said.

"Who with?"

"She's accompanied Grayson Earle upon occasion. And Raymond O'Doole. There were a few others."

He grudgingly gave me their names, which I noted in my memo book. When we were done, I tossed the remaining flyers in the trash and stood up. "It's been a pleasure, Dick. A little advice? Loosen up. One day you're gonna sneeze and your head's gonna explode."

His eyes narrowed. "Piss off, asshole."

I laughed all the way back to the office.

* * * *

Tracking down the men whose names he'd given me turned out to be an exercise in frustration, and I hate exercise. Though they were well-known public figures they were pretty well insulated; I don't know if they gave the slip to every private eye looking for dirt, or if it was just me, but I was blocked at every turn. Neither charm nor bribery did any good, and I tried plenty of both. Damn economy had everyone so afraid for their jobs they wouldn't let slip even a peep.

Eventually the pints down at the Savage sang their siren song, and I was headed out the door when I caught sight of one of the pictures of Lily that I'd printed. She lay on her face in bed, sleeping, her rounded butt jutting proudly in the air.

At her studio. Not her home. *Her studio.*

I plopped back down and started pecking at the keyboard.

* * * *

The apartment was registered to Ainsley Pierce. That took me a while to figure out, and it was dark by the time I arrived in front of the apartment complex in Shreve Island, not far from her home.

A narrow sidewalk led around back to her unit. I knocked without result and was studying the lock when her door suddenly opened inward and a man dressed in dark clothing ran headlong into me.

I managed to get my dukes up just as he slammed a knee into my crotch. My eyes jumped out a couple of inches and I swear I heard my balls rattle around in my skull. Another shot to the groin and my legs seemed to retract into my body. I fell heavily and the man raced around the side of the building out of sight. A car engine roared and faded into the distance.

I lay there for a while, taking a little breather. After ten or fifteen minutes I decided that if I ever wanted to walk again, I'd better get started. So I gingerly got my legs under me and eased myself to my feet.

The apartment was nearly empty of furniture. The living room held only a flea market sofa and a pockmarked coffee table. A queen sized bed filled most of the tiny bedroom. At its foot stood a tripod-mounted camera, with a cord leading to the closet, where I guessed she had her internet server.

A suitcase was open on the bed, clothes heaped in it haphazardly. It looked as though I'd interrupted someone packing to leave.

Lying next to it was a man fully dressed in a pinstripe suit. I recognized the Roman nose, bushy eyebrows, and noble mane of Grayson Earle.

The bloody lump on his temple, that was new.

"Now we're getting somewhere," I said.

I flipped open my cell and tapped out a number. After listening to a few minutes of bitching and moaning I had what I needed. I hung up and dialed the Old Man. "Boss," I said. "Get Peter Grant down to the office first thing tomorrow morning. We need to talk."

When I'd finished, I made another call, my last of the night.

* * * *

They had already assembled when I arrived next morning. Sheila was there, steno pad in hand, wearing a lime green skirt, with a matching purse slung over her shoulder. "Dave, Mr. Grant, Sheila," I said nodding to each in turn. I turned to the man who'd walked in with me. "You know Inspector Lennart, don't you, boss?"

"Yes, of course," he said, but his eyes said *What the hell are you doing?*

The rest of us gathered in front of the Old Man's desk, Grant and I in the chairs, Lennart standing between and just behind us. Sheila took a seat to one side. I cleared my throat. "I suppose you're wondering why I've asked you here today…"

"I think we've got a pretty good idea," said David. "Where is Lily?"

That got Grant started. "Yes, where is she? You said the other night that she'd be along, but I haven't seen her, heard from her—"

Lennart nudged his elbow. "Keep quiet, you."

"Where's Lily?" I said, hamming it up. "That's the question, isn't it? One of you knows the answer. One of you is a stalker, and damn near a killer, and I know who. But don't take my word for it." I looked over at the door and said, "Okay, come on it."

The door opened and Lily stepped through. She'd dyed her hair black but it was still as thick and lustrous as ever. I wondered if she'd taken that disguise below the belt.

"That's him!" she said, pointing. "That's the son of a bitch who attacked me!"

David, the Old Man, look around at each of us. "What?" he said. "That is totally ridiculous! What reason would I have to attack her? We've never even met!"

Lily wasn't finished. "That motherfucking pervert had the doll with him. He said he'd seen my website and couldn't stop thinking about me. Said he wanted a threesome with him and his 'girlfriend.' He offered me money. I told him to fuck off and he got pissed. We struggled. I ended up with the doll and slung it at him, and the leg came off in my hand. I didn't wait around to see what he would do next."

"This is an obvious setup," said David, fuming. "I'm not going to stand for it. I know people on the force, people more senior than you, Lennart, and they're going to hear from me, count on it."

"You're forgetting something." I pulled a sheaf of folded papers from my inside coat pocket. "You found out where Lily had her pad, and last night you went by, but someone was already there. Lily had called up Grayson Earle, a close friend of hers, and had him go pick up some clothes. He was nearly done when you surprised him. Damn, Dave, what kind of pussy beats up an old man?"

I threw the papers in his face, and they scattered across the desk. The light wasn't as good as in the other photographs from Lily's camera, but you could clearly see two men struggling, one falling on the bed. As the other ran he stared straight into the camera. David Evans.

For once, the Old Man looked old. He pressed his hands to his face, then let them drop in his lap. The he opened the drawer of his desk and pulled out a revolver.

"Don't do it!" cried Grant. "Don't shoot yourself!"

I saw the look of tight-lipped desperation on Evan's face and said, "I don't think that's what he has in mind."

"Nobody move," he said. He stood and slid around the side of the desk. "I'm leaving, and if you try to follow, I'll kill you."

"David, please," said Grant. "Do the right thing and give yourself up."

"Shut up, Peter. If you hadn't been such a fool none of this would have happened. Oh, and by the way, I'm telling your wife about you and Lily."

"Now you're just being petty," I said.

Suddenly Sheila stood up. "David," she said breathily. "Before you go, there's something I've always wanted to do." She pressed herself against him and planted a kiss right on his lips.

We were all as stunned as David was. Then I saw Sheila's hand snake down into her purse and emerge wrapped around a pair of brass knuckles. She pushed David away and snapped a sharp uppercut under his chin. His eyes rolled back and he slumped to the floor.

I could have kissed her then, and would have, too, if she hadn't been armed.

After Lennart had left with a dazed David Evans, I caught Lily staring at me. "I don't leave my camera on when I'm not working," she said. "Did those come from my apartment?"

"Oh, hell no," I said, laughing. "Well, not really. I called Lennart over to your studio last night, and after we got Earle packed off to the hospital, we staged a fight and got some pics. I Photoshopped Dave's face on later."

"How is Grayson? Is he going to be okay?"

"That's what the doctors say. He had a concussion. That was pretty slick, getting the Winchester to register you as Miss Ainsley Earle. I guess old Grayson pays well for discretion." I made a mental note to visit Dick the concierge for a little talk when I had some free time.

Lily smiled and stepped closer. "I really appreciate all you've done," she said, as the sweet smell of her perfume surrounded us. "I'd like to show you how much it means to me sometime."

My face got as red as a baboon's ass. "Well, the thing is, I really do have a girlfriend, and she's got a temper. If she found out I cheated on her, she'd break it off, and I don't mean our relationship. I'm sorry—you have *no idea* how sorry—but…"

Lily laid a finger across my lips and smiled serenely. "Bring her," she said.

For once, I was speechless.

✗

Graham Powell was born in Austin and has lived all over Texas. A fan of private eye stories as far back as the Hardy Boys, his work has appeared in *Fedora 3, Thrilling Detective, Plots with Guns, Needle Magazine,* and the recent anthology *The Eyes of Texas. Bad Men,* his collection of crime stories, is available from Amazon.

SHOW AND ZELLER

GORDON LINZNER

Gregson Harris stopped just before passing through the glass doors of Annie Moore's. Something spooked him. A reflection in the glass, perhaps. It wasn't the dripping overhead air conditioner, or the reckless cyclist tearing along the sidewalk. It certainly wasn't me. Had he realized the nondescript, slightly overweight middle-aged matron across the street was following him, I'd have known, and one of my subordinates would take over.

It wouldn't be the first time I, Dorian Zeller, had been outed by an observant subject or a bit of bad luck.

But this was only the first day of a new case, and I'd barely been tracking Harris for a quarter hour from his office through the streets of midtown Manhattan. Even the most careless private investigator would have to go out of his way to be spotted among the milling lunchtime crowds.

Annie Moore's was a relatively cozy Irish pub on East 41st Street, near Madison Avenue. If his wife's suspicions were correct, Harris was likely meeting his lover here for lunch.

He only hesitated an instant, but I recognized the stance. I shrank back in my post across the street, trying to blend in with a plain metal wall, pretending to take a picture with my phone of one of the metal placards embedded in the sidewalk, adopting my best ignore-the-tourist pose. Julys in New York were increasingly hot and humid; I couldn't carry much in the way of changing my appearance. A low profile was essential.

Harris abruptly spun around and dashed across the street toward me. An irate cab driver braked with a screech and a honk. I doubled down on my photography. Harris raced past me, across Fifth Avenue, and up the wide steps between the marble lions guarding the main entrance of the Mid-Manhattan library. Patience and Fortitude, they were named, a fitting mantra for a private investigator as well.

I started after him, got only a few paces when I heard the shouting. Another man, muscular and mustachioed, in his late fifties, wearing a black T-shirt and jeans, chased after Harris.

Either Cassandra Harris hedged her bets, hiring a second detective agency to also keep tabs on her husband—a bad idea, as she'd claimed to be strapped for cash, and two investigators were more than likely to get in each other's way—or a third party was interested in Mr. Harris' movements.

In any case, the newcomer was a rank amateur.

If I were made, or thought I'd been made, I'd simply return to the office. I still combed my hair forward to cover faint scars from the first (and last) time I tried pursuing a job anyway. And that was after the self-defense classes.

I focused on the man in black. Obviously his cover was blown. If I tried outpacing him, I'd reveal myself to both him and Harris. Should he manage to get eyes on Harris again, and keep from being spotted a second time, he could be my buffer as he led me to my subject. More likely, he'd lose Harris entirely, which would at least provide me with an opportunity to find out what he wanted. In any case, the lunch date, whether innocent or salacious, was off the table.

If Gregson Harris was smart, he'd head straight for the side exit on 42nd Street and disappear into Bryant Park. If he were smarter, he'd hide in the lobby, wait for his pursuer to enter, then slip back out again.

I positioned myself near the building's northeast corner. This provided a decent if less than ideal view of both main and side entrances.

Minutes later, the man in black stomped back down the marble steps, scowling in frustration. The guard in the doorway seemed none too cheerful, either.

I watched him slowly retrace his steps across Fifth Avenue and, unexpectedly, enter Annie Moore's.

* * * *

In front of the pub's floor-to-ceiling windows frontage, I stopped, pretending to answer a text. My new subject took a stool near the front of the bar beside a much younger man. They obviously knew each other. The latter did not look pleased. Annie's old location, on 43rd Street, had many crannies inside where one could stand unnoticed, but an office tower had taken its place, so I remained outside until the pair seemed fully engrossed. Then, phone in hand, I slipped within.

Engrossed was too weak a word. Their discussion quickly became a shouting match. The bartender hurried over, but before he could intervene the younger man stormed out. Phrases like "twice your age" and "your mother's condition" stood out.

Some customers shifted further down the bar, leaving me an opening. Typing, I perched one stool away, muttered "Guinness" as the bartender cleared away the lad's half-finished IPA. Said bartender then raised the glass in front of my subject and said, "This is on your tab." Not a question. A statement.

The man sighed, slumped, and dropped his Visa card on the bar. I read the name Sanchez as the bartender snatched it up.

"Bourbon. Neat." His tone reeked of defeat.

I finished play-typing, laid my phone face down on the bar. "Kids," I muttered.

He turned. "You say something?"

I sighed. "My daughter. Been texting all day. Why don't I pick up? Why can't we talk more? She says I'm a terrible listener. She broke up with her boyfriend and is blaming me." I shrugged. "You have children?"

He grimaced. "You saw how well we get along."

"That was your son? Wow."

"It took my wife and I a while to accept his sexual preferences. He still doesn't trust us."

I cupped a hand behind one ear to indicate I couldn't hear clearly, then slid over to the stool beside him, ready to continue our conversation. As I'd planned.

"I warned Katie her guy was a narcissist," I confided. "She might've dumped him earlier I'd kept my mouth shut."

Sanchez nodded. "Peter's got a crush on an executive where he's interning, a man twenty plus years his senior. I'd hoped to confront that man today. He keeps dodging me."

"I'm sure you'll have other opportunities." I reached for the menu. I knew better than to push, while still leaving myself open should he voluntarily wish to say more.

"I'm just looking out for my boy..." Sanchez began.

My imaginary daughter would be proud. Poor listener? Ha!

* * * *

Many investigators find computer searches tedious. To me, they're simply another kind of surveillance, with less risk of being noticed. A post-lunch session in the library's computer room proved more productive, and less adrenaline-inducing, than my earlier time on the street. Nothing disappears from the internet, if one knows where and how to look.

In a now defunct social media site called AllPlanet, by reading between the lines on his posts from the late 1990s, I found definite hints that college-age Gregson Harris was at least intrigued by the possibility of exploring alternate sexuality options. Peter Sanchez had outed himself long before attaining legal drinking age; his father had confirmed that much. What Rafe Sanchez omitted was his own arrest record; as a teenager with a short temper, he'd been accused of involvement in the death of a rival street gang member. Lack of evidence, and a really good lawyer, got him a plea deal of six months in prison and three years' probation.

"So you're positive," Cassie Harris repeated, when I called to update her, "that my husband is not spending our thousands on an affair with another woman, or some young stud, or a neighbor's Great Dane...?"

I resisted the urge to respond with a joke of my own. Let her relieve her frustration whatever way works.

"Not so far as I've determined. I'm looking at some other avenues, but marital cheating looks increasingly unlikely."

"Then what has he been doing with our money over the past year? Is he being blackmailed for some other shady activity? Has he acquired a gambling habit?"

"I'm investigating all possibilities. I've arranged for a pair of very discreet colleagues to meet your husband and his friends, separately, casually. That should give me more to go on. We'll have your answers by the end of the week..."

"Not sooner? I remind you, my resources are running low."

"We'll have answers," I repeated, and hung up. Whether those answers would prove useful was another issue.

I returned to Harris's workplace that afternoon to continue my surveillance. At five minutes to six, he sauntered out of the building, stopped for a quick drink at a nearby bar—not Annie's—then headed downtown to the Tribeca loft he shared with his wife. My cab had no problem following his.

I took in the fancy brickwork of the former factory, then decided my day was done; the rest of the evening, he'd be Cassandra's problem.

The next day, a bigger problem arose.

* * * *

Though I sub-contracted the task of uncovering hidden financial transactions to a more experienced colleague, I spent most of the morning in my air-conditioned Upper West Side apartment, which doubled as my office, trying to track Gregson Harris's money myself. Sometimes a less skilled researcher can stumble across a detail missed or ignored by the expert; it happened to me twice, often enough that I didn't mind the redundancy. Neither I nor my colleague were having any success, which in itself was suspicious. Why would a man draining his own funds, even if jointly held with his wife, go through so much trouble to hide his tracks? How did he do it so well?

Around eleven I pushed the keyboard aside, rubbing my eyes. I needed to go downtown for a few more hours of surveillance, assuming Harris didn't eat lunch in.

My preparations were immediately interrupted by a visitor: Cassandra Harris.

Her eyes were red and puffy; her hair mussed. I decided not to press for an explanation. She seemed otherwise fairly composed as she took a check from her purse. "I believe this is the amount you quoted me for two days. I added an extra ten percent for additional expenses. Plus any inconvenience."

I took the check. I'm not an idiot. "Have my services not been satisfactory?" I asked, even as I used my phone to deposit the amount directly into my business account.

"They were. But they are no longer required."

"Did you find your missing funds? You're still entitled to my efforts until the end of the day, should you wish..."

She shook her head. "That is no longer a concern."

I nodded. "You realize, I can accept no responsibility if Mr. Harris continues depleting his—your—accounts."

"That won't be happening. Mr. Harris is dead."

I widened my eyes, waiting for the punchline.

"He left our place on Hudson Street around one this morning, as far as I can tell," she added. "His body was found behind a dumpster on Staple Street, two blocks from our loft. One shot, through the forehead. He died...instantly, the police said. No suffering." She rubbed her dry, reddened eyes.

"A mugging gone wrong?" I mused aloud. "A bookie tired of waiting? A blackmailer?" Neither of the latter were likely; people demanding money don't kill the prospective source. And the timing for a mugging seemed rather coincidental, even given the area's high crime rate. "They're sure it's him?"

"I identified the body myself. The police caught the man. I've got that consolation, at least. I still blame myself."

"Oh?"

"You mentioned the man at the bar. I told Greg I knew about it, didn't say how, and said he should man up, meet this Rafe Sanchez character, reassure him he was just mentoring his boy. I had no idea he'd do it that same night."

"I didn't give you Sanchez's name."

"The police did. Sanchez had been texting Greg vague threats over the past week or so. Probably got the number from his son. My husband used that number to send a text, at my unwitting instigation, asking that they meet that night to clear the air. The police tracked the number to Sanchez. No doubt they'll find witnesses to put this low-life at the scene."

The picture she painted of Rafe Sanchez didn't quite fit my impression. I let that slide. "And the several hundred thousand dollars you may have floating around?"

"Really, Miss Zeller! Stop bringing that up!"

"My apologies." Despite years of self-training, from time to time my low-end Asperger's pops up. "Although that was why you hired me."

"As far as I'm concerned, that money is gone. I don't care how foolishly my husband may have spent it. His life insurance will tide me over for now. I ask again, for my own peace of mind, that you drop your investigation."

A ping from my bank confirmed that her check had cleared. "You're the client. I'll comply with your request at once. I am no longer working on your behalf."

"That's all I ask."

"If you need me to follow up later..."

"I doubt it. Have a good day, Miss Zeller. I have funeral arrangements to make."

I shook her hand and saw her out. I had arrangements of my own to make. Such as meeting a potential new client.

* * * *

Three days later our paths crossed again, this time at her loft in Tribeca. I'd been summoned there at her request.

"I ordered you to stop investigating my case."

"I'm not working on your case. I have a new client. Rafe Sanchez."

"I know," she snapped. "You're the one who got my husband's killer released! Do you know what that feels like?"

"He didn't kill your husband. You know that."

"I don't even know how he can afford your rates!"

"I do pro bono as well. When appropriate." I settled into a too-soft settee as the widow paced angrily in front of me. "See it from my point of view, Mrs. Harris. Peter Sanchez, Rafe's son, confirmed he'd told his mentor, your husband, about his father's past. Gregson Harris was reluctant to face any physical threat, real or imagined. So reluctant he scurried away from meeting Rafe Sanchez on a crowded street, in midtown, in the middle of the day. Yet he apparently was fine with setting up a meeting that same evening on a little-used side street in the dead of night.

"Similarly, you felt compelled to nag him about his cowardice within hours of learning of it, yet for a year didn't even hint at your concern over depleted bank accounts."

The woman stopped pacing. "Maybe my husband intended to murder Sanchez himself, get him out of his life. Or not murder, but to scare him off by brandishing a gun."

"You told the police your husband didn't own a gun. Nor was there any sign of a struggle during which Rafe Sanchez could have taken the gun from your husband."

"You have been busy, haven't you? I told them only that I didn't know about a gun. My husband is dead! Could you stop besmirching his character? You've nothing to gain by it."

"Except to establish a man's innocence. Rafe Sanchez may have a temper, might even kill someone in a rage, but for him to cold-bloodedly and with forethought shoot a man in the head at point-blank range? I think not. The police agreed."

"He was seen in the area. Explain that."

"He'd gotten a text that your husband wished to meet him. He waited an hour for Mr. Harris, then went home."

"You've only his word."

"And the word he texted on leaving. 'Cobarde.' Coward."

"Fine. Your client had the best motive, but let's say someone else got to my husband first. A bookie to whom he owed thousands. A blackmailer he tried to get rid of. A fellow worker whose dark secret he was about to reveal. Show me who else would want Gregson dead."

"You've been watching too much television, Mrs. Harris. Only one person had a strong motive for killing your husband. A person who squirreled away hundreds of thousands of dollars from your joint accounts, and knew Gregson was about to find out."

"You're accusing me? I'll ruin you, Zeller!"

"You can try."

"You have no proof or you'd have given it to the police. They'd be here now."

"Oh, it's there. Give it time. Your husband's cellphone, for example, that he allegedly texted Sanchez from. Forensics was able to access its information with minimal contact. Whoever used that phone last left fingerprints. If they aren't your husband's, who else could they belong to?"

She stared coldly, licking her lips, not speaking.

"One could have used gloves, but that's difficult on such a tiny keyboard. Or done a voice to text conversion, but that might leave a record. Or tapped out the letters with, say, a hairpin. Provided one thought that far ahead."

"You're bluffing. How would you know?"

"I'm off the job, remember? The police may or may not have enough to pursue a case against you. I do know one thing for certain."

Her glare deepened.

"If one cent of the money your husband supposedly took from your accounts turns up, and they trace it back to you...well, there's the motive. It's pure speculation until then."

Cassandra Harris strode to the non-working fireplace and grasped one of the decorative andirons.

"Here's some speculation for you," she snapped. "Suppose an intruder makes her way into a grieving widow's home. At least, an unwelcome guest. A person she fired. Threatens blackmail. Maybe threatens her life. Wouldn't she fight back?"

I got to my feet. "Bad idea. I'm trained in self-defense. More importantly," I pulled my cellphone out of my purse, "every word we've spoken has been forwarded to the NYPD. And uploaded to the Cloud, for good measure."

"I admitted nothing."

"That's the spirit!" I turned and left the loft as Cassandra Harris slowly, ever so slowly, lowered her andiron.

It wasn't a complete win. Not yet. But satisfying enough, for now.

Gordon Linzner is founder and former editor of *Space and Time Magazine*, and author of three published novels and dozens of short stories in *F&SF*, *Twilight Zone*, *Sherlock Holmes Mystery Magazine*, and numerous other magazines and anthologies, including *Footprints in the Stars, The Mountains of Madness Revealed,* and *Across the Universe.* He is a lifetime member of SFWA.

MUSTANG SALLY

JOHN M. FLOYD

My client, a red-haired young woman in jeans and a yellow T-shirt, sat silently in the chair on the other side of my desk and inspected my office. I hadn't even heard her come in over the sound of the ceiling fan; my door's always open, and when I looked up from my morning paper, there she was. She of course wasn't yet a client, since she had yet to speak to me, but I hoped she would be. I needed the work.

Her gaze had settled on my window, and she seemed to study the trees in the park across the street a moment before turning to face me. She had green eyes.

"Thomas Langford?" she said.

"That's me."

"Your ad said you're a private detective."

"Investigator." I folded my paper and took my feet down off the desktop. "And your name is . . ."

"Sally Marshall."

Her cheeks, I noticed, were almost as red as her hair. I figured she was either embarrassed or overheated. Maybe both. This was, after all, summertime, and even though fish were jumping and the cotton was high, the living wasn't necessarily easy. It was hot as the hinges of hell, even at ten in the morning, and the A/C in my building wasn't the best. That's why I kept the fan on and the door open.

"Want a cup of coffee?"

"It's too hot for coffee," she said.

"You're right." I leaned back and put on what I hoped was a professional face. "How can I help you, Ms. Marshall?"

A word of explanation. At the time that I met Sally Marshall, I'd already been in this job a few years. I wasn't as smart as Holmes or as brave as Spenser or as handsome as Magnum, but I was a former cop and a pretty good investigator. And I thought I'd heard it all: *my supposedly disabled employee is teaching an aerobics class, I think my Russian brother-in-law has bugged my apartment, my neighbor's cat keeps peeing in my flowerbeds, my husband ran off with my best friend and I miss her.*

But I'd never heard anything like this.

"My ex-boyfriend's father's dog," she said, "ate my diamond ring."

I stared at her a minute. "It's also too hot to be April Fool's Day."

"I'm not fooling," she said.

But she admitted her story was strange. Ms. Marshall, it turned out, was a freelance writer and had taken a taxi earlier this morning to the home of a Mr. George Neely to pick up a car she had loaned a week earlier to his son Wilson—the aforementioned boyfriend. "Will parked it in the barn," Neely told her. "Stay here, I'll back it out." They said nothing more; she and the old man had never liked each other. It was while she waited in the driveway, she said, that a skinny black-and-white spotted dog with one ear missing popped up out of nowhere and approached her, growling and baring its teeth. She backed away, suddenly aware that there was no place to run. Then she remembered her heavy, hard-soled sandals. Slowly she bent her left leg and reached down with her right hand to slip off a shoe while at the same time holding her left palm out in a stop-right-there gesture to the dog. In a terrified but soothing voice she said, "Take it easy, doggie. Good doggie—"

And it lunged forward and bit her.

"On the hand?" I asked. My eyes immediately went to her left hand, expecting to see the ragged stub of a ring finger. But her hand looked fine—not even a bandage.

"I was lucky," she said. "Technically he bit me—his jaws snapped shut on my fingers—but the ring must've got in the way. It was brand new and loose anyway, and when I snatched my hand out of his mouth, his teeth dragged it right off my finger." She held up her hand, and I could see a long pink mark above the nail of her ring finger. "Probably one chance in a million, but that's what happened."

"So, this ring—you're sure the dog swallowed it?"

"Positive. Gulped it right down. I think it scared him—might've scratched his throat—because he jumped back for a second, and when he did, I whacked him in the nose with my shoe, and he yipped and took off running around the side of the house."

"What happened then?"

"Mr. Neely backed my car out and pulled up beside me. He looked at me a little funny when he got out—I mean, I was standing there shaking and sweating and holding one shoe in my hand—but he didn't say anything. I'm pretty sure he hadn't seen what happened with the dog."

"And you didn't tell him?"

"No. I was pretty flustered, and old George wouldn't have done anything about it if I had. I just hopped into the car and drove off. He probably thought *good riddance*."

"And you came straight here?"

"Not at first. I drove around awhile, thinking. I'd seen your ad someplace, a week or two ago, and for some reason I remembered it."

Probably my stunning photo. But right now, I was wishing she hadn't seen it at all.

"You sure this dog belongs to George Neely?"

"I'm assuming he does. It was there at his house."

"But you never saw him before, right? The dog, I mean."

"No. This was only the second time I've been to George's house. It's pretty close to my apartment. Wilson lives on the other side of town."

I paused a moment, thinking. None of my thoughts were good. I studied her face, which seemed a little less flushed now. Her red curls stirred in the breeze from the ceiling fan.

"You said this was a diamond ring?"

"Two carats," she said.

"A wedding ring? I thought you said—"

"Engagement. Wilson and I were supposed to get married."

"Supposed to?"

"We broke up," she said. "Two nights ago."

Which explained the *ex*-boyfriend. "But you kept the ring."

"Damn right I did."

"Even though you're no longer engaged."

Her eyes hardened. "He gave it to me. It's mine now."

"Did Wilson agree with that?"

"Doesn't matter if he did or not. He has plenty more where that came from." She paused then and focused on me. "So, are you gonna take the case, or what?"

"Get your ring back, you mean?"

"That's what I mean. That's why I'm here."

"And how do you propose I do that?"

She shrugged. "That's up to you. You're the investigator. My suggestion would be to get the dog and keep him until he . . . well . . ."

"Produces the goods."

"Right."

I drew in a long breath and let it out. "Ms. Marshall, have you considered talking to the police about this? Or maybe Animal Control? I mean, the dog did attack you, and they could—"

"No police," Sally said. "No dogcatchers, no veterinarians, none of that."

"Why not?"

"I have my reasons." Her face had reddened again. "Are you gonna help me or not?"

We stared at each other awhile, and I heaved another sigh. I guess nobody ever said this job was easy.

I took a minute to give her the standard spiel about daily rates and expenses, but both of us knew they wouldn't apply. What had to be done here would probably have to be done today, over the next few hours. Instead we agreed on a one-time fee of two thousand dollars, payable if and when I deliver the ring. I felt like one of those bloodsucking, ambulance-chasing lawyers—you pay us only if we win the case.

Sally Marshall and I shook hands across the desk. Then she stood up, we exchanged a final frown—smiles had not been part of our meeting today—and she left. I watched, from my window, as she crossed the street and climbed into a bright red Mustang. It looked a little like my Camaro in the parking lot behind the building, though mine was older and plainer and had trouble getting started. Like me.

I tucked George Neely's address into my pocket, sat again at my desk, and Googled several sources describing the average dog's digestive tract and how long it might take an ingested foreign object to pass from point A to point B. I saw nothing encouraging and many things disgusting, but I was now at least armed with some basic information. I figured I had from six to twenty hours to locate and secure the treasure. Anything longer than that, my quest would be over and my modest reward lost.

My last thoughts, as I locked the office and headed down the stairs, were about business opportunities and life decisions and taking pride in one's chosen career. I had studied accounting in college, for cryin' out loud. I could be doing someone's taxes right now.

My car started on the third try.

* * * *

My first stop was Walmart, where I bought a packet of latex gloves, a sturdy leash, a small Igloo cooler, a bag of ice, and a fat sirloin steak. If I couldn't find the dog, I would at least have a good meal. I dumped the ice and the steak into the cooler, piled it and the rest of my purchases onto the passenger seat, and took off. En route, I phoned my longtime and infinitely patient girlfriend, Debra Jo Wells, and left her a message that I might be late for our date tonight. I didn't tell her why. We never shared details about our work with each other anyway—she was a paralegal at a law firm five blocks from my office—and I sure didn't plan to start now.

George Neely's home was a tired-looking ranch house at the edge of a patch of woods just south of town. I parked in the gravel driveway and waded through weeds to the front door with a cautious eye on the shrubbery. For all I knew, it might be hiding a mean, one-eared dog.

The man who answered the door looked like John Huston, the late actor/director. Big guy, bags under his eyes, long face, maybe seventy. I introduced myself and shook his hand. Unlike what I'd expected, he seemed friendly.

"What can I do for you?" he said.

And I gave him the only story I could think of, the first part of which was true.

"I'm working for a young lady who says she came to see you this morning," I said. "Sally Marshall. Says she knows your son."

"Yep. Sally and Will was a big thing for a while there. Thought they was gonna get hitched. Don't know the whys and wherefores, but things didn't work out. Can't say I'm sorry—that gal's a little odd. Anyhow, she came today to pick up the car she'd loaned him."

"You don't mind me asking, why'd she loan it to him?" Something, I only just realized, that I should've asked her myself.

He shook his head. "Beats me. Maybe his was in the shop."

"And why would he leave the car here for her, instead of taking it back to her place?"

"'Cause they broke up, I guess. All I know is, Will left it here yesterday, said since Sally lives close by, she could pick it up whenever she wanted."

"Sounds like the two of them didn't split up on good terms."

"I can't say, there. My chillun don't tell me much."

"What does he do, your son? For a living."

"You know, I ain't really sure, no more. Don't see him nor talk to him often. These kids, they got their own lives now, too busy for the old folks. He does well, though, moneywise."

"I believe you," I said. Two-carat diamonds don't come cheap. Actually I was beginning to give some serious thought to Wilson Neely. I was fairly sure I'd seen or heard the name before. "Anyway—what I really came here for was to ask if I could borrow your dog for a day or so. I got a leash in the car. I'd be happy to pay you for the favor."

I don't think I could've surprised him more if I'd told him I'd just beamed in from Mars.

"You want to borrow my dog?"

"More like rent him. Just for a while. The thing is, Sally says she saw him here yesterday, the spotted one with a missing ear, and she's being paid to write a piece for the paper about a new dog park here in town, and she wants to go spend some time there but she needs a dog to take with her, and well, you see where I'm going, here . . ."

He let out a laugh. "You're going back emptyhanded, is where you're going. I seen that one-eared dog, too, earlier today, but he ain't mine. Don't know whose he is or where he belongs. In fact, last I saw of him he was headed out to them woods over there, about the time Sally left."

Whoa. "So you don't have any idea where I might find him."

"Not a clue. It'd be a needle in a haystack, I expect." He shrugged. "Sorry."

Oh well. So much for my Frodo Finds the Ring adventure. There was just one more thing.

"That car of hers," I said. "It's a red Mustang, right?"

"Yep. A twenty-ten, I think."

* * * *

Sally Marshall's apartment house was less than a mile west, but I headed north instead, to my office. Several things were nagging at my mind, and though I could've probably found the answers via my phone, the computer on my desktop would be easier.

One thing that bothered me was the name Wilson Neely. It was definitely familiar, and the faint bell it rang in my mind was more an alarm than a jingle. The other thing was, if Sally's former boyfriend was so well-off, financially, why borrow her car for a week, and why drop it off at his father's place when he was done? Even more to the point, why hide it in the barn?

And why had Sally been so dead set against involving the police?

Finding what I needed didn't take long. The online editions of recent newspapers gave me the story I wanted. One of the biggest jewelry stores in the city had been robbed by a masked gunman five days ago—I vaguely remembered hearing about it—and the local TV stations' websites said the suspect was still at large and unidentified. And a call to my old buddy Ronnie Robertson at police headquarters gave me two facts that the news stories hadn't included: (1) Wilson J. Neely was a convicted felon, having served time in the state pen for fraud, assault, and assorted other crimes, and (2) a red fifth-generation Ford Mustang had been spotted leaving the jewelry store the night of the crime and had also been seen parked in the area twice in the two days prior to the robbery. Sally had been right when she mentioned something about her ex-boyfriend not needing her ring because he had "plenty more where that came from." He probably had a bagful.

Wilson Neely's father might not know what shenanigans his son was up to—I somehow believed him there—but I had a feeling Sally did know.

Even so, she was my client, and I felt I owed her a report. First things first.

I drove across town for the second time that day, the leash and other dog-catching supplies still lying unused on the passenger seat, and found Sally sitting on the little patio in front of her apartment building. I pulled up a chair and told her the bad news. The dog that bit her was a stray, he didn't belong to George Neely, and he was gone with the wind. So was her ring. Although by this time I knew, and so did she, that it wasn't hers at all, and hadn't been Wilson's either. I shook her hand one last time, put the chair back where I'd found it, and left.

I turned right on Magnolia, not far from her apartment and about halfway between her place and George Neely's, and had aimed my Camaro north toward home and was thinking about lunch when I saw the dog. Skinny, black-and-white spotted, one ear missing. He was sitting in a clearing beside the road, calmly watching the passing traffic as if taking a count.

I pulled over and parked. He was still there. Holding my breath, I took the cut of steak from the cooler, picked up the leash, got out, and walked toward him.

* * * *

That night Debra Jo and I met for a late dinner, downtown. As we climbed out of our cars my cell phone buzzed, so I stayed outside the restaurant to take the call while she went in and found a table and looked over the menu. I joined her five minutes later, and we had no other interruptions. After dessert and coffee we strolled the two blocks to the park across the street from my office building and sat together on one of the wooden benches. It was still humid—we were used to that—but the nighttime temperature was down to something at least reasonable. A warm breeze riffled the leaves of the oaks that lined the sidewalks.

"Who was it on the phone, earlier?" she asked me.

I turned to study her profile in the dim light of the streetlamps.

"Ron Robertson. He was working late."

"Your old partner?"

I nodded. "He called to say they'd caught the guy who robbed that jewelry store the other day. Recovered most of what was stolen. Came from an anonymous tip, phoned in to Ronnie this afternoon. Says he's a hero now." What I didn't add was that Ronnie also assured me that Sally Marshall would be kept out of the story. I had told him that she'd almost certainly known about what happened, but only after the fact. And keeping her out of it would keep me out as well. I doubted George Neely would remember my name, if he even remembered my visit.

"I'm happy for Ronnie," Debra Jo said. "But I'm also happy you're not there anymore. On the force, I mean."

"Me too," I said.

She snuggled into my shoulder. It was quiet in the park. Overhead, visible through the leafy branches. a quarter moon floated in and out of the clouds.

"Thanks again for the ring," she whispered. "It's beautiful."

"I should've done it a long time ago."

She raised her left hand, turned it a little to catch the light. "Where'd you get it?" she asked.

I smiled into the darkness, enjoying the smell of her hair, and the trees, and the city around us. I'd had my share of bad smells, this afternoon.

"You wouldn't believe me," I said, "if I told you."

John M. Floyd's short fiction has appeared in *Alfred Hitchcock's Mystery Magazine, Ellery Queen's Mystery Magazine, The Strand Magazine, Mississippi Noir, The Saturday Evening Post,* and many other publications. His stories have also been selected for inclusion in three editions of *The Best American Mystery Stories* and have been optioned for film. A former Air Force captain and IBM systems engineer, John is an Edgar nominee, a four-time Derringer Award winner, a recipient of the Edward D. Hoch Memorial Golden Derringer Award for lifetime achievement, and the author of eight books.

FUNERAL POTATOES

E.E. KING

I live in Hollywood. Not up in the Knolls, where the scent of money is stronger than night-blooming Jasmine, or near the Boulevard, where hawkers dress like Superman or Marilyn Monroe and pose with the tourists, but over on the flatlands, on Barham. It's near the freeway. The constant whoosh of cars is like an ocean, but fishier.

I don't often get away from the city. But, for the first time in years, I was taking a vacation from smog, dirt, and murder.

I'm a PI, a private investigator. I had just finished a nasty case. I'd found a missing child and a nest of human vipers. It was the kind of case that made you feel as if you'd never be clean again. I wanted to wash my hands and my soul. I wanted to forget the whole rotten human race.

So, I went up to Alta to clean my wounds and my memory. Alta's a small town high up in the mountains above Salt Lake City. In the winter it's a popular ski resort, but the rest of the year it's almost deserted. It's the Alps on steroids. America's answer to Switzerland, bigger, higher, and so full of flowers the paths look like earthbound rainbows. It's a place perpetually stuck in the early 1950s. An America I'd thought never existed outside the imagination of advertisements and TV shows. The place made me nostalgic for a time I'd never known.

* * * *

It's difficult to believe that the state is one of the driest in the nation because here, in the heights, it's lousy with water—lakes, streams, and waterfalls, cold as melted snow, which isn't surprising because that's what they are. It's dry in another way though, heavily Mormon and morally teetotalling. You can get beer at the grocery or 7-11, unless you want it with alcohol. You can only get alcohol at the State Liquor Stores, which are carefully hidden, and even there you can't get it cold.

Utah beer is 3.2% alcohol and tastes like weak piss. I didn't care. I wasn't here for the nightlife, which was good, since it consisted mostly of bats and owls.

I was staying at the Silver Fork Lodge, a rustic B&B with a view of the whole valley and the mountains beyond. I'm not much for long hikes, but I enjoy putting on my waders and fly-fishing. I seldom catch anything, but that's not the point. There's a special peace to standing alone mid-stream, cut off from the world. To casting a line into space and watching it arch into gently flowing water.

I was the only overnight guest at the Silver Fork, though lots of locals came in for lunch and dinner. On Friday, a couple of Chicago Paddies moved in— Peggy and Mac, a red-faced, couple in their mid-fifties, as hearty as lager stew.

"Ya know," Mac, said, "Peggy and I are takin' the time we never had, to see each and every state."

"Exploring just as if it were a foreign country," Peggy added.

"And it is! Three-two beer and no whiskey for sale except in pubs or state stores."

"And the food," Peggy laughed. "Oh lord it's awful, but the mountains are fierce, and the folks are friendlier than a smile."

"We plan to go to a Mormon potluck on Sunday," Mac said. "Care to join us?"

"No thanks," I said.

"We'll bring you back a doggie bag," Peggy said.

"Woof," I said.

She giggled.

After breakfast, they left to survey the state like the alien country it was. I left to submerge myself in the serenity of the stream. I went to bed early and woke late. There was nothing, nothing but time and the river.

It was ten a.m. when I went for breakfast. I sat on the deck watching hummingbirds dive bomb interlopers. Hummers are a possessive lot, amazingly pugnacious for something so tiny, midget hell raisers with wings.

Tammie, my usual waitress, didn't come to the table—three days, and I was already hidebound.

Tammie was one of those pretty, healthy girls they specialize in up here. She always seemed ecstatic to see me. Being a waitress from Utah is a high fructose combination.

Most of the kids who worked here were local, a healthy, good-looking bunch that were clean, cheerful and sweet smelling, even if they'd just finished hiking.

Utah's a good place to escape to. Everyone's polite and vigorous. Everyplace is tidy. Everybody seems prosperous. You don't fear walking dark night streets. The only uninvited visitors are missionaries, and the only truly dangerous thing is the food, which owes most of its substance to Campbell's Cream of Chicken soup, Jell-O, and fat.

There's a Stepford wives' quality about the place. The waitresses all have names like Chrissie, or Katie, or Kathy. They're skiers, hikers, and mountain bikers. They have strong teeth, wide smiles, muscular legs—no acne, cavities, or original thoughts. They're good kids—even the bad ones. Bad is relative. In Utah it might mean having a drink, a smoke, or shopping on Sunday. Where I come from bad kids are really bad—murder, gang warfare, rape, and vandalism on Sunday. It's difficult for me to get excited about a few drinks or some fooling around.

I guessed Tammie must be having a day off, probably running a marathon. Instead, Christie, one of the other regulars, came to take my order. Her face was red and raw like she'd been crying—and she had. Her nose was running so violently I was afraid she'd drip snot into my water glass. If the Utah niceness was catching and she was contagious, I'd have to find a new line of work. Maybe it wouldn't be so bad. I'd join the church, get bonded for life to some sweet, sweet thing and have twenty children. There's a joke they tell up here. Why do Mormons stop having kids at thirty-five? It's a good number.

"What's wrong?" I asked Christie. I really didn't want to know. I didn't care if her dog had died, her boyfriend had left her, or if she'd discovered she had herpes. All I wanted was a cheese omelet, a cold beer, and to be left alone. But it's hard to ignore a snotting waitress.

"Tammie's dead," she sniffed. She began sobbing, long and hysterically, gasping for air between gulps, like a swimmer caught in the undertow.

"She died last night," she howled. I raised an eyebrow, motioning to the seat across from me. Christie's legs buckled. She collapsed into it, pouring out her grief in inarticulate sobs, as if I'd asked her to.

"She was fine last night," Christie wailed. "We went out after work and had a few drinks at the Canyon Inn."

I guessed Tammie and Christie were what they called the Jack—or maybe in their case Jill—Mormons, gals who'd been raised in the faith but had fallen away. Some were still believers, but didn't like all the rules; no alcohol, caffeine, cigarettes, or sex and lots of home teaching. But in Utah even the apostates were syrup sweet and too wholesome.

"We didn't drink much," Christie sobbed on, just as if I'd been paying attention, instead of imagining casting my leader far off into still waters—not to mention my cold beer and cheese omelet.

"In fact, I don't even think she'd finished one, when she said she had a stomachache. Then she doubled right over, fell on the floor, and curled into a li-li-little b-b-ball." She sniffed. "We rushed her to the emergency room, but she d-d-d-died about half an hour later."

Burrowing her face in her hands, Christie fled howling into the kitchen.

Another server came to the table to take care of me. His nametag read "Greg."

"I'm awfully sorry about that Mr.," he said. "It's been a real tough day."

I nodded and ordered my food. After I finished, I went up to my room, grabbed my gear and headed out to the Mill Creek River.

It was a lovely day, blue skies; such as you never get in the city, white fluffy clouds, and bird song. But I couldn't stop thinking about Tammie—she'd been a sweet kid, which seemed the norm here. In LA she'd probably have received sainthood. Why would she just die? A poisoned drink? It didn't seem likely.

I left the stream after an hour. Despite the chirping birds and gently moving water I couldn't find peace. I was going to visit the coroner. Then I was going to track down Tammie's whereabouts on the day she'd died. It was just what the doctor ordered, another nonpaying case.

Driving down into the city, the blue, blue skies dimmed to grey. The Great Salt Lake lay before me, an inland ocean, but much more saline. Gangsters could never have invaded the city because it's practically impossible to sink a body in Salt Lake. Even cement overshoes float.

I had a little trouble finding the place because the city and its environs have very few street names, only addresses. These are laid out in a grid stemming from the central temple. Every address marks how far you are from the temple. At 9088 South 43265 East, I was very far indeed, but I knew that anyway.

Utah drivers are surprisingly rude, I guessed all that treacle politeness must damage their car seats, because they shed it when locked inside their urban attack vehicles. I'd never seen so many SUV's, except in LA where they are necessary to traverse the rough terrain of uncertain prestige.

"Can I help you?" asked a smiling, blond clerk in the coroner's office. Her desk plate read "Pammie Truly."

I showed her my card. "I'd like to talk to the coroner," I said. "There was a death last night that I'm investigating, and I have some questions."

She checked out my credentials and put in a call to Blake Edwards, a friend at the FBI.

"Do you know a Mr. Eddie Evers," she asked. "Uh hum. Yes. Un hum. Oh certainly! Thank you, Mr. Collins.

"He says to afford you any help we can," she squealed. "To think that you know the head of the FBI!"

The coroner was a plump, doughy woman named Mrs. Smoot, who seemed like she would have been more at home in a bakery. She was practically salivating with the excitement of answering my questions. I was a big time PI here—I'd worked with the LAPD and the FBI. She didn't know that I'd been rubbing two dollars together for a month, just trying to get them to mate. She didn't know that I barely made enough to pay for my nasty little dive on Barham. She didn't know that the only thing I could reliably afford was self-denial. But it didn't matter. It's difficult to be altruistic when all you can think about is how to pay rent—but the last case I'd done had set me up for at least a month or two. And Tammie had polluted my trout stream with her demise.

Mrs. Smoot's report only heightened the mystery. Tammie appeared to be in perfect health, except for the fact that her liver had dissolved. Even if she'd been a heavy drinker for fifty years, instead of a twenty-two-year-old who'd had a few drinks on weekends, that kind of damage just wasn't natural. You need some serious toxins to liquidate a liver.

I thanked Mrs. Smoot and left. I began to retrace Tammie's steps. The day she'd died she'd gone to a potluck with her family—mother, father, boyfriend Ray, four sisters and three brothers, it was a typical Mormon family. It didn't seem possible anything at the potluck could have been the culprit, because there'd been at least twenty people there. But I found the name of the guy who had arranged it, Elder Loveless, and paid him a visit.

Loveless' house was modest by Utah standards. It would have been a mansion in LA. It was a neat affair, picket fence and cropped, weed-less lawn. I don't know what they do to weeds in Utah, but I swear I'd never seen so many perfect greens outside of Pebble Beach.

Loveless greeted me at the door. He wore a white shirt, black pants, black shoes, black tie, and a constant smile.

"Greetings neighbor," he said. "What can I do for you today?"

"Well," I said, pulling out my card. "I'd like to talk about the potluck you gave the other day."

"Certainly," he said. "I'd be glad to. I host these gatherings at least twice a week or so and they're fine. But you don't need to be a private investigator to come to the next one," he chuckled. "Just bring an open heart, a willing spirit, and an empty belly.

"In fact, I'm having another one down in Moroni Park after church tomorrow at 2:00. The park's on 8409 South 2609 East."

"Thanks, Elder Loveless," I said. "But I'm actually calling because one of the people at your party, Tammie Darling, died rather suddenly yesterday. It seems like it must have been some kind of poison. I'm trying to track down everything she ate."

"Well," he said, pulling his lips down in a facsimile of sorrow. "Isn't that just terrible! Such a sweet, sweet spirit, bless her heart. I must go see her folks. They're good people. How on earth did she die?"

"Her liver dissolved," I said.

"Well, that's just horrible," he said. "But the good lord must have his reasons, which we poor sinners cannot yet fathom. I'm sure she's in a better place."

"No doubt," I said, looking around at Loveless's décor. Plastic runners covered his light beige carpets and his beige couches were coated in plastic slipcovers. A picture of some guy kneeling before an angel, who was zapping him with gold light beams, graced one wall. The other had a portrait of Jesus, who bore a striking resemblance to Fabio.

"Could you tell me what was served at the potluck?" I asked.

"Well surely, Mr. Evers," he smiled again, displaying every one of his perfect teeth. They must have a lot of dentists in Utah.

"Since I'm hosting another tomorrow, to which you are invited, I can do better than that. I can show you the spread. But it is a potluck you know. I supply the main dishes, but I can't tell you exactly what everyone else brought to share."

"That'll be fine." I said. I followed him down the plastic path to a spotless white kitchen. Every counter was covered with Mormon delicacies. There were crudités topped with cheese wiz, slices of Velveeta and white bread. There were potato chips complimented by a dip of Cheese Wiz, Philadelphia cream cheese, evaporated milk, and sweet pickles. There were a kaleidoscopic variety of Jell-Os with otherworldly suspensions of shredded carrots, peas, and cubed ham floating in them like a science experiment gone bad. There was Frog's Eye Salad, an ambrosial addition to any potluck. It was made from small pasta balls mixed with a tub of whipped topping, canned crushed pineapple, and canned mandarin oranges. There were Hawaiian haystacks, a tasty concoction of white rice and refrigerator scraps exotically set on leaves of iceberg lettuce.

The pièce de résistance was a dish they called Funeral Potatoes. It was casserole of shredded potatoes submerged in a can of Campbell's Cream of Chicken soup, topped with sour cream, crowned with cornflakes and baked until molten.

"And I make mine special," Loveless grinned. "I add some mushrooms to the mix."

"Delicious," I said. "If there's one thing that recipe was lacking it was fungus."

"The Sisters usually bring dessert," he smiled. "Sister Hunsaker makes the finest divinity fudge you'll ever taste."

"I'm sure of that," I said.

"What's this," I pointed to some peculiar red lumpy red and green confections stacked on a plate by the immaculate sink.

"Popcorn balls," He smiled. "It's mini-marshmallows, corn syrup, salted nuts, chocolate chips, Jell-O, and popcorn. Would you care for one? There're truly delicious."

"I really shouldn't dilute your potluck supplies," I said. "Besides, I just ate." I hadn't, but I'd lost my appetite somewhere around the Frog's Eye Salad.

Mormons replace caffeine, nicotine, alcohol, and sex, with Jell-O, cheesy casseroles, economy desserts, and secret underwear. Everyone needs opiates.

"Did you know that Funeral Potatoes and green Jell-O, were immortalized in a set of collectible pins from the 2002 Winter Olympics?" Loveless beamed.

"That's a bit of useful knowledge of which I was ignorant," I said.

I left him in his doorway, smiling, waving, and re-inviting me to his Sunday potluck. "And bring your friends!"

I continued retracing Tammie's activities. The food seemed toxic, but not lethal—not liver dissolving.

I visited the Canyon Inn. At about three p.m. mid-week, it was almost empty. Just a few busty smiling barmaids and a couple of old men clutching drinks in their withered hands, waiting for the second coming. The barmaid had heard about Tammie but offered no insight.

I visited Tammie's grieving family but didn't stay long. Her parents greeted me and invited me in. I wondered how, with nine kids, they kept their place so clean. Their carpets were bare, but like Loveless, their furniture was shrouded in clear plastic. I wondered if neatness and tackiness were dominant genetic traits among Mormons, along with strong legs, good teeth, and horrendous recipes. I watched their external politeness battle their internal anguish. Mrs. Darling brought forth cookies and tears. Mr. Darling apologized for her display of waterworks. I hated battering words against the wall of their misery. What did I hope to discover? Tammie's death was a mystery and would remain so. People dropped dead every day for no explicable reason. I returned to the Silver Fork, sat on the deck, and watched the sun sink into the haze over the Great Salt Lake.

I spent the next day, Sunday, in the river, watching the water flow around me like liquid peace.

When I returned to have dinner at the Silver Fork the entry was blocked by two police cars, red and blue lights flashing. An ambulance was screeching away down the canyon. I wondered if some overly ambitious rock climber had fallen from the heights, or if someone had been swept away in one of the torrential rivers. In LA it would have been gang warfare, here it was more likely to be an irate moose—still, dead is dead. What did it matter where you had met your end, in a dirty back alley or scaling a marble mountain above flowing waters? You were gone, no longer concerned by anything. Wind or smog, water, or fire, all were equal now. You were past caring.

I parked a ways from the Silver Fork and walked toward the door. The police were leaving when I got there. I knew better than to ask what had happened. Police don't like to talk to strangers, especially large ones from the big bad city.

Greg, Christie, and the rest of the staff were there. It was crowded. The Silver Fork was a popular place to hang out and watch the sun paint the mountains gold. Though the room was packed, it was quiet as a deathbed.

"What happened?" I asked Greg.

"It was Peggy and Mac, that nice couple from Chicago," he said.

"They were so sweet," Christie sniffed. "Such kind, good people bless their hearts."

"Are they...?" I let the sentence dangle. Greg looked at his shoes, minutely examining the laces as if searching for an answer there. "I don't know. They're taking them to the hospital but..."

"Th-they had just come back from their potluck," Christie wailed. "They sat down and ordered two beers, but before I could even bring it th-th-they j-j-just c-c-collapsed."

"Do you know what else they did today?" I asked.

Greg slowly shook his head. "They asked where there was a church, a Catholic church. Mac said he wasn't that religious. But Peggy liked to go on Sundays and take communion."

"She said it w-w-was like wearing clean un-un-underwear in c-c-case you were hit by a c-c-car." Christie sobbed. "They looked just like Tammy did before s-s-she..."

Greg awkwardly patted her arm. "Why don't you go home now, Christie," he said. "It's been a long day."

She fled into the kitchen, nose dripping onto the wooden floor, leaving a damp trail of sorrow behind her.

"After church they went to Elder Loveless's potluck. They were just like two kids," he shook his head, "invited to a picnic. They seemed fine when they came in. Said what a nice time they'd had, and then, well it was just like Christie said.

"It all happened very fast. They complained of stomach pains and collapsed on the floor. I called 911. I think they were still breathing, but they didn't look good." He shook his head again and sighed. "Poor Christie. She's all shook up."

There didn't seem anything to do. I wanted to go to the hospital and see how they were, but I'd just have been in the way. I sat out on the deck and watched the sun streaking violent colors across the sky, like a child finger-painting. I wondered if it was Peggy and Mac's final sunset.

It was. I found out the next morning and returned to Mrs. Smoot, the friendly mortician, for a chat.

"It's really odd," she said. "I've never seen anything like it, and now three cases in three days.

"They both appeared to have been very healthy. The man had had a slight heart murmur, but nothing worth worrying about. And just like that girl, their livers were total mush."

"Any idea what might have caused it?" I asked.

"Nope," she said, shaking her head, "It's a real mystery."

I drove back through the gridded streets of Salt Lake to Elder Loveless's door.

He was there, and apparently happy to see me, if smiles are evidence of joy. He seemed to be wearing the same black pants, shoes, and tie as yesterday and a duplicate starched white shirt. But the pants seemed too spotless and pressed and the shoes too polished not to be new. Maybe he had a closet full of identical clothes.

Once again, he was shocked and dismayed to hear of the deaths. Once again, he had nothing to offer but an invitation to another potluck.

Three days later there was another death. Everyone at the Silver Fork was talking about it. Salt Lake has a population of almost 200,000, but because of the pervasive religion it has the feel of a small town. Mormons, and their children, whether Jacks or Jills, share a common culture and many know each other from the endless meetings, ward parities, and home teachings.

This time it was Elder Doolittle who had met his maker. He was high up in the church, a president or a prophet or something. He'd been a hale and healthy fifty-six-year-old, married, with nine children. According to all he never drank, smoked, swore, or shopped on Sundays.

The trout stream had lost its calm. I smelled something funny, and it wasn't burnt Jell-O.

I went down to the morgue.

"Why Mr. Evers," said Mrs. Smoot. "It's so peculiar. He seems like he was in perfect health, but his liver has completely dissolved. I just don't know what's happening."

There didn't seem to be anything else to say. I left and went to Doolittle's house. It was about the last place I wanted to go, but something didn't add up.

Doolittle lived in a house that was a giant copy of the others I'd seen. The door was opened by a pretty girl of nineteen or so. She had blond hair, fine cheekbones, and a nice pair of legs. But her eyes were red and puffy from weeping.

"Yes," she said. "Can I help you?"

"I'm very sorry to disturb you," I said. "I'm a private investagator, working with the police. I'm trying to discover what caused your father's death."

Her eyes wided, as if I'd told her I was a magician.

"You're a private eye," she breathed. "Hold on let me get my mom."

I waited on the doorstep feeling like the fraud I was. A soft, round woman in a neat, flowered housecoat wandered out.

"Hello, I'm Mrs. Dolittle," she said holding out her hand. "Peggie says you are working with the police?" I nodded. "Mr...?"

"Evers," I said.

"Evers," she repeated. "I'll be happy to assist you in any way I can, of course. Please come in and sit down."

We sat on her beige, plastic-covered couch which could have been a big brother to Loveless's. Maybe the Mormons have figured out how to get furniture to reproduce. It would explain a lot.

Four small faces peered around the doorway, examining me with the interest a scientist might show for a new species of mold. I grinned at them and they vanished.

"May I get you anything?" Mrs. Doolittle said. "Some soda, or cookies maybe?"

"That would be great ma'am," I said. I didn't want anything except a little time. As soon as she had gone, I raced down the hall. Another small face peered at me from one of the doorways. But I bared my teeth and it vamoosed.

I found what I hoped was the master bedroom. The drawers were full of neatly folded undergarments. The clothes hanging in the closet were color coded, dark to light, waiting tidily for Mr. Doolittle, who was never coming back.

Beneath the bed, stacked in neat rows, like tiny green soldiers, were dozens and dozens of NyQuil bottles. I heard a noise behind me and straightened up. Peggy stood in the doorway watching. I grinned what I hoped was a *just doin' my job,* look and slithered past her.

I slid onto the couch, reaching home plate just as Mrs. Doolittle wobbled through the door balancing a cup of something orange, a plate of Rice Krispies squares and what may have been a few cookies, though all that was visable was a thick coat of hard pink hard frosting topped with multi-colored sprinkles.

I smiled and sipped the orange stuff. It was orange juice cut with Tang. "Did Mr. Doolittle suffer any health problems that you knew about?" I asked.

She sighed. "No, he was healthy as a horse, except for his throat."

"His throat?" I asked.

"His throat," she said. "That poor man was just cursed with a sore gullet. He went through a bottle or two of cough syrup every night. It was the only way he could get to sleep." She sniffed and wiped her eyes.

"What did you do yesterday, before Elder Doolittle was taken ill?" I asked.

"Well, we went to church, just like always. Then usually we go to temple to perform endowments."

"Endowments?"

"Yes, like, you know, vicarious baptism for our deceased ancesters."

Not only didn't I know, I didn't want to.

"Did you go yesterday?"

"No, yesterday we went to a lovely potluck in the park with the family. It was such a nice day, and Elder Loveless is such a sweet spirit. It seemed rightous. But maybe if we had gone to church and done the endowments…" She sobbed silently and blew her nose noisily.

"I'm sure that you are not to blame ma'am," I said, and I was. But she was right. If they had gone to the temple to baptize the dead, Doolittle would probably not have joined them.

"Thank you," I said, rising from the couch. It was so soft I had to grip the arm to propel myself upward. The plastic clung to the back of my legs, making a farting sound as I broke free. "You've been most helpful," I said, "but I've taken up enough of your time."

"You haven't even had a cookie," she protested.

I pulled out my phone and stared at it. "I'd love to," I lied. "But duty calls."

I drove to Loveless, navigating the grid of clean neat streets that had as much character as a Walmart.

I was welcomed in by the smiling Elder, who was horrified to discover that Doolittle had gone to meet his maker.

"Such a pious man," he said, "and so healthy. Whoever would have thought he'd go so suddenly? It's the good Lord's will, but hard on the family. I must pay them a visit. Would you care to sit down and have something to eat?"

"No thanks, I just ate," I said. I hadn't, but I was pretty sure that his culinary delights would send me straight to somewhere nasty, maybe just to the bathroom, but more probably to hell.

"The thing is Elder Loveless, Doolittle died in exactly the same way Tammie and Peggy and Mac did. His liver dissolved. That's not even close to common. And the only link I can find is that they all attended potlucks you gave."

"So were about thirty other fine souls," he smiled tightly. "The Lord works in mysterious ways."

"But it wasn't the Lord at work here, was it Elder Loveless, nor was it mysterious, at least not to you, was it?" I said. "It was the *Coprinopsis atramentaria*, also known as Tippler's Bane, that you added to the funeral potatoes. Interesting isn't it? A mushroom whose poisons are only toxic when combined with alcohol. They're perfectly harmless, unless you've had alcohol within seventy-two hours of consumption. And they all did, Tammie the night before, Mac and Peggy at communion, and Doolittle in his nightly Nyquil."

"The Catholic church is the great and abominable satan, which is the whore of all the earth. And the imbibing of alcohol is against the word of wisdom. But all the departed can still get into heaven," he said, holding out his palms and spreading his plump fingers wide. "It's never too late for that. That's why we baptize the dead.

"Besides, I didn't think it would kill them," Loveless said. "Just make them a little ill, ill enough to teach them a lesson, ill enough to consider repentance."

"But the deaths didn't stop you did they?" I said. "Some people are affected more strongly by poison than others. Even peanuts can be deadly if you're allergic."

"God made their constitutions weak. I was just his instrument."

"Well I hope next time he chooses a harp. You're off key and out of tune, but you'll have a lot of time to practice in prison."

"I will gladly serve time, if the Lord so decides," he smiled again.

I called the police. When they got there I went up to the Silver Fork to pack. It was time to get back to the city, where the criminals snarl.

I prefer them that way.

E.E. King is a painter, performer, writer, and biologist who has won numerous awards and fellowships for art, writing, and environmental research. She's been published widely, most recently in *Clarkesworld* and Flametree. Her books include *Dirk Quigby's Guide to the Afterlife* and *Electric Detective.* Her landmark mural, *A Meeting of the Mind*s (121' x 33') can be seen on Mercado La Paloma in Los Angeles. Visit her online at elizabetheveking.com.

THE MAKINGS OF A KILLER

ROBERT JESCHONEK

When Morgan Vane walked into the crowded French hotel room, everyone turned to look his way except the dead man in the bathtub.

Vane could practically feel the sudden inhalation of breath from the six cops in the room...the communal gasp of surprise as they took in his familiar form. They all recognized his iconic outfit, of course, from the maroon leather jacket stretched over his broad shoulders to the black turtleneck sweater and black jeans underneath. Though he'd never met a single one of them, his six-foot, five-inch frame was well known to them all, as was his oval face, olive complexion, and glossy black cap of hair. How many times had his deep mahogany eyes stared out at each of them from a TV screen, website, or book cover?

Every one of them was thrilled to see him—not just happy, but *thrilled*—and he knew it. And he relished their reaction, as always.

It was *good* to be *God*. Or a world-famous American author/TV star/private detective, at least.

"Monsieur Vane?" The first person to speak, a slender, silver-haired woman in the bathroom doorway, frowned at him. "Is it really you?"

Vane's impulse was to grin and spread his arms, soaking up the adulation... but instead he nodded grimly. "I wish I were here under better circumstances." After all, he had a job to do.

The female cop walked toward him, eyes fixed on his face. Vane was certain from the way the other cops hung back that she was the highest-ranking officer among them, in charge of the crime scene. He could also tell from her tone, expression, and movements that she was not in a good mood.

"How did you know?" She tipped her head toward the bathroom. "Did an alert go out over the TV detective hotline that there had been a suspicious death here tonight in Saint-Malo?"

Vane shook his head. "I happen to be staying in this very hotel, *Capitaine*. All part of my latest book tour."

"Just 'Lieutenant.'" She stuck out her left hand. "Lieutenant Loire."

"My pleasure," said Vane as he shook her hand. "Shall I assume you're familiar with my work?"

"Familiar with *you*." She said it with an edge in her voice, as if she didn't mean it in a good way, entirely.

"Perhaps I should go." Vane said it carefully, since it was the exact opposite of what he wanted to do. "Let you get to it."

Just then, a tall, gray-haired man with a hook nose and a black trench coat stalked into the room. He took one look at Vane, and his bushy eyebrows shot up. "*Morgan Vane?*"

Vane acted like he didn't know who the man was. "Yes?"

Loire stiffened as the man approached. "Monsieur Vane, this is my commanding officer, Capitaine Claude Beuzec. Capitaine, this is..."

Beuzec cut her off and lunged forward, extending a hand to Vane. "You have come to solve our case, I take it?"

Vane shook his hand and shrugged. "I just happened by, actually. It seems Lieutenant Loire has things well under..."

"Yes, yes." Beuzec sneered. "Her competence is well known...but we would be *most* honored if a great detective like *yourself* would choose to lend a hand."

Vane shot a glance at Loire. Her rigid body language spoke volumes. "Thank you, Captain, but..."

"Please, Monsieur Vane. We *need* you." Beuzec leaned close and threw an arm around his shoulders. "If, of course, you'll see fit to waive your usual fee, as our budget is extraordinarily tight these days. Though perhaps we could take the fee out of Lieutenant Loire's salary."

Vane hesitated. "Very well. I will investigate on a pro bono basis, free of charge, at least for..."

"Excellent!" Beuzec clapped him on the back. "I am certain my people will learn a *great deal* from someone as accomplished as you." He grinned at Loire. "*Especially* the lieutenant here."

With that, Beuzec spun away from him and charged out the door without another word.

Loire watched him go with obvious hatred in her eyes, then sighed and turned to Vane. "This way." She slouched toward the bathroom.

"*Merci.*" Vane fell in step behind her, secretly exulting that he'd gained admission...not that there had ever been any doubt. He was a man who got what he wanted, right down the line.

And right now, he wanted to solve the murder of the man in the bathtub.

"Ma'am. Monsieur Vane." A bald young cop in a navy blue windbreaker and rose-tinted granny glasses pushed toward Loire. He spoke with an accent that was very different from hers—the kind that came from living in the Brittany region and speaking the native Breton language in addition to French. "We have found trace evidence in the tub drain." He beamed at Vane as he held up a sealed evidence baggie with strands of blond hair curled inside. He had a familiar look on his face, one that Vane had seen often—the look of a fan.

"*C'est bon,* Officer Cunoval." Loire squinted at the baggie and nodded. "If it does not yield a killer, perhaps it will at least help us identify our victim."

Vane frowned at the naked body sprawled in the tub. The victim looked to be in his fifties, short and paunchy, with light brown skin and no hair visible anywhere on his body. "You don't know who he is yet?"

Loire shook her head. "No wallet, no mobile phone, no luggage. He checked in to the hotel three days ago under the name Silas Gardiner and paid for two weeks in advance with cash."

"Strange, isn't it?" As Vane said his patented catchphrase, he reached into a pocket of his jacket and drew out his trademark prop: a solid gold toothpick. Smoothly, he slid it between the teeth on the right side of his mouth, further setting the stage for his performance.

"Very strange, yes." Cunoval grinned, then caught himself and cleared his throat. "Perhaps the autopsy will tell us something."

"I'm curious." Vane narrowed his eyes as he gazed down at the corpse in the tub. "How exactly did you determine this was a murder and not a mere accident?"

"It did look like an accident at first," said Loire. "A slip-and-fall."

"Then, we found this." Cunoval held up an evidence-collection swab in a sealed plastic tube. "Teflon silicone spray, applied to the surface of the tub."

"Lubricant." Vane raised his eyebrows and nodded. "He was *made* to fall."

"That is certainly how it appears, Monsieur Vane," said Loire. "Now we must figure out who helped him along."

"Will you be assisting us on this case?" Cunoval grinned eagerly. "Providing consultation, perhaps?"

"Capitaine Beuzec wants him on the team," said Loire.

"And what about you?" asked Vane.

"I do not have any choice, do I?" said Loire.

Vane met her stare. "But what if you did?"

Loire sighed. "Perhaps you may yet be helpful." She raised an index finger. "*If* you do not withhold any facts that could be pertinent in the resolution of this case."

"That goes without saying," said Vane...though of course he was already withholding certain pertinent facts.

For example, he already knew the identity of the hairless dead man in the tub. Of everyone in the room, Vane alone knew the man's real name and background.

And he was keeping it to himself, no matter what Loire had said.

As Loire turned away to speak to another officer, Cunoval suddenly pushed close, lowering his voice so only Vane could hear. "What does your gut tell you so far? Are you confident you can solve this case?"

"Absolutely." Vane used his tongue to shift the gold toothpick from the right side of his mouth to the left. "No doubt whatsoever."

He could say it with such conviction because he'd already solved the case. He already knew the killer and every detail of what he'd done.

Not that he was going to let that spoil his investigation. After all, he might know who'd killed the man, but the hardest part of his job still lay ahead...his favorite part, truth be told.

He still had to pick the "true" murderer and convince the world that he was to blame. Or she.

And he had to make it all interesting enough to support his next book, TV episode, and online pay-per-view special.

* * * *

Loire got a call on her cell phone and stalked out of the room. Vane took the initiative and followed along uninvited.

"Finally." Loire stopped at the elevator and hit the button to summon a car. "We may have a bit of *bonne chance* in this case."

"Good luck?" said Vane as the door opened in front of them. "How's that?"

Loire pushed into the elevator and jabbed a button on the control panel. "A delivery for Monsieur Gardiner."

When they got to the ground floor, she led the way across the gleaming lobby. As Vane followed, he noted the gleaming brass fixtures, black-veined marble, and rich, dark wood of the furnishings. Everything was new; the *Oceanique Majestique* hotel and spa had just opened three weeks ago, a glittering new jewel along the waterfront of the tourist town of Saint-Malo.

"*Où est-il?*" Loire snapped out the words as she hurtled toward the reception desk. *Where is it?*

Two young women stood behind the desk, looking nervous in their smart black blazers and red neckties. They were both on the tall side, just under six feet, and had shoulder-length blond hair.

The taller of the two had a nametag that read *Mirrin*. "Right here, ma'am."

"It's over here." The other girl's nametag read *Jilli*.

They also had similar accents—Australian or Kiwi, both equally thick.

As Loire hurtled around the side of the desk, both girls scrambled toward a red suitcase sitting against the wall. They both grabbed it at the same time, tipping it back and wheeling it along the walkway behind the desk.

Loire held out both hands, impatiently flexing her fingers against her palms. "And where is the individual who delivered it?"

The girls stopped pushing the case and looked at each other with wide, worried eyes.

"Gone, ma'am," said Jilli. "We didn't know..."

"Should we have told him to wait?" asked Mirrin.

Loire gestured for the luggage again. "Was there a receipt, at least? Some kind of paperwork?"

Both girls shook their heads at once.

"All right, all right." Loire pushed through the swinging door behind the desk, grabbed the suitcase handle, and dragged the bag out on her own. "You two, don't go anywhere."

"We won't, ma'am," Jilli said earnestly.

"Anything to help, ma'am," added Mirrin.

Loire rolled the bag past Vane and heaved it up onto a low glass table with no apparent fear that the table might break. "This came from Air France, you say?"

"Yes, ma'am," said Jilli.

"Late luggage, apparently," said Mirrin.

Loire pulled a pair of latex gloves from her pants pocket and tugged them on. Then, she grabbed the zipper and yanked it around the edge of the bag. "And Mr. Gardiner has been checked in for three days, has he not?"

"Yes, ma'am." Jilli and Mirrin said it in unison.

Loire finished unzipping and flipped open the lid of the bag. Vane watched with what he hoped was a convincing look of great suspense, then a look of surprise as the contents of the bag became evident.

"Porn." Loire picked up one of the DVDs from the bag and glared at its lurid cover. "With children."

"Indeed." Vane glanced at the bag's contents and looked away in disgust.

Loire sighed. "This still doesn't tell us who he is." She opened the DVD case and examined it, then clapped it shut and dropped it on the table.

"Maybe there's something in another disk," suggested Vane.

"Or deeper in the suitcase." Loire pulled out handfuls of DVDs and stacked them on the table. When the bag was empty, she felt along the bottom and sides, pressing her fingertips into the lining. "Yes. There is something inside."

Digging into a corner of the bag, she pulled open a hidden flap secured with Velcro. When the flap was peeled all the way back, a stack of papers lay exposed, about an inch high, bound with brown cord.

"What are these, pray tell?" Loire held up the stack with a scowl.

Vane looked closer. "Bearer bonds, I believe."

"Is that so?" asked Loire.

"Worth a fortune, from what I can see," said Vane. "If, indeed, they are genuine."

"Hm." Loire flipped through the pages. "The question is, what was a child pornography smuggler doing with a stack of bearer bonds hidden in his suitcase?"

"Not to mention, who is he?" added Vane.

"We will have the answer soon enough." Loire dropped the bonds on top of the pile of porn. "It is only a matter of time, now that our victim has begun giving up his secrets."

Want to bet? That was what Vane wanted to say, though he settled for this: "I'm sure you're right."

* * * *

According to hotel surveillance footage, "Silas Gardiner" had spent most of his time out of the building, leaving at dawn and returning around midnight each night. Cameras showed him walking toward the waterfront and turning left on his daily travels, heading toward the walled city at the heart of Saint-Malo.

Loire and Vane followed in his footsteps, walking out as the sun set, leaving the criminal scientists to scour the dead man's porn, bonds, and luggage.

It was a pleasant June evening, warm enough for shirt sleeves. Vane breathed deep, relishing the salt sea air carried to him on the gentle breeze.

Loire, however, didn't seem to be enjoying the sea breeze at all. Her mood still struck him as sour; he was starting to think her grouchiness might be perpetual.

"Where did he spend his time, I wonder?" Loire walked slowly, staring at the brick sidewalk underfoot and the waist-high gray block seawall on the right. "Where did he go each day?"

"Where everyone else goes, I would guess." Vane pointed at the rooftops in the distance, surrounded by high granite ramparts. "The walled city."

As if in support of his comment, a middle-aged couple hurried past, heading in the direction he was pointing. There were plenty of people taking the same route, clusters of tourists heading for late suppers among the city's multitude of restaurants.

"*Peut-être*," she said. *Perhaps*. "Though there are plenty of other places to go, yes?" She gestured at the other side of the street, across from the seawall and sidewalk. "Many blocks between the hotel and the walled city. More than enough trouble for him to get into."

"You think so?" said Vane.

She snorted. "I have been a police officer in Saint-Malo for the past twenty years. I know this town's underbelly all too well."

"Lots of vice for the tourists?" asked Vane.

"For the locals, as well." Loire stopped and leaned her arms on the seawall, taking a long look below. Rows of rough-cut posts jutted from the sand, their rugged tips rising to the level of the wall—a tidebreak of twisted driftwood, like a forest out of a bad dream.

Vane eased in beside her and also cast his gaze downward. "Twenty years you've been a cop in this town?" The sand had taken on a rosy tint in the light of the setting sun. "Are you a native?"

Loire shook her head. "Not native to Saint-Malo, *non*. My people are from Quimper, to the west." She pronounced it *cam-pear*. "Also a tourist town."

"Also Breton," said Vane. "So you have lived in Brittany all your life."

"I have."

"And do you love it here?" he asked. "Is that why you've stayed?"

"I did stay because of love." She rubbed her eyes. "Though now, it's more like the *opposite* of love."

"Ah." Vane had already studied her past, though he could have deduced certain facts simply by studying her behavior at the crime scene. "Capitaine Beuzec. You were married to him, yes?"

Loire flashed a look of surprise in his direction. "How did you..."

Vane kept pushing ahead. "He left you for another woman?"

Loire scowled and looked away. "That is none of your business."

"Whatever happened, your marriage ended badly, didn't it?" asked Vane. "But he's still your boss, and he's making your life miserable."

Loire glared silently but didn't deny it.

"Then why don't you leave?" said Vane. "Get a fresh start somewhere else."

"At my age?" Loire waved dismissively. "Fifty is too old for such a fresh start."

"No it isn't," said Vane. "You have plenty of time to begin a new career."

Loire turned to him. "As what? Police work is all I have ever known."

Vane shrugged. "Then stay with it. There are other jobs in other places."

"And *he* will never let me go," snapped Loire. "He told me so when I asked about a transfer. He said he will give me a bad reference or make up some lies about me for a background check. He's enjoying himself too much, making every day of my life an exercise in abuse and futility."

Vane stared at her. The pain on her face and in her voice was clear. "So you wouldn't leave if given the opportunity? If, say, a promotion came along in another town, and it didn't depend on Beuzec's recommendation?"

Loire looked at him, then turned her gaze to the sand below. "As if that would ever happen."

"But what if it did?" asked Vane.

Suddenly, Loire pushed forward. Something on the sand had caught her eye. "Do you see that?" She pointed.

Vane squinted. "No."

"Right there." She pointed more emphatically. "Something shiny."

Vane did see it, then...because he'd put it there. "Looks like a crushed soda can to me."

"Come on." Loire spun and took off. There was a stairway half a block closer to the walled city, and she headed straight for it.

Down on the sand, the two of them threaded their way through the forest of gnarled posts, which seemed much taller from below. Loire zeroed in on the item she'd spotted from the wall and rushed right up to it.

"Well, well." She pulled out a latex glove and used it to scoop up the object. "What have we here?"

Vane leaned close and nodded. "A can of Teflon silicone lubricant."

"That is correct." Loire raised one eyebrow. "This could be our murder weapon, yes?"

"It does seem likely," said Vane. "I wonder what secrets it will yield in the lab?"

Loire shook the can and smirked. "It is *already* telling me a story, Monsieur Vane."

* * * *

"*Oui*, I sell that product here." The beefy shopkeeper nodded once, then shook his head. "*Non*, I did not sell it to a killer."

"That you know of." Loire dangled an evidence bag in front of him, containing the lubricant can.

The shopkeeper clenched his teeth behind his thick brown mustache and kept his massive arms folded over his black polo shirt. "I have done nothing wrong, Lieutenant." As he said it, his eyes shifted to Vane, who stood behind Loire. Was he more worried about the celebrity detective than the local investigator?

"Your hardware store is the only one that stocks this particular brand," said Loire. "We have checked around, Monsieur Bouchard."

"Have you checked with every mechanic and builder in town, too?" Bouchard's voice was deep and gruff. "Perhaps the killer stole the spray from one of them, as they have all bought some from me at one time or another."

Loire shoved the evidence bag at Bouchard's face. "This is a brand-new can, Yann. It was purchased recently, and you know it."

Bouchard pushed the bag away with both hands. "*If* your killer bought this here, I would not have sold it to him with the knowledge that it would be used in the commission of a crime."

"*C'est des conneries!*" Loire snapped out the curse with disgust. "You most certainly would!"

Bouchard's eyes shifted to Vane, then back to Loire. The scowl on his face seemed to lack conviction. "Listen here..."

Loire turned to Vane. "Don't let this man fool you. His name has a habit of coming up in connection with criminal activities."

Vane smiled. "You don't say."

"It is never *him* who goes to jail, though," said Loire. "But as they say, there is a first time for everything, yes?"

Bouchard sighed and rolled his eyes. "Would it kill you to try a new tune one day, Madeleine?"

"'Lieutenant,'" corrected Loire. "Now tell us who bought the lubricant."

"A bum," said Bouchard.

Loire frowned. "Someone you dislike, you mean?"

"I mean a bum." Bouchard shrugged. "An actual bum. What he wanted a can of Teflon silicone lubricant for, I had no idea, and I didn't ask. He smelled awful, but he paid in cash."

Loire's frown deepened. "And you didn't know this bum?"

Bouchard shook his head. "I make it a practice not to look at bums in the street if I can avoid it."

"A mystery bum." Vane nodded slowly. "Strange, isn't it?"

But the truth was, it wasn't the least bit strange to him.

* * * *

"This so-called bum," said Loire on the walk back to the *Oceanique Majestique*. "We will look for him on the hotel's security video. Then, we will go out and find him on the street, wherever he is."

"Unless he was in disguise," said Vane. "In which case, he might not be so easy to find, eh?"

Loire walked through the revolving door into the hotel's lobby without answering.

Once she and Vane were inside, the familiar voice of Cunoval called out to them. "Lieutenant! We have news!"

Loire stopped. "What now?"

"Two things." Cunoval raised two fingers as he hurried up to her. "First, the victim's toilet was plugged. By this." He held up an evidence bag containing a wadded-up red cloth napkin. "It is embroidered with the logo of *Le Phare*."

"An upscale restaurant in the walled city." Loire said it for Vane's benefit. "And the rest?"

"Second, we have video of an unknown male leaving the victim's room after the estimated time of the murder," said Cunoval. "The male in question wore a hooded sweatshirt and kept his head down, out of view of the camera. He left via the stairwell, in which no cameras are yet functional."

"Of course they aren't." Loire rubbed her left temple as if she had a headache.

Suddenly, the elevator dinged, and the door slid open with the sound of laughter—male and female together.

Turning toward it, Vane saw someone he knew all too well emerging into the lobby. Her high heels clacked a familiar rhythm across the marble floor.

"What's this now?" asked Loire.

"Oh my God." Cunoval sounded like he might have a stroke from excessive excitement. "It's *her*."

A young blond woman in a tight white knee-length dress approached, followed by Capitaine Beuzec. She smiled warmly and waggled her fingers in a friendly wave.

Vane knew that wave was meant for him.

"Look who just turned up." Beuzec grinned. "A colleague of Monsieur Vane's has offered to lend a hand."

Vane winced at the use of the word "colleague."

"You are expecting her, of course," said Beuzec. "Mademoiselle Kitty Fox."

Kitty glided over and pecked Vane on both cheeks. "Hello, Morgan." Her book covers didn't do her justice. Her long blond hair framed a face of exquisite beauty, complete with deep dimples, a single perfect mole above her left lip, and a gently curved elfin nose. "Sorry I'm late."

Vane turned a look of surprise into a tight-lipped smile. "Hello, Kitty."

Loire frowned. "Another famous investigator? Is there a convention nearby?"

When Kitty giggled, complete with crinkled nose, she looked closer to twenty-one than her actual age, which was twenty-eight and change. "Didn't Morgan tell you? We've been seeing each other, haven't we?" She blinked her beautiful ice blue eyes.

It wasn't true, but Vane didn't say so. If he'd denied the relationship, she would have just spun her usual web of fact-free fantasy.

"Vane of Justice and the Crimefox." Cunoval blew out his breath in admiration. "Until now, I've only heard rumors..."

Vane kept a straight face in spite of himself. "We'd like this to remain a rumor for now, if you don't mind."

"Oh, of course." Cunoval nodded enthusiastically. "I promise the utmost discretion."

Kitty stepped over to Beuzec and patted his shoulder. "Claude here has agreed to let me participate in the case, Morgan. Two consultants for the price of one."

"How could I say no to such a beautiful woman?" Beuzec flashed a special look in Loire's direction as he chuckled.

Loire glared. "Perhaps if you explained that we already have more than enough support on this..."

"You're the one who's always yapping about insufficient resources," snapped Beuzec. "Well, this time, you've got more than enough!"

Loire fell silent.

"Don't you want me to help, sweetheart?" Kitty batted her eyelashes. "I promise I'll be good."

Vane gave Kitty the reaction she seemed to expect: irritated resistance. "Too many cooks spoil the soup, Kitty dear."

"But we *do* make an excellent team." Kitty winked. "Gibraltar proved that once and for all, wouldn't you say?"

Vane's blood curdled at the mention of that place. It was Gibraltar where he'd first met Kitty, two years ago. It was there that she'd brazenly stolen the spotlight by solving a murder out from under him...bringing in the actual killer instead of the suspect Vane was planning to frame, in other words.

How could he ever forget all that, especially when she'd used it as the launchpad for a very successful celebrity detective career much like his own? A career that might yet eclipse his, if the right case came along that gave her the juice she needed to exceed him.

"You never miss out on an opportunity, do you?" asked Vane. "To work together, that is."

Kitty raised an eyebrow. "Can you blame me?" The look she gave him spoke volumes; their history, their rivalry, and her intention to win at any cost were all wrapped up in that icy blue gaze of hers.

Vane didn't bother broadcasting his own intentions. There was simply no need for it...and anyway, more pressing work was at hand. "Lieutenant?" He turned to Loire. "Perhaps we should pay a visit to that restaurant, *Le Phare*?"

"With me, you mean?" asked Kitty.

"Of course." Vane smiled with false civility. "Let's go solve this case, my dear."

"That's the spirit!" Beuzec clapped him on the back and headed for the door. "Two great detectives teaming up under my command!"

Loire watched him go with undisguised disgust. "*Le Phare* it is." She pulled out her phone and thumbed the screen. "Just let me call ahead first. I would hate to show up without a reservation."

* * * *

Loire drove the mile or so from the hotel to the walled city—Kitty in the front seat and Vane squeezed into the back. En route, Kitty pumped Loire for information about the case...though Loire, to her credit, didn't seem thrilled about giving it to her.

Loire parked her black Volkswagen outside the Porte St-Vincent gate, the main entrance to the city. She got out of the car and led the way at a brisk pace as Vane and Kitty followed a few paces behind her.

"Don't I get a proper hello?" Kitty kept her voice low though Loire was out of earshot.

"I thought I'd already given you one," said Vane. "Are you angry that I've left out the parade?"

"Being inhospitable won't earn you any points." Kitty leaned in and jabbed him in the side with an elbow. "Do you *want* to look like an ass when my camera crew gets here?"

Vane snorted. "Turning it into a three-ring circus, are we?"

"With you as the chief clown." Kitty laughed. "But there's still time to become my sideshow, instead."

Vane smirked. "How did *you* know that's my lifelong ambition?"

"I'm just saying." Kitty wobbled as her heel caught on a cobblestone, then quickly recovered. "Washed up is washed up, old man. People want their true crime from a pretty face, not one that's pretty *ugly*."

Vane used his tongue to move the gold toothpick from the left side of his mouth to the right. "Now is that any way to talk to the modern-day Sherlock Holmes?"

"It is if I'm the modern-day Moriarty," said Kitty.

Vane laughed as he followed Loire through the gate into the walled city. The notion of Kitty as any kind of Moriarty figure was hilarious.

* * * *

The Porte St-Vincent opened onto a broad street that was one of the busiest in the walled city—the Place Chateaubriand.

The lights of restaurants blazed away the evening gloom, each café, bistro, or brasserie teeming with tourists. Every available outdoor seat was filled; every waiter was running with trays in hand. The air was thick with chatter, laughter, and the clatter of plates and silverware.

"What a crowd." Four men in business suits at a nearby café table waved at Kitty, and Kitty waved back. "But it's good to see my fans are here."

"Remind me to avoid that café," said Vane. "If they're *your* fans, we know they have terrible taste."

Suddenly, Loire stopped and spun to face them. "Are the two of you having a spat?" She frowned. "Because you certainly don't sound very loving to me, right now."

"It's just our patented repartee," said Kitty. "Isn't that right, Morgan?"

Vane did not offer comment.

Loire stared at them both for a moment. Then, she continued along the street, which followed the curve of the city wall.

Kitty shook her head at Vane, then hurried to walk alongside Loire. That left Vane bringing up the rear, which was fine with him.

As the three of them followed the bend of Place Chateaubriand, Vane scanned passing faces for anyone he might recognize. He pricked up his ears, too, soaking in the babble of language rushing around him—more British-inflected English than anything else.

The demographics were well-known to him. Saint-Malo, a short ferry ride across the Channel from England, was a favorite destination of British tourists. They came for the beaches by day and the restaurants and clubs by night, saturating the local economy with British pounds. Other Europeans went there, too, with occasional Americans in the mix...but Saint-Malo was biggest with the Brits, laying on the hospitality and entertainment to keep them coming back for more.

Even now, Vane heard the sound of a live rock band not far away, playing an electronically amplified classic. The music was coming from around the bend, somewhere beyond the thickening crowd drawn to see the musicians up close.

Vane and the others would reach *Le Phare* before the crowd got too heavy. Vane knew the street well; he'd studied it, and the rest of the walled city and all of Saint-Malo, before embarking on this latest venture. Above all else, he believed in preparation as a means of attaining his goals.

Not that he was prepared for a chair to come crashing out of the window of *Le Phare*.

Just as the place came into view, glass shattered over the crowd, blasted from a front window by the hurtling chair. Suddenly, the happy babble turned into a medley of cries and shouts as tourists reacted to the barrage.

The crowd parted fast enough that the chair hit the street instead of a person. From there, everyone parted even further and faster, giving *Le Phare* a wide berth in case something else flew out of it.

At which point, Loire was already running for the restaurant's front door. So was Vane, though Kitty hung back.

As Vane charged into *Le Phare* behind Loire, he quickly saw the cause of the ruckus. A full-blown brawl was raging in the solarium, a knock-down-drag-out between middle-aged men in track suits and rugby shirts.

"Break it up!" Loire waded in without hesitation, pulling two men apart with such force that both of them stumbled and fell. "I said stop! *Arrêt! Arrêt!*"

The other men ignored her and kept swinging at each other. Grunting like animals, the two burliest ones wrestled through a doorway, tumbling from the solarium into the restaurant proper.

Bucking the tide of customers evacuating the place, Vane stormed after the burly wrestlers. As the gray-bearded men tumbled into a booth, Vane quickly pocketed his gold toothpick and barreled toward them.

With a hammer-blow kidney punch, he loosened the grip of the man on top, then dragged him off the other man by the scruff of his neck.

Tossing the first wrestler to the floor like a sack of trash, Vane went after the other. He didn't bother with conversation or offer surrender as an option; he just plucked the man from the leather-upholstered seat with one hand and rabbit-punched him in the face with the other.

As the man went limp, Vane dropped him and headed for the solarium. At first, in the muddle of fighting men and upended furniture, he didn't see Loire.

Then, as a bruiser snarled and charged him, Loire reappeared, clubbing the bruiser in the head with a table leg. The man fell hard, and Loire threw her make-shift club down on top of him.

Without a word, then, she and Vane proceeded to break up the rest of the brawl.

* * * *

Soon, the floor of *Le Phare* was littered with twelve bruised men in torn track suits and rugby shirts, hands bound behind their backs with white zip ties from Loire's pockets.

"You." Loire pointed at the most dignified-looking among them, a tall man with finely chiseled features and silver hair clipped in a tight, neat cut. "Explain this."

The man she'd singled out looked around at the others, then turned his gaze to Loire. "My name is Hull. Corliss Hull." His accent was American...Bostonian, Vane decided. "My friends and I were having an argument, and it got out of hand."

"Obviously," snapped Loire. "Now tell us *why*."

"That one." Hull jabbed his chin at one of the two gray-bearded wrestlers whom Vane had broken up. "Rab McKay. It's *his* fault."

McKay thrashed on the floor, making a show of wanting to go after Hull. "Come over *here* and say that, ye lummox!" His accent was Scottish.

"Whoa, boys." Kitty chose that moment to intercede, stepping out of the solarium doorway in her tight white dress with hands raised. "Is this how you'd want to be seen on international TV?"

The twelve men gaped at her with newfound interest. "You're Kitty Fox!" said one of them.

"Are we on camera right now?" blurted another.

"Not just yet." Kitty grinned and flicked a finger back and forth. "But wouldn't you rather put your best foot forward and be ready when the camera gets here?"

Suddenly, all twelve men were sitting straighter and looking friendlier.

"What's the story here, fellas?" Kitty planted her fists on her hips.

"We all played rugby together in college," said Hull. "At Harvard. We're all Harvard graduates."

"Harvard?" Kitty beamed. "I *thought* the I.Q. seemed high in here."

"Once a year, we meet up somewhere in the world for a reunion game," said Hull. "We've been here for a week, working out, getting ready...but now we're down a player, all because Rab over there couldn't keep his mouth shut."

"I did the same as I *always* do," said McKay. "Veej knew to expect it! He was just as good as I am at dishin' it out."

"You had to keep on him about the *alopecia*, didn't you?" Hull shook his head with disgust.

"Wait a minute." Kitty's eyes widened. "Did you say *alopecia*? As in the condition that leaves someone without any hair on his body?"

"That's the one." Hull nodded. "Vijay had it all his life. He used to wear a wig, but he stopped doing even that a while back."

Kitty looked at Loire, who in turn looked at Vane. Vane nodded once to confirm he understood the significance.

According to Hull, Vijay had no hair anywhere on his body...just like the dead man in the tub at the *Oceanique Majestique*.

"Hmm," said Kitty. "Strange, isn't it?"

* * * *

It was well after midnight when Vane sat down with Loire and Kitty at the police station, which was right across the street from the *Oceanique Majestique* hotel.

They stared at each other across a square table in one of the interrogation rooms, blinking in the jittery fluorescent light. A patrolman brought coffee, but Vane and Kitty had a kind of standoff and wouldn't touch it, as if to prove that neither of them needed it.

"So Silas Gardiner is Vijay Patel." Loire shrugged. "At least we know that much."

Vane nodded. The body had been positively identified by the rugby players, who'd been brought in for booking for their disorderly conduct.

"The problem is, we don't know much else," said Loire.

"We have the murder weapon," said Vane.

Kitty tapped one perfectly manicured nail on the table. "The Teflon silicone spray."

"We have the suitcase," said Vane.

"So what?" Loire sipped her coffee. "*Et alors?*"

"Kiddie porn and bearer bonds." Kitty tapped the table again. "The mark of a true scumbag."

"The bonds provide an untraceable means of payment," said Vane. "A perfect instrument for high-value illicit transactions."

"Again, *et alors?*" Loire got up from the table and paced across the room. "We still have no idea who killed our scumbag, do we?"

"You're right," said Vane. "What suspects do we have? The unidentified male leaving Patel's room on the security video? The mystery bum who bought the lubricant?"

"The rugby players?" Loire pulled back a window blind and peered out at the night. "Each of them has eleven alibis, as the team members claim they were together on the night of the murder."

"What about the trace evidence from the crime scene?" asked Kitty. "The hair from the tub drain?"

"Results will be some time yet. We had to send the hair to a forensic lab in Paris." Loire let the window blind fall and paced back across the room. "Meanwhile, the clock is ticking. The murderer moves further from our grasp."

"Not necessarily." Kitty tapped her finger once more. "I believe I can solve this mystery, Lieutenant...if you don't mind, of course, Morgan."

"Please." Vane bowed his head. "Be my guest."

Gratified, Kitty smiled. "The key to this murder is quite simple." She shrugged. "It's rather obvious, really."

Loire growled with impatience. "So what *is* it?"

Kitty arched an eyebrow. "The second suitcase."

Loire planted her hands on her hips and stared down at Kitty. "What second suitcase?"

"Patel's, of course." Kitty leaned back and crossed her legs.

"But Air France sent only one," said Loire.

Kitty raised a finger. "Incorrect. I called them, pretending to work for the hotel, and they told me they sent *two* bags for Mr. Gardiner, not just one."

"If there was a second suitcase, what happened to it?" asked Loire.

"I believe I can solve that mystery, too." Kitty flashed a look of amused delight at Vane. "Who notified you of the first bag's arrival?"

"The receptionists at the hotel's front desk," said Loire.

"Exactly," said Kitty. "And did you know that one of them has a criminal record?"

Loire hesitated, perhaps because she realized she'd missed a step in her investigation. "Which one?"

"Mirrin Daugherty." Kitty nodded. "I took the liberty of reaching out to a friend at Interpol, and he turned up quite a rap sheet on Mirrin. A dozen arrests, mostly for drug possession in Australia...even some jail time."

Loire looked rattled, then gathered herself up and shifted back to professional cop mode. "And I suppose this Mirrin stole the second suitcase?"

"She was there when it arrived," said Kitty. "She had the opportunity to tuck it away somewhere...and she had the motive, too. Scuttlebutt around the hotel has it that Mirrin is behind a rash of recent thefts, and she's working with a *partner*."

Loire narrowed her eyes. "Who's her partner? The other girl, Jilli?"

Kitty shook her head. "They say it's someone outside the hotel."

"'They?'" Loire grimaced. "Who are 'they?'"

"Hotel staff," said Kitty. "Maids, maintenance men, cooks, bartenders...you know. They're some of my biggest fans."

"And whom do 'they' say is Mirrin's partner?" asked Loire.

Kitty shrugged. "That's all I've got at this point. My famous face will only get me so far, you know."

Vane tried, and failed, to hold back a sarcastic comment. "Then you haven't really solved the case, have you?"

"Better than *you* did," snapped Kitty.

"Well, it's a lead," said Loire.

"Unless it isn't," said Vane.

"And the only way we'll know is a good, old-fashioned stakeout." Loire grabbed her coffee and headed for the door.

* * * *

Mirrin emerged from the hotel at four in the morning, two hours before the end of her shift. Sure enough, she was pulling a red suitcase along behind her—the twin of the one delivered earlier that day for "Silas Gardiner."

Casting a quick look at the police station across the street, she turned right, heading for the waterfront. Then, she followed the route Vane and Loire had taken earlier that evening, crossing the street to the seawall and going left toward the walled city.

Meanwhile, Vane, Loire, and Kitty followed down a side street running parallel to the sea. Lights off, Loire drove quietly down the blocks, pausing at intersections to make sure Mirrin hadn't veered off somewhere.

"She's meeting her partner." Kitty, who'd switched her white dress for a chunky black sweater, tights, and knit cap, sat in the front passenger seat, glued to each glimpse of Mirrin out the side window. "She has to be."

"Or maybe she's cut him loose," suggested Vane. "Maybe she's skipping town with the goodies."

"More kiddie porn and bearer bonds?" said Loire.

"I wish I knew." Kitty sounded more excited than anyone in the car. "I can't wait to find out."

"You'll know soon enough," said Loire.

"I just hope you're not disappointed," said Vane. "Things don't always turn out the way you expect."

"That's right, they don't," snapped Kitty. "Case in point, Gibraltar."

Vane didn't answer. He just sat in the back seat and waited, a small smile playing over his lips.

As for Mirrin, she kept marching along the cobblestone sidewalk toward the walled city, lit by the occasional glow of traffic lights along the street. Her blond hair whipped behind her in the wind off the sea, fluttering like gold ribbons against the darkling horizon of the English Channel.

After walking a mile, she reached the end of the path and stopped. The walled city sprawled on her left, its ramparts illuminated from below.

Vane and the others parked at the mouth of the side street they'd been traversing, awaiting her next move. The Volkswagen's diesel engine automatically switched off instead of idling; it was programmed to start back up as soon as the driver stepped on the accelerator pedal.

"So what do we do now?" Kitty was still excited. "Leave the car here and follow her into the city on foot?"

"Most likely," said Loire. "At least, that's what I'll be doing. You two will wait here."

"No way!" Kitty grabbed the door handle on her side and started to pull it. "If you're going into the city, so am I."

"Neither of you are." Vane reached between the seats and pointed toward the cobblestone walk. "Look."

Mirrin wasn't standing at the end of the path anymore, and she wasn't walking toward the walled city, either. She was nowhere in sight.

"*Merde!*" Loire stomped the accelerator, restarting the engine, and swung the VW out of the side street. "Where is she?"

There was still no sign of Mirrin as the VW bolted across the road and jerked to a stop. Loire and Kitty leaped out first and ran.

When Vane caught up with them, they were gazing over the seawall. Loire pointed, but she didn't need to. Vane could see where Mirrin had gone.

When the tide was out, as it was now, it was possible to walk across the sand to two islands near the walled city—Grand Be and Petit Be. That was exactly what Mirrin was doing, dragging the suitcase toward those rocky humps.

"This is it," said Kitty. "She's making her connection."

"Or hiding her loot," said Vane. "Those islands are mostly submerged at high tide."

"Either way, we've got her." Kitty headed for a nearby stairway cut into the seawall. "I'm about to crack this case wide open."

* * * *

As Kitty, Loire, and Vane crossed the beach, Loire drew a gun from the holster under her jacket. The three of them were dangerously exposed, with no means of concealment between the seawall and the islands.

Fortunately, Mirrin never looked back. She was far ahead, completely focused on dragging the suitcase and reaching her destination. Whatever noise her pursuers made was carried away from her on the ocean breeze.

"She's heading for Petit Be." Loire spoke in a loud whisper, though she didn't need to.

Vane could see the blonde was giving the larger island, Grand Be, a wide berth. Her course was aimed at the smaller of the two, which was a little farther out across the sand.

At least that gave him and his companions options. They could use the rocky base of Grand Be for cover in case Mirrin finally looked back. Then, as she closed in on one side of Petit Be, they could hurry across the gap and skirt the other side of that smaller island.

Unfortunately, Kitty didn't seem to have any interest in such a strategy. Before Vane could discuss it with her, she broke into a jog, distancing herself from him and Loire.

"Damn." Loire ran after her, not that it would do any good. Kitty kept jogging faster and would clear Grand Be before she could reach her.

Vane, for his part, hung back in the shadows of Grand Be. He was ready, now that his group had splintered, to put his own plan into action.

* * * *

As Kitty and Loire ran after Mirrin, Vane approached the opposite side of Petit Be. Employing all the stealth at his command, he quietly climbed the rocky slope, taking care not to slip on the wet stones.

When he reached the top, he stayed low and worked his way to the central building, the Fort du Petit Be...the *only* building on the island. Reaching the corner of one turret at the front of the fort, he stopped. He could hear voices on the other side, carried on the ocean breeze.

One, as expected, belonged to Mirrin. "I love seeing you so happy."

The other was a man's voice, deep and gruff. "And I love *being* happy, *mon amour*. All because of *you*."

Monsieur Bouchard. It was the hardware store owner, the one who'd sold the lubricant to the mystery bum.

"Do you realize what this means?" asked Bouchard. "What it means to *us*?"

"Money?" said Mirrin.

"A future together," said Bouchard. "Now we can be together always, living as we choose. Never again will we have to worry that poverty might come between us."

"Oh, Yann," said Mirrin, and then they were both silent for a while.

Peering around the corner, Vane saw the reason why. They were kissing passionately with the suitcase at their feet.

Suddenly, a third voice pierced the night. "You are absolutely right!" It was Kitty, storming out from behind a rocky hill. "You *won't* have to worry about poverty. You'll both be very well taken care of *in prison*!"

Bouchard and Mirrin broke their embrace and gawked.

"Whatever's in that suitcase, I hope it was worth killing for," said Kitty.

"I've killed no one!" Reaching behind him, Bouchard pulled something from the waist of his blue jeans—a pistol, which he swung around to point at Kitty. "Until now!"

Vane didn't hesitate. Bolting around the corner, he charged Bouchard, plowing into him with a flying tackle.

The gun went off on the way down, firing into the air. Then, as the two men landed, Vane grabbed Bouchard's wrist and bashed his gun hand on the rocky ground.

It took four blows for the gun to pop free, at which point Kitty grabbed it. Meanwhile, Bouchard kept thrashing, putting up a fight though Vane's greater bulk and superior leverage kept him firmly in place.

"Yann Bouchard!" Kitty pointed the gun at Bouchard. "You are under arrest for the murder of Vijay Patel!"

Bouchard stopped fighting. "Who?"

Just then, Loire swooped in and snatched the pistol away from Kitty. "That's enough." She also had a tight grip on the arm of Mirrin, whom she'd corralled while Vane and Kitty were busy with Bouchard. "You are *not* a police officer, and you cannot conduct an arrest."

"But who solved the murder?" Kitty smirked. "Not the *police*, that's for sure."

"We didn't kill anyone!" said Mirrin.

Kitty scowled. "Playing dumb won't help you."

"Who's playing?" shouted Bouchard. "And who the hell is Vijay Patel?"

* * * *

"Admit it," said Kitty. "I blow your mind, don't I?"

Vane, who was pouring a cup of coffee from a fresh pot, didn't answer. Kitty was finding new ways to get on his nerves with each passing minute; she'd been bouncing off the walls ever since they'd returned to the police station from Petit Be.

"I make you think about getting out of the game." She smiled as she smoothed the front of her tight white dress, which she'd put back on after the stakeout. "No one else has ever made you feel as inadequate as I do."

Vane smirked. "I wouldn't put it in those words, exactly."

"Poor Morgan. Always afraid to talk about feelings." She patted his cheek. "There, there."

Vane sipped his coffee. It was good...delicious, in fact. Or maybe the taste was colored somewhat by his own anticipation of what was about to happen.

Because in truth, he was at least as excited as Kitty...but for different reasons.

"This will all be over soon, dear." Kitty nodded. "My camera crew is setting up right now in the squad room. Then, you'll be free of all this...responsibility."

"Is that so?" said Vane.

"You won't have to worry about being the Number One Detective in the world anymore." Kitty hopped up and kissed him on the tip of his nose, then twirled away. "You're welcome."

With that, she scooted off to join her crew.

Just then, Loire shuffled into the break room, looking exhausted. "She loves putting on a show, doesn't she?"

Vane snorted. "Children."

Loire smiled tiredly and reached for the coffee pot. "Long day, *oui?*"

Vane nodded. "How goes the questioning? Are Bouchard and Mirrin still denying any role in Patel's murder?"

"Other than selling lubricant to our mystery bum." Loire filled a paper cup with steaming black coffee. "Though the suitcase full of heroin in their possession does suggest they are not to be trusted."

Vane narrowed his eyes. "And what do you think?"

Loire returned the pot to the warmer and met his gaze. "I do not trust them," she said, "but I believe them."

"You do?"

"I believe they are opportunists, nothing more." Loire sighed. "Mirrin saw the suitcase of heroin arrive, and she told her boyfriend, Bouchard, who has a long history of dirty dealings...but not fatal ones. He arranged a financial transaction, to be conducted by night on Petit Be. A skiff was due to arrive, at which time a business acquaintance would accept the drugs, and the purchase price would be deposited in Bouchard's hands." She shrugged. "That was the plan, anyway. Both Mirrin and Bouchard corroborate this story."

"I see." Vane drained his coffee cup and tossed it in the trash bin.

"You're not surprised?" Loire frowned. "You're not going to say 'Strange, isn't it?'"

"Why would I?" Vane drew a gold toothpick from his jacket pocket. "There's nothing strange about it."

"What makes you say that?"

At that moment, Officer Cunoval flashed into the room, carrying a fistful of papers. His eyes were wide, his face flushed, his breathing rapid.

"I believe you are about to find out," said Vane, and then he inserted the gold toothpick into his mouth.

* * * *

When Vane, Loire, and Cunoval walked into the squad room, Kitty was shooting a stand-up segment with a three-person video crew while Beuzec watched. All three crew members wielded high-end gear; Vane could see that the camera, sound equipment, and lights were all top of the line. The crew themselves were all young, fresh out of university or close to it, and focused with grim intensity on their work.

As for Kitty, she wore the cool, smooth demeanor of a seasoned TV host, gliding and gesturing gracefully among the empty desks. "Working closely with local law enforcement, I have investigated this murder with all the skills and experience at my disposal. I was determined to persevere until the victim was identified and the killer brought to justice...at any cost."

Vane stood along the wall with Loire and Cunoval, out of shot and away from Beuzec, and watched Kitty's performance. He had to hand it to her; she was great in front of a camera...better than he was, probably. Her many flaws were not evident when she stood before a lens.

Not yet, anyway.

"At last, my work has paid off," she said. "I have told you the secrets of the previously unknown victim, Vijay Patel." Kitty nodded for dramatic effect. "Now, as this special edition of *Crimefox Files* continues, I am about to tell you the name of the killer."

As Kitty gazed into the camera with her icy blue eyes, Vane felt Loire and Cunoval tensing on either side of him. Loire started to move, but Vane shot out an arm to hold her back.

Loire frowned with annoyance. Vane, in reply, held up a single index finger, signifying that she should wait.

Hands clasped loosely at her waist, Kitty slowly crossed the squad room. "Who would murder Vijay Patel? To get to that answer, we must first answer another question: *why* would someone kill him?" Never breaking eye contact with the camera, she stopped and leaned against a desk. "The answer, I have discovered, is *greed*, plain and simple."

Again, Loire started to move, and again, Vane held her back. He wanted the moment to be perfect, just perfect.

"Vijay Patel was a smuggler of drugs and child pornography," said Kitty. "He planned to transport a fortune in both to Saint-Malo, under the cover of a rugby reunion match. But his luggage was delayed by the airline, and his plan fell apart. By the time the luggage showed up at his hotel, he was dead." She paused thoughtfully, tipping her head to one side. "Part of that luggage ended up in the hands of police...and the rest, when I found it, was in the possession of local crime lord Yann Bouchard and his lover, Mirrin Daugherty.

"This is the very same Yann Bouchard who admitted that the Teflon silicone lubricant used to murder Vijay Patel came from his shop. What does this tell us?" Kitty pushed away from the desk and crossed slowly to the camera, gesturing with both hands. "It tells us that this crime lord Bouchard must have been Patel's local connection...that he arranged to murder Patel when he showed up without the contraband...and that his lover, Mirrin Daugherty, used her position as hotel receptionist to retrieve said contraband when it was delivered after Patel's murder.

"After extensive research and investigation, I have concluded that this sequence of events must be true. And the evidence backs me up." Kitty clasped her hands together and nodded. "After all, *blond* hair was found in the drain of the tub where Patel died...and Mirrin Daugherty *is* a blonde."

Suddenly, Vane called out. "But not the *only* blonde."

The moment, at last, was perfect.

Kitty spun to gape at him with a look of supreme annoyance. "Excuse me?"

Vane stepped out from between Loire and Cunoval. "Wouldn't you agree that there are other blondes involved in this case, Kitty?"

Kitty glared. "Are you referring to the other hotel receptionist, Jilli Swanson?"

Vane joined Kitty in front of the camera and shook his head. "Only if that was Jilli's hair in the tub drain."

Just then, Cunoval spoke up. "Which it wasn't!" His timing was unplanned but perfect. He marched over to join Kitty and Vane, shaking his fistful of papers. "Jilli Swanson is innocent!"

"Cunoval!" shouted Beuzec. "What are you doing? Get out of her shot!"

Scowling, Kitty drew a finger across her throat for the benefit of the crew—the universal signal to stop shooting video.

"Don't you *dare* turn that camera off." Vane said it sternly, his tone coiling with menace.

"I said *cut*!" snapped Kitty.

The cameraman, sound man, and light technician exchanged looks...then came to an unspoken agreement and went back to work.

The show, it seemed, would go on.

"You're fired!" said Kitty. "All three of you!"

"Now then." Vane cleared his throat. "Is there anything else you can tell us about that blond hair from the drain, Officer Cunoval?"

"*Oui*." Cunoval held up the papers in his hand. "According to the forensics report..."

"Cunoval!" Beuzec stepped forward, looking livid. "Enough of this! You are interfering with a..."

For once, Loire got to cut *him* off. "Let him continue, *sir*." She swooped over and stood in his path. "*Trust* me, you're going to want to hear this."

Beuzec scowled as if he might charge past her anyway...but then he took a half-step back and folded his arms over his chest.

Cunoval cleared his throat and picked up where he'd left off. "According to the forensics report, which arrived thirty minutes ago from the ENFSI crime lab in Paris, the blond hairs retrieved from the tub drain match a donor sample from the ENFSI archives."

Vane switched his gold toothpick to the other side of his mouth. "And whom did the donor sample belong to, pray tell?"

"Someone who had donated biological samples as part of a past criminal case," said Cunoval. "Elimination samples, as the donor had visited an important crime scene during an investigation."

"Anything else you can tell us about this donor?" asked Vane.

"Yes." Cunoval stared dramatically at the camera. "Fingerprints from the same donor were also found on the murder weapon—the can of lubricant."

Vane nodded. "Who *was* this mysterious donor, Officer Cunoval?"

"Kitty Fox." Loire chose that moment to march over with a pair of open handcuffs. "You are under arrest for the murder of Vijay Patel."

Beuzec gasped. "*What*?"

Kitty backed away, a look of panic spreading over her features as she realized Vane was doing much more than upstaging her. "Oh my God! This is insane!"

"Not at all," said Vane. "It is, in fact, *perfectly* sane. And I theorize it is only the *latest* in a *long* line of murders linked to Ms. Fox." He turned to focus on the camera. "How else to explain her meteoric rise? What better way could there be for someone so young and inexperienced to advance her career as a media crime expert?" He looked at her and shook his head. "This way, she would never be wrong in identifying a perpetrator."

"Because *she* always decided whom to *frame*," added Cunoval.

Kitty continued to back away from Loire. "No! It's him!" She jabbed a finger at Vane. "*He's* framing *me*!"

"Is that so?" asked Loire. "Then how do you explain the prints on the lubricant, Mademoiselle Fox? That can was sent off to the lab before your arrival. You could not possibly have touched it unless you did so *before* we took it into custody."

"But I didn't!" Kitty was sliding toward hysteria as the extent of her predicament became clear.

"Likewise, we retrieved your hair from the drain before your involvement in the investigation." Loire shook her head slowly. "It could only have been deposited there *before* Mr. Patel's body was found."

"*Mon dieu*," said Beuzec. "This is incredible!"

"It's all circumstantial!" Kitty angled herself so she was backing toward an exit. "I didn't do it!"

"We will let the courts determine that," said Loire.

Suddenly, Kitty whirled as if to make a run for it...only to bump into Vane, who'd slipped around to block the exit.

He grabbed her by the shoulders and locked eyes with her. "How many of your other cases did you rig, you phony?" His voice and expression oozed with contempt. "How many lives have you destroyed in your rush to glory?"

"Let go of me!" Kitty thrashed in his grip. "*You* planted that evidence!"

"Blaming others right up to the end," said Vane. "You sicken me."

"Now then." Loire hooked a cuff around Kitty's right wrist and snapped it tight. "Where were we?" She did the same to Kitty's left wrist. "Kitty Fox, you are under arrest for the murder of Vijay Patel."

Vane couldn't resist making one more contribution. "Her real name isn't Kitty Fox," he said as Loire led her prisoner away. "It's Agnes Butts of Peckerhead, Ohio."

"Agnes Butts?" Beuzec winced. "Really?"

"Shut up!" howled Kitty. "Shut your mouth! And it's *Pepperhead*!"

Vane pulled the gold toothpick from between his teeth and pointed it at the camera, raising one eyebrow for effect. "Strange, isn't it?"

* * * *

Later, when the dust had settled, Vane slipped out of the police station. While everyone's attention was focused elsewhere, he walked to the seawall, where a middle-aged man with a rail-thin body and gaunt features awaited him.

"*Bonjour*." The man, who wore a loose brown shirt and tattered blue jeans, waved him over. "Good to see you, Monsieur Vane." His thin, dark hair fluttered in the sea breeze.

"You, too." Vane held out his hand for a shake. "It's been a busy day. I had an important case to solve."

The man took his hand. "And you solved it?"

"Of course." Vane grinned. "Would you expect anything less?"

The man closed his eyes. "Thank God. Oh, thank God." Then, he opened them and flung his arms around Vane. "And thank *you*. From the bottom of my soul, thank *you*."

At that moment, Vane caught sight of Loire crossing the street toward them. "I'm very glad everything worked out for you." He patted the man's back, then pushed him away. "Now I really must return to my duties."

The man saw where Vane was looking and understood. "*Merci*, and *au revoir*." With one final wave, he hurried off down the cobblestone walk, heading in the opposite direction from the walled city.

Loire watched as he rushed away. "Who was that?"

"A fan." Vane sighed. "Pouring his heart out about what I've meant to him."

"Ah." Loire turned and leaned on the seawall. Her mood seemed lighter than usual. "You make a big impression, don't you?"

"That's true." Vane leaned beside her, gazing out at the sapphire sea as it glittered under the midday sun. "Though I suppose you could say the same of Kitty Fox."

"A big impression, yes." Loire clucked. "But nothing underneath."

"The perfect celebrity." Vane smirked.

Loire shook her head. "What a pity. Such a waste."

"Don't feel too bad for her," said Vane. "She'll use this to her advantage, you'll see. Just wait till she writes her next book from behind bars." He rolled his eyes. "It'll be a smash, I promise you."

Loire scowled. "What kind of person does it take to do something like this? To kill for fame and fortune, then place the blame on the innocent?"

"That's a difficult question," said Vane, though it wasn't, really. What kind of person did it take? Someone exactly like him.

For that was what he'd done with Kitty—framed her for the murder of Patel. He'd left samples of her hair at the crime scene, hair he'd been saving since their first encounter at Gibraltar. He'd been saving her fingerprints, too, and had transferred them to the can of lubricant...no easy task if done right, but as with so many things, he was an expert in the practice. Right from the start, she'd been his target, his patsy; she was a rival, a nuisance, a threat, and he'd taken her off the game board...at least for now, at least until some judge or jury decided the evidence against her was too circumstantial.

But there was more to it than that, more at stake than discrediting Kitty. There always was, when Vane worked his magic. He loved the challenge of "solving" the very crimes he'd committed in a way that was believable to the authorities and his audience alike. The thrill of arranging the perfect frame-up while cutting a giant figure in the public eye was one of the things he lived for.

But none of it would be complete if his victims weren't so richly deserving.

"Some people just have a darkness inside them," he told Loire. "A darkness that takes over when certain opportunities present themselves."

"She didn't *need* such opportunities, though, did she?" asked Loire. "She seemed to me a woman who already had everything."

Vane shrugged. "There must have been more to it."

There certainly was, as the man who'd hugged him moments ago could have attested. For that man's daughter had been brutally raped one year ago by Patel. The girl had killed herself after that, after Patel had escaped punishment on a technicality.

But Patel's great escape had ended in Saint-Malo. With meticulous planning and the help of the girl's father—aka the "mystery bum," the Air France luggage delivery man, and the man in the hoodie on the security footage—Vane had ended Patel's days of guilt-free evasion.

And Patel had died under a cloud. Though he'd avoided punishment for the crime he *had* committed, the world would always think of him as dying for *other* crimes...ironically, ones he *hadn't* committed. Thanks to Vane planting evidence in the late-arriving luggage, Patel would always be known as a smuggler of drugs and kiddie porn, a reprehensible lowlife who'd gotten what was coming to him.

Which was, in every way that mattered, perfectly accurate.

"So." Loire bumped elbows with Vane and smiled. Her mood really *had* improved. "*Que faire?* What next for you, Monsieur Vane?"

"The usual," said Vane. "Write a book, make a TV show. What about you?"

Loire rested her chin on her folded hands. "The usual. Back to rounding up drunken tourists."

"Staying in town?" asked Vane. "I thought all this excitement might have given you the urge to leave."

Loire shrugged. "It is too late for that. I am too old to start over."

"But you've got the juice now," said Vane. "You closed a case that will lead to the conviction of an international celebrity."

"And what happens when a potential employer runs a background check? What happens when they talk to Capitaine Beuzec?" She scowled and shook her head. "He will continue to punish me, and I will remain trapped here."

"But..."

She raised a hand to cut him off. "Better to not even try, Monsieur Vane."

Vane started to say something, then stopped. For a long moment, he and Loire stared out at the rolling surf.

"Maybe you'll change your mind someday," he said finally. "Stranger things have happened."

Loire sighed. "My mind is made up."

"If you *do* change it, though..." Vane reached into the breast pocket of his maroon jacket. "Perhaps this will be of some help." He drew out a small silver case, the length and width of his pinky finger, and handed it over.

Loire flicked the tiny catch and lifted the lid, then stared at the contents without a word.

"My private number is inscribed on the case," said Vane.

"But are you sure you mean to give me what is *inside* the case?" Frowning, Loire drew out the object that was tucked into the case's black velvet lining. It was a twin of his famous gold toothpick.

"Of course." Vane smiled. "From one investigator to another."

"I cannot accept this." She put the toothpick back into the case and closed it, then pushed it toward him. "It is too extravagant."

"You deserve it." Vane nodded. "I know potential when I see it. You might yet go far, if you put your mind to it." He pushed the case back to her. "And this could give you an edge. It could open doors for you."

Loire gazed at the case, turning it over in her hands. "But I might never use it that way."

"Think of it as a memento, then," said Vane. "A souvenir of our first case together, as well as an ace in the hole."

The toothpick was more than that, though. Something was hidden inside it, something that would make it an ace in the hole for Vane himself if Loire ever rose through the ranks.

A microtransmitter. The tiniest radio that money could buy was hidden inside it, set to be activated if she ever got close to the kind of intelligence he might need.

"Good luck," said Vane, giving her shoulder an affectionate squeeze. "May you go very far indeed."

Robert Jeschonek is an envelope-pushing, *USA Today*-bestselling author. His stories have appeared in *Pulphouse Fiction Magazine, Fiction River, Postscripts, Pulp Literature*, and other publications around the world. His crime tale, "The Messiah Business," appeared in *Fiction River: Risk Takers* and was named an honorable mention in *Year's Best Crime and Mystery Stories 2016*. His novels have won the International Book Award, the Forward National Literature Award, and the Scribe Award. Visit him online at robertjeschonek.com. You can also find him on Facebook and follow him as @TheFictioneer on Twitter.

LOOSE ENDS
FLETCHER FLORA

Our classic reprint this issue is by Fletcher Flora, who is no stranger to the pages of BCMM, having appeared in our first issue with another classic reprint. "Loose Ends" first appeared in *Manhunt* magazine, August 1958.

CHAPTER 1.

A woman wanted to see me about a job. Her name, she said, was Faith Salem. She lived, she said, in a certain apartment in a certain apartment building, and she told me the number of the apartment and the floor it was on and the name and the address of the building it was in. She said she wanted me to come there and see her at three o'clock that afternoon, the same day she called on the telephone, and I went and saw her, and it was three o'clock when I got there.

The door was opened by a maid with a face like half a walnut. You may think it's impossible for a face to look like half a walnut, and I suppose it is, if you want to be literal, but half a walnut is, nevertheless, all I can think of as a comparison when I think of the face of this maid. She wasn't young, and she probably wasn't old. She was, as they say, an indeterminate age. Her eyes smiled, but not her lips, and she nodded her head three times as if she had checked me swiftly on three salient points and was satisfied on every one. This gave me confidence.

"I'm Percy Hand," I said. "I have an appointment with Miss Salem."

"This way," she said. Following her out of a vestibule, I waded through a couple acres of thick wood pile in crossing two wide rooms, and then I crossed, in a third room, another acre of black and white tile that made me feel, by contrast, as if I were taking steps a yard high, and finally I got out onto a terrace in the sunlight, and Faith Salem got up off her stomach and faced me. She had been lying on a soft pad covered with bright yellow material that might have been silk or nylon or something, and she was wearing in a couple of places a very little bit of more material that was just as shining and soft and might have been the same kind, except that it was white instead of yellow. Sunbathing was what she was doing, and I was glad. Her skin was firm and golden brown, and it gave the impression of consistency all over, and I was willing to bet that the little bit of white in a couple of places was only a concession to present company. Nine times out of ten, when someone tries to describe a woman who is fairly tall and has a slim and pliant and beautiful body, he will say that she is willowy, and that's what I say. I say that Faith Salem was willowy. I also say that her hair was almost the identical color of the rest of her, and this seemed somehow too perfect to have been accomplished deliberately by design, but it may have been. You had to look at her face for a long time before you became aware that she was certainly a number of years older than you'd thought at first she was.

"Mr. Hand has arrived, Miss Faith," the maid said.

"Thank you. Maria," Faith Salem said.

I stepped twice, and she stepped twice, and we met and shook hands. Her grip was firm. I liked the way her fingers took hold of my fingers and held them and were in no hurry to drop them.

"Thank you for coming, Mr. Hand," she said. "You must excuse me for receiving you this way, but the sun is on this terrace for only a short while each afternoon, and I didn't want to miss any of it."

"I'd have been sorry to have missed it myself," I said.

She smiled gravely, taking my meaning, and then released my fingers and walked over to a yellow chaise lounge on which a white hip-length coat had been left lying. She put on the coat and moved to a wrought iron and glass table where there was a single tall tumbler with alternating red and yellow stripes. The tumbler was empty. Holding it against the light, she stared through it wistfully as if she were regretting its emptiness, and I watched her do this with pleasure and no regrets whatever. There is a kind of legerdemain about a short coat over something shorter. It creates the illusion, even when you have evidence to the contrary, that it's all there is, there isn't any more.

"I like you, Mr. Hand," she said. "I like your looks."

"Thanks. I like yours too."

"Would you care for a drink?"

"Why not? It's a warm day."

"I had a gin and tonic before you came. Do you drink gin and tonic?"

"When it's offered. A gin and tonic would be fine."

She set the red and yellow tumbler on the glass top of the table and turned slightly in the direction of the entrance to the black and white tiled room.

"Gin and tonic, Maria," she said. I had thought that the indeterminate maid with a face like half a walnut had gone away, and I felt a slight shock of surprise to discover that she had been standing all the while behind me. Now she nodded three times exactly, a repetition of the gesture she had made at the door, and backed away into the apartment and out of sight. Faith Salem sat down in a low wicker chair and crossed her feet at the ankles and stared at her long golden legs. I stared at them too.

"Please sit down, Mr. Hand," she said. "Maria will bring the gin and tonics in a moment. In the meanwhile, if you like, I can begin explaining why I asked you to come here."

"I'd appreciate it." I folded myself into her chair's mate. "I've been wondering, of course."

"Naturally." The full lower lip protruded a little, giving to her face a suggestion of darkness and brooding. "Let me begin by asking a question. Do you know Graham Markley?"

"Not personally. Like everyone else who reads the papers, I know something about him. Quondam boy-wonder of finance. No boy any longer. If he's still a wonder, he doesn't work at it quite so hard. Works harder nowadays, from reports, at spending some of what he's made. Unless, of course, there's another Graham Markley."

"He's the one. Graham and I have an understanding."

There was, before the last word, a barely perceptible hesitation that gave to her statement a subtle and significant shading. She had explained in a breath, or in the briefest holding of a breath, the acres of pile and tile in this lavish stone and steel tower with terraces that caught the afternoon sun for at least a little while. Delicately, she had told me who paid the rent.

"That's nice," I said. "Congratulations."

"It's entirely informal at present, but it may not remain so. He's asked me to marry him. Not immediately, which is impossible, but eventually."

"That'll be even better. Or will it?"

"It will. A certain amount of security attaches to marriage. There are certain compensations if the marriage fails." She smiled slowly, the smile beginning and growing and forcing from her face the dark and almost petulant expression of brooding, and in her eyes, which were brown, there was instantly a gleam of cynical good humor which was the effect, as it turned out, of a kind of casual compatibility she had developed with herself. "I haven't always had the good things that money buys, Mr. Hand, but I've learned from experience to live with them naturally. I don't think I would care now to live with less. With these good things that money buys, I'm perfectly willing to accept my share of the bad things that money seems invariably to entail. Is my position clear?"

"Yes, it is." I said. "It couldn't be clearer."

At that moment, Maria returned with a pair of gin and tonics in red and yellow glasses on a tray. She served one of them to Faith Salem and the other to me, and then she completed the three nods routine and went away again. The three nods, I now realized, was not a gesture of approval but an involuntary reaction to any situation to be handled, as my arrival earlier, or any situation already handled, as the serving of the drinks. I drank some of my tonic and liked it. There was a kind of astringency in the faintly bitter taste of the quinine. There was also, I thought now that it had been suggested to me, a kind of astringency in Faith Salem. A faintly bitter quality. A clean and refreshing tautness in her lean and lovely body and in her uncompromised compatibility with herself.

"Did you know Graham's wife?" she asked suddenly.

"Which one?" I said.

"The last one. Number three, I think."

"It doesn't matter. There was no purpose in my asking for the distinction. I didn't know number three, or two, or one. Graham Markley's wives and I didn't move in the same circles."

"I thought perhaps you might have met her professionally."

"As an employer or subject of investigation?"

"Either way."

"Neither, as a matter of fact. And if I had, I couldn't tell you."

"Ethics? I heard that about you. Someone told me you were honorable and discreet. I believe it."

"Thanks. Also thanks to someone."

"That's why I called you. I'm glad now that I did."

"I know. You like my looks, and I like yours. We admire each other."

"Are you always so flippant?"

"Scarcely ever. The truth is, I'm very serious, and I take my work seriously. Do you have some work for me to do?"

She swallowed some more of her tonic and held the glass in her lap with both hands. Her expression was again rather darkly brooding, and she seemed for a moment uncertain of herself.

"Perhaps you won't want the job," she said.

I nodded. "It's possible."

"We'll see." She swallowed more of the tonic and looked suddenly more decisive. "Do you remember what happened to Graham's third wife?"

"I seem to remember that she left him, which wasn't surprising. So did number one. So did number two. Excuse me if I'm being offensive."

"Not at all. You're not required to like Graham. Many people don't. I confess that there are times when I don't like him very much myself. I did like his third wife, however. We were in college together, as a matter of fact. We shared an apartment one year. Her name was Constance Vaughan then. I left school that year, the year we shared the apartment, and we never saw each other again."

"You mean you never knew her as Mrs. Graham Markley?"

"Yes. I didn't know she'd married. In college she didn't seem, somehow, like the kind of girl who would ever marry anyone at all, let alone someone like Graham. That was a good many years ago, of course, and people change, I suppose. Anyhow, it was rather odd, wasn't it? I came here about a year ago from Europe, where I had been living with my second husband, who is not my husband any longer, and I met Graham and after a while entered into our present arrangement, which is comfortable but not altogether satisfactory, and then I learned that he had been married to Constance, whom I had known all that time ago. Don't you think that was quite odd?"

"It seems to meet the requirements of the term."

"Yes. The truth is, it made me feel rather strange. Especially when I discovered that she had simply disappeared about a year before."

"Disappeared?"

"Simply vanished. She hasn't been seen since by anyone who knew her here. You'll have to admit that it's peculiar. Numbers one and two left Graham and divorced him and tapped him for alimony, which he probably deserved, and this was sensible. It was not sensible, however, simply to disappear without a trace and never sue for divorce and alimony, or even separate maintenance. Do you think so?"

"Off hand, I don't. There may have been good reasons. Surely an attempt was made to locate her."

"Oh, yes. Of course. Her disappearance was reported to the police, and they made an effort to find her, but it was kept pretty quiet, and I don't think anyone tried very hard. Because of the circumstances, you see."

"No, I don't see. What circumstances?"

"Well, Constance had a baby. A little boy that got to be almost two years old and died. Constance loved him intensely. That's the way she was about anyone or anything she loved. Very intense. It was rather frightening, in a way. Anyhow, when the little boy died, she seemed to be going right out of her mind with grief, and Graham was no consolation or comfort, of course, and then she met Regis Lawler. Psychologically, she was just ready for him, completely vulnerable, and she fell in love with him, and apparently they had an affair. To get to the point about circumstances, Regis Lawler disappeared the same night that Constance did, and that's why no one got too excited or concerned. It was assumed that they'd gone away together."

"Don't you believe that they did?"

"I don't know. I think I do. What do you think?"

"On the surface, it seems a reasonable assumption, but it leaves a lot of loose ends."

"That's it. That's what disturbs me. Too many loose ends. I don't like loose ends, Mr. Hand. Will you try to tie them up for me?"

"Find out where Constance Markley went?"

"Yes."

"I'm sorry."

"You mean you won't?"

"I mean I probably couldn't. Look at it this way. The police have far greater facilities for this kind of thing than any private detective, and they've tried without success. Or if they did find out where Constance Markley went, it was obviously not police business and was quietly dropped. Either way, I'd be wasting my time and your money to try to find her now."

"Don't worry about wasting my money."

"All right. I'll just worry about wasting my time."

"Is it wasted if it's paid for?"

"That's a good point. If you want to buy my time for a fee, why should I drag my heels? Maybe I'm too ethical."

"Does that mean you accept?"

"No. Not yet. Be reasonable, Miss Salem. If Constance Markley and Regis Lawler went off together, they might be anywhere in the country or out of it. The West Coast. South America. Europe. Just about anywhere on earth."

She finished her tonic, lit a cigarette, and let her head fall slowly against the back of the wicker chair as if she were suddenly very tired. With her eyes closed, the shadows of her lashes on her cheeks, she seemed to be asleep in an instant, except for the thin blue plume of smoke expelled slowly from her lungs. After a few moments, her eyes still closed, she spoke again.

"Why should they do that? Why disappear? Why run away at all? Women are leaving husbands every day. Men are leaving wives. They simply leave. Why didn't Constance?"

"People do queer things sometimes. Usually there are reasons that seem good to the people. You said Mrs. Markley was an intense sort of person. You said she'd suffered a tragedy that nearly unbalanced her mentally. You implied that she hadn't been happy with Graham Markley. Maybe she just wanted to go away clean—no connections, no repercussions, nothing at all left of the old life but a man she loved and the few things she'd have to remember because she couldn't forget."

"I know. I've thought of that, and it's something that Constance might possibly have done, as I remember her."

"How do you remember her?"

"Well, as I said, she was intense. She was always excited or depressed, and I could never quite understand what she was excited or depressed about. Ideas that occurred to her or were passed on to her by someone. Impressions and suggestions. Things like that. Little things that would never have influenced most people in the least. She was pretty, in a way, but it took quite a while before you realized it. She had a kind of delicacy or fragility about her, but I don't believe that she was actually fragile physically. It was just an impression. She didn't appeal to men, and I never thought that men appealed to her. In the year we lived together, she never went out with a man that I can recall. Her parents had money. That's why I lived with her. I had practically no money at all then, and she took a fancy to me and wanted to rent an apartment for us, and so she did, and I stayed with her until near the end of the school year. I married a boy who also had money. Never mind me, though. The point is, we went away from school, and I didn't see Constance again. She was angry with me and refused to say good-bye, I've always been sorry."

"How did she happen to meet and marry Graham Markley?"

"I don't know. Graham is susceptible to variety in women. Probably her particular kind of intangible prettiness, her fragility, something happened to appeal to him at the time they met. I imagine their marriage was one of those sudden, impulsive things that usually should never happen."

"I see. How did you learn so much about her? Not back there in the beginning. I mean after she married Markley. About her baby, her affair with Lawler, those things."

"Oh, I picked up bits from various sources, but most of it I learned from Maria. She was maid to Constance, you see, when Constance and Graham were living together. When I came along and moved into this apartment, I sort of acquired her. Graham still had her and didn't know what to do with her, so he sent her over to me. Isn't that strange?"

"Convenient, I'd say. Did Maria see Constance Markley the night of her disappearance?"

"Yes. She helped Constance dress. Apparently she was the last person that Constance spoke to."

"May I speak with her for a moment?"

"If you wish. I'll get her."

CHAPTER 2.

She got up and walked barefooted off the terrace into the black and white tiled room, and I drank the last of my gin and tonic and wished for another, and in about three minutes, not longer, she returned with Maria. She sat down again and told Maria that she could also sit down if she pleased, but Maria preferred to stand. Her small brown face was perfectly composed, and expressionless.

"What do you want me to tell you?" she said.

"I want you to answer a few questions about Mrs. Markley," I said. "Constance Markley, that is. Will you do that?"

"If I can."

"Miss Salem says that you saw Mrs. Markley the night she disappeared. Is that so?"

"It's so. I helped her dress for the evening."

"Did she go out alone?"

"Yes. Alone."

"Do you know where she was going?"

"I assumed that she was going to see Mr. Lawler. She didn't tell me."

"Did she go to see Mr. Lawler often?"

"Twice a week, maybe. Sometimes more."

"How do you know? Did she confide in you?"

"More in me than anyone else. She had to talk to someone."

"I see. Were you devoted to Mrs. Markley?"

"Yes. She was very kind, very unhappy. I pitied her."

"Because of the death of her child?"

"Partly because of that. I don't know. She was not happy."

"Did you approve of her affair with Mr. Lawler?"

"Not approve, exactly. I understood it. She needed a special kind of love. A kind of attention."

"Mr. Lawler gave her this?"

"He must have given it to her. Otherwise, she wouldn't have gone on with him. That's reasonable."

"Yes, it is. It's reasonable. And so are you, Maria. You're a very reasonable woman. Tell me. What was your impression of her the night she disappeared?"

"Pardon?"

"Her emotional state, I mean. Was she depressed? Cheerful?"

"Not depressed. Not cheerful. She was eager. There's a difference between eagerness and cheerfulness."

"That's true. Besides being reasonable, Maria, you are also perceptive. Did she seem excessively agitated in any way?"

"Just eager. She was always eager when she went to see Mr. Lawler."

"Do you think that Mr. Markley was aware of the relationship between his wife and Lawler?"

"I don't know. He didn't show much interest in anything Mrs. Markley did. Not even when the child died."

"All right. Just one more question. Maria. What time did Mrs. Markley leave here?"

"About eight. Perhaps a few minutes before or after."

"Thank you, Maria."

Maria turned her still brown face toward Faith Salem, who smiled and nodded. The maid nodded in return, three times, and went away. Faith Salem stood up abruptly, standing with her legs spread and her hands rammed into the patch pockets of the short white coat.

"Well?" she said.

"It looks hopeless," I said. "You'd be wasting your money."

"Perhaps so. If I don't waste it on you, I'll waste it on someone else."

"In that case, it might as well be me."

"You agree, then? You'll take the job?"

Looking up at her, I was beginning to feel dominated, which was not good, so I removed the feeling by standing.

"Tentatively," I said.

"What do you mean, tentatively?"

"I'll make a preliminary investigation. If anything significant or interesting comes out of it, I'll go ahead. If not, I'll quit. You'll pay my expenses and twenty-five dollars a day. Are those terms acceptable?"

"Yes. I accept."

"Another thing. I'm to be allowed to talk with whomever I think necessary. Is that also agreed?"

"Yes, of course." She hesitated, her soft lower lip protruding again in the darkly brooding expression. "You mean Graham, I suppose. I'd prefer, naturally, that he not know whom you're working for."

"I won't tell him unless I think it's advisable. I promise that much."

"That's good enough. I have confidence in your word, Mr. Hand."

"Ethical. Someone told you, and you believe it, and that's what I am. I'll begin my investigation, it you don't mind, by asking you one more question. What are you afraid of?"

"Afraid? I'm afraid of nothing. I honestly believe that I've never been afraid of anything in my life."

"I'm ready to concede that you probably haven't. Let me put it differently. What disturbs you about Constance Markley's disappearance?"

"I've explained that. I don't like loose ends. Graham has asked me to marry him. For my own reasons, I want to accept. First, however, he has to get a divorce. He can get it, I suppose, on grounds of desertion. I only want to know that it really was desertion."

"That's not quite convincing. What alternative to desertion, specifically, do you have in mind?"

"You said you would ask one more question, Mr. Hand. You've asked two."

"Excuse me. You can see how dedicated I become to my work."

"I should appreciate that, of course, and I do. I honestly have no specific alternative in mind. I just don't like the situation as it stands. There's another thing, however. I knew Constance, and I liked her, and now by an exceptional turn of events I'm in the position of appropriating something that was hers. I want to know that it's all right. I want to know where she went, and why she went wherever she did, and that everything is all right there and will be all right here, whatever happens."

I believed her. I believed everything she told me. She was a woman I could not doubt or condemn or even criticize. If I had been as rich as Graham Markley, I'd have taken her away, later if not then, and I'd have kept her, and there would have been between us, in the end, more than the money which would have been essential in the beginning.

"I'll see what I can do," I said. "Do you have a photograph of Constance Markley that I can take along?"

"Yes. There's one here that Maria brought. I'll get it for you."

She went inside and was gone for a few minutes and came back with the photograph. I took it from her and put it into the side pocket of my coat without looking at it. There would be plenty of time later to look at it, and now, in the last seconds of our first meeting, I wanted to look at Faith Salem.

"Goodbye," I said. "I'll see you again in a few days and let you know if I intend to go ahead."

"Call before you come," she said.

"Yes," I said. "Certainly."

"I'll see you to the door."

"No. Don't bother. You'd better stay here in the sun. In another half hour, it'll be gone."

"Yes. So it will." She looked up at the white disk in the sky beyond a ridge of tooled stone. "Goodbye, then. I'll be waiting to hear from you."

She offered me her hand, and I took it and held it and released it. In the middle of the black and white acre, I paused and looked back. She had already removed the short white coat and was lying on her stomach on the yellow pad. Her face was buried in the crook of an elbow.

I went on out and back to my office and put my feet on the desk and thought about her lying there in the sun. There was no sun in my office. In front of me was a blank wall, and behind me was a narrow window, and outside the narrow window was a narrow alley. Whenever I got tired of looking at the wall I could get up and stand by the window and look down into the alley, and whenever I got tired of looking into the alley I could sit down and look at the wall again, and whenever I got tired of looking at both the wall and the alley, which was frequently, I could go out somewhere and look at something else. Now I simply closed my eyes and saw clearly behind the lids a lean brown body interrupted in two places by the briefest of white hiatuses.

This was pleasant but not of the first importance. It was more important, though less pleasant, to think about Graham Markley. Conceding the priority of importance, I began reluctantly to think about him, and after a few minutes of reluctant thinking, I lowered my feet and reached for a telephone directory. After locating his name and number, I dialed the number and waited through a couple of rings, and then a voice came on that made me feel with its first careful syllable as if I'd neglected recently to bathe and clean my fingernails.

"Graham Markley's residence," the voice said.

"This is Percival Hand," I said. "I'm a private detective. I'd like to speak with Mr. Markley." Ordinarily I use the abbreviated version of my name, just plain Percy, but I felt compelled by the voice to be as proper and impressive as possible. As it was, in the exorbitantly long pause that followed, I felt as if I had been unpardonably offensive.

"If you will just hold the wire," the voice said at last, "I shall see if Mr. Markley is at home." Which meant, of course, that Mr. Markley was certainly at home, but that it remained to be seen if he would be so irresponsible as to talk with a private detective on the telephone, which was surely unlikely. I held the wire and waited. I inspected my nails and found them clean. I tried to smell myself and couldn't. Another voice came on abruptly, and it was, as it developed, the voice of Graham Markley.

"Graham Markley speaking. What can I do for you, Mr. Hand?"

"I'd like to make an appointment to see you personally, if possible."

"About what?"

I had already considered the relative advantages in this particular instance of candor and deception, and I had decided that there was probably little or nothing to choose between them. In cases where deception gains me nothing, I'm always prepared to be candid, and that's what I was now.

"About your wife. Your third wife, that is."

"I can't imagine why my wife should be a point of discussion between you and me, Mr. Hand."

"I thought you might be able to give me some useful information." There was a moment of waiting. The wire sang softly in the interim.

"For what purpose?" he said. "Am I to understand that you're investigating my wife's disappearance?"

"That's right."

"At whose request?"

"I'm not at liberty to say at the moment."

"Come, Mr. Hand. If you expect any cooperation from me, you'll have to be less reticent."

"I haven't received any cooperation from you yet, Mr. Markley."

"It was reasonably apparent to everyone, including the police and myself, why my wife went away. I confess that I can't see any use in stirring up an unpleasant matter that I had hoped was forgotten. Do you know anything that would justify it?"

Again I evaluated the advantages of candor and deception, and this time I chose deception. The advantages in its favor seemed so palpable, as a matter of fact, that the evaluation required no more than a second.

"I've learned something," I lied, "that I think will interest you."

"Perhaps you had better tell me what it is."

"Sorry. I'd rather not discuss it over the telephone."

"I can't see you today. It's impossible."

"Tomorrow will do. If you'll set a time, I'll be happy to call on you."

"That won't be necessary. I'll come to your office."

"I don't want to inconvenience you."

"Thank you for your consideration. However, I prefer to see you in your office. How about two o'clock tomorrow afternoon?"

"Good. I'll be expecting you."

I told him where my office was, and we said good-bye and hung up. Hocking back in my chair, I elevated my feet again and closed my eyes. Faith Salem was still lying in the sun. I watched her for a few moments and then opened my eyes and lit a cigarette and began thinking about Regis Lawler. I didn't accomplish much by this, for I didn't have much material for thought to start with. I had met him casually a few times quite a while ago, in this or that place we had both gone to, but most of what I knew about him was incidental to what I knew about his brother, who was older and generally more important and had more about him worth knowing.

The brother's name was Silas. After long and precarious apprentice years in a number of illegal operations, he had begun slowly to achieve a kind of acceptance, even respectability, that increased in ratio to the measure of his security. Now he was the owner of a fine restaurant. At least, it was a restaurant among other things, and it was that equally, if not primarily. When you went there, it was assumed that you had come for good food, and that's what you got. You got it in rich and quiet surroundings to the music of a string quartet that sometimes played Beethoven as well as Fritz Kreisler and Johann Strauss. The chefs were the best that Lawler could hire, and the best that Lawler could hire were as good as any and better than most. On the correct principle that good food should tolerate no distractions, the service was performed by elderly colored waiters who were artists in the difficult technique of being solicitous without being obtrusive.

If you wanted distractions, you went downstairs, below street level. This was known as the Apache Room, a little bit of the Left Bank transplanted, and it was phony and made no pretense of being anything else, and it was frankly for people who liked it that way. There were red-checked cloths on the tables, pretty girls with pretty legs who serviced the tables, a small orchestra with the peculiar quality that is supposed to be peculiarly Parisian, and murals all around the walls of girls in black stockings doing the can-can alternating with other murals of other girls being maltreated by Apaches and always showing quite a lot of one white thigh above a fancy garter in the deep slit of a tight skirt.

On the floor above the restaurant, up one flight of carpeted stairs, you could go to gamble if you chose. In a series of three large rooms muffled in drapes and carpets, you could play roulette or poker or blackjack or shoot dice, and sometimes you might even win at one or the other or all, but more often, of course, you lost and were expected to lose graciously. If you did not, as sometimes happened, you were escorted outside by a brace of hard-handed gentlemen in evening clothes, and you were thereafter *persona non grata* until you received absolution and clearance from Silas Lawler himself. The games were reputed to be honest, and, all things considered, they probably were.

In the basement, you could dance and make moderate love and get drunk, if you wished, on expensive drinks. In the restaurant, you did not get drunk or dance or make love or look at naughty murals. In the game rooms, you gambled quietly with no limit except your own judgment and bank account, and you saved everything else for some other place and some other time. Patrons passed as they pleased from one level to another, but the atmosphere was never permitted to go with them. The basement never climbed the stairs, nor did the upper floors descend.

Silas Lawler was, in brief, not a man to be taken lightly, or a man who would take lightly any transgression against himself or his interests. It was, I reflected, wholly incredible that he would be indifferent to the disappearance of a brother. Whatever the reason for the disappearance, whatever the technique of its execution, Silas Lawler knew it, or thought he knew it, and he might be prevailed upon to tell me in confidence, or he might not, but in any event it would be necessary for me to talk with him as soon as I could, which would probably be tomorrow. I would see Graham Markley at two, and later I would try to see Silas Lawler, and if nothing significant came of these two meetings I would go again to see Faith Salem, which would be a pleasure, and terminate our relationship, which would not.

Having thought my way back to Faith Salem, I closed my eyes and tried to find her, but the sun had left the terrace, and so had she. Opening my eyes, I lowered my feet and stood up. I had determined an agenda of sorts, and now there seemed to be nothing of importance left to do on this particular day. Besides, it was getting rather late, and I was getting rather hungry, and so I went out and patronized a steak house and afterward spent one-third of the night doing things that were not important and not related to anything that had gone before. About ten o'clock I returned to the room and bath and hot plate that I euphemistically called home. I went to bed and slept well.

CHAPTER 3.

I woke up at seven in the morning, which is a nasty habit of mine that endures through indiscretions and hangovers and intermittent periods of irregular living. In the bathroom, I shaved and necessarily looked at my face in the mirror. *I like you, Mr. Hand,* Faith Salem had said. *I like your looks.* Well, it was an ambiguous expression. You could like the looks of a Collie dog or a pair of shoes or a Shoebill stork. It could mean that you were inspired by confidence or amusement or the urge to be a sister. Looking at my face, I was not deluded. I decided that I was probably somewhere between the dog and the stork. I finished shaving and dressed and went out for breakfast and arrived in due time at my office, where nothing happened all morning.

Two o'clock came, but Graham Markley didn't. At ten after, he did.

I heard him enter the little cubbyhole in which my clients wait when there is another client ahead of them, which is something that should happen oftener than it does, and when I got to the door to meet him, he was standing there looking antiseptic among the germs. His expression included me with the others.

"Mr. Hand?" he said.

"That's right. You're Mr. Markley, I suppose?"

"Yes. I'm sorry to be late."

"Think nothing of it. In this office, ten minutes late is early. Come in, please."

He walked past me and sat down in the client's chair beside the desk. Because I felt he would consider it an imposition, I didn't offer to shake hands. I felt that he might even ignore or reject the offer, which would have made me indignant or even indiscreet. Resuming my place in the chair behind the desk, I made a quick inventory and acquired an impression. He sat rigidly, with his knees together and his hat on his knees. His straight black hair was receding but still had a majority present. His face was narrow, his nose was long, his lips were thin. Arrogance was implicit. He looked something like the guy who used to play Sherlock Holmes in the movies. Maybe he looked like Sherlock Holmes.

"Precisely what do you want to tell me, Mr. Hand?" he said.

"Well," I said, "that isn't quite my position. What I want is for you to tell me something."

"Indeed? I gathered from our conversation on the telephone yesterday that you were in possession of some new information regarding my wife."

"Did I infer that? It isn't exactly true. What I meant to suggest was that the available information isn't adequate. It leaves too much unexplained."

"Do you think so? The police apparently didn't. As a matter of fact, it was quite clear to everyone what my wife had done. It was, as you may realize, an embarrassing affair for me, and there seemed to be no good purpose in giving it undue publicity or in pursuing it indefinitely."

"Do you still feel that way? That there is no purpose in pursuing it any further?"

"Until yesterday I did. Now I'm not so sure. I don't wish to interfere with whatever kind of life my wife is trying to establish for herself, nor do I wish to restore any kind of contact between her and me, but since our telephone conversation I've begun to feel that it would be better for several reasons if she could be located."

"Are you prepared to help?"

"Conditionally."

"What conditions?"

"Are you, for your part, prepared to tell me who initiated this investigation?"

"What action would you consider taking if I were to tell you?"

"None. The truth is, I'm certain that I know. I merely want to verify it."

"You're probably right."

"Miss Salem? I thought so. Well, it's understandable. Under the circumstances of our relationship, she's naturally concerned. She urged me once previously to try again to locate my wife, but I wasn't inclined to reopen what was, as I said, an unpleasant and embarrassing affair. Apparently I underestimated the strength of her feeling."

"You don't resent her action, then?"

"Certainly not. I'm particularly anxious to settle any uneasiness she may feel. I'm even willing to assume the payment of your fee."

"That's between you and her, of course. Will you tell me why you think your wife disappeared?"

"As to why she disappeared, I can only speculate. As to why she left, which is something else, I'm certain. She was having an affair with a man named Regis Lawler. They went away together. The relationship between my wife and me had deteriorated by that time to such an extent that I really didn't care. I considered it a satisfactory solution to our problem."

"Satisfactory? You said painful and embarrassing."

"Painful and embarrassing because it was humiliating. Any husband whose wife runs away with another man looks rather ridiculous. I mean that I had no sense of loss."

"I see. Did she give you any idea that she was leaving before she went? "

"None. We didn't see each other often the last few months we lived together. When we did see each other, we found very little to say."

"You said you could only speculate as to why she disappeared instead of leaving openly. I'd like to hear your speculation."

"You would need to have known her before you could understand. She was, to put it kindly, rather unstable. Less kindly, she was neurotic. She may have been almost psychotic at times. I don't know. I don't understand the subtle distinctions between these things. Anyhow, she had had a bad time when our child died. At first, after the initial shock, she became withdrawn and depressed, totally uninterested in living. Later there was a reaction. A kind of hysterical appetite for activity and experiences. It was then that she met Regis Lawler. It's my opinion that she disappeared because she wanted to cut herself off completely from the life that had included our marriage and the death of our child. It's difficult to believe, I know."

"I wouldn't say so. Not so difficult. I've already considered that motivation, as a matter of fact. It seems to fit in with the little I know about her. There's another point, however, that bothers me. Was Regis Lawler the kind of man to fall in with such a scheme?

"I can't answer that. If he was devoted to her, it's fair to assume that he would do as she wished, especially if she convinced him that it was something she desperately needed."

"Possibly. I didn't know Lawler well enough to have an idea. Miss Salem said that Mrs. Markley's family had quite a lot of money. Did Mrs. Markley herself have any?"

"No. Her mother and father were both dead when we married. If they had money at one time, which I believe was so, it had been dissipated. The estate, I understand, did little more than pay the claims against it."

"Then your wife had no personal financial matters to settle before she left?"

"Not to my knowledge."

"Was Regis Lawler a wealthy man?"

"I have no idea. His brother apparently is."

"Well, you can see what I'm getting at. It would not be a simple matter for a man of wealth to disappear. It would certainly entail the liquidation of assets—securities, property, things like that. He'd have to convert his wealth to negotiable paper that he could carry with him. If he wanted to assure his not being traced through them, he'd have to convert to cash. Do you know if Regis Lawler did any such thing?"

"No. But the police surely made such an obvious investigation. Since it was not an issue, it follows that Lawler did do something of the sort, that he had no holdings to convert."

"Right. If Lawler had left much behind, the police wouldn't have quit investigating. They'd have smelled more than a love affair. As you say, he either converted or had nothing to convert. At any rate, he must have had considerable cash in hand. Running away with a woman, I mean, wouldn't be any two-dollar tour. Unless he had a job arranged somewhere, an assured income, he must have been, putting it mildly, damn well heeled."

"Oh, I think it's safe to assume that he had at least enough cash to last a while. I can't imagine that. Regis Lawler was a pauper."

His tone implied that no one but a simpleton, specifically me, would waste time speculating about it. I was beginning to think he was right. That was okay, though. I had been convinced from the beginning that I was wasting my time on the whole case. That was okay too, since I was doing it for a fee.

"How long ago was it that Mrs. Markley left?" I said.

"Two years ago next month."

"Did she take anything with her? Any clothes, for example? I know from talking with her maid that she took nothing when she left home that night, but I'm thinking she might have taken or sent luggage ahead to be picked up later. She'd have done something like that, I imagine, if she was being secretive."

"No doubt. On the other hand, if you accept the theory that she intended to make a complete break, she might not have wanted to keep any of her old possessions, not even her clothes. I don't find this incredible in her case. Anyhow, I honestly don't know if she took anything. She had closets full of clothes, of course. If anything was missing, I wouldn't know."

"How about the maid?"

"She thought that nothing was missing, but she wasn't positive." He looked at his wrist watch and stood up abruptly, his knees still together as they had been all the time he was sitting, and he had, looking down at me, a kind of stiff, military bearing and collateral arrogance. "I'm sorry to end this interview, Mr. Hand, but I have another appointment. You'll have to excuse me."

"Certainly," I said. "I was running out of questions, anyhow. Thanks very much for coming in."

"I'm afraid I haven't been very helpful."

"You never know. It doesn't sound like much now, but it may mean something later."

I walked around the desk and with him to the door. I didn't offer to shake hands, and nether did he.

"Please inform Miss Salem or me of any progress," he said.

"I'm not optimistic," I said.

The door closed between us, and I went back and sat down. As far as I was concerned, I was still wasting time.

CHAPTER 4.

From street level I went up two shallow steps into a spacious hall. The floor was carpeted. The walls were paneled with dark and lustrous walnut. At the far end of the hall, a broad sweep of stairs ascended. To my right as I entered was the dining room. The floor was carpeted in there also, and the walls were also walnut paneled. Tables were covered with snowy cloths and set with shining silver. A few early diners were dining. The string quartet was playing something softly that I remembered by sound and remembered after a moment by name. *Stars in My Eyes*. By Fritz Kreisler. A very pretty tune.

I looked right. A cocktail lounge was over that way, beyond a wide entrance and down a step. A number of people were drinking cocktails. There was no music. I recognized a martini, which was all right, a Manhattan, which was better, and an Alexander, which you can have. Everything was very elegant, very sedate. Maybe someone saw me, maybe not. No one spoke to me or tried to stop me. I walked down the hall and up the stairs.

The carpet went up with me, but the walnut stayed below. The hall upstairs ran a gauntlet of closed doors recessed in plaster. It was nice plaster, though, rough textured and painted a soft shade of brown. Cinnamon or Nutmeg or one of the names that brown acquires when it becomes a decorator color. It was too early for the games, and the rooms behind the doors were quiet. All, that is, except the last room behind the last door, which was the private room of Silas Lawler. Someone in there was playing a piano. A Chopin waltz was being played. I thought at first it was a recording, but then I decided it wasn't. It was good, but not good enough.

I opened the door softly and stepped inside and closed the door behind me. It was Silas Lawler himself at the piano. He turned his face toward me, but his eyes had the kind of blind glaze that the eyes of a man may have when he is listening to good music or looking at his mistress or thinking of something a long way off. A pretty girl was sitting in a deep chair, one hand on the back of her neck. She had short black hair and smoky eyes and a small red petulant mouth. She was facing the door and me directly, and her eyes moved over me lazily without interest. Otherwise, she did not move in the slightest, and she did not speak.

Lawler finished the Chopin waltz, and the girl said, "That was nice, Lover." She moved nothing but her lips, in shaping the words, and her eyes, which she rolled toward him in her head. She didn't sound as if she meant what she said, and Lawler didn't look as if he believed her. He didn't even look as if he heard her. He was still staring at me, and the glaze was dissolving in his eyes.

"Who are you?" he said.

"Percy Hand," I said. "We've met."

"That's right," he said. "I remember you. Don't you believe in knocking?"

"I didn't want to interrupt the music. I like Chopin."

"Do you? It's better when it's played right."

"You play it fine. I thought at first it was Brailowsky."

"If you thought it was Brailowsky, you've never heard him."

"I've heard him, all right. I went to a concert once. I got a couple records."

"In that case, you've got no ear for music. Brailowsky and I don't sound alike."

"Maybe not. Maybe it was just the shock of hearing you play at all. I never figured Silas Lawler for a pianist."

"I was a deprived kid. I had secret hungers. I made some money and took lessons."

"So was I. So had I. I didn't."

"Make money or take lessons?"

"Both."

"You can see he's poor," the girl said. "He wears ready-made suits."

"Botany 500," I said. "Sixty-five bucks."

Lawler looked at her levelly across the grand. I could have sworn that there was an expression of distaste on his face. The deprived kid business was on the level, I thought. He remembered the time. He didn't like people who made cracks about the poor.

"This is Robin Robbins," he said carefully. "She's pretty, but she's got no manners. That isn't her real name, by the way. She didn't think the one she had was good enough. The man you're trying to insult, honey, is Percy Hand, a fairly good private detective."

"He looks like Jack Palance," she said.

"Jack Palance is ugly," I said, "God, he's ugly."

"So are you," she said.

"Thanks," I said.

"In a nice way," she said. "Jack Palance is ugly in a nice way, and so are you. I don't really care if you're poor."

"Just as long as you're good in bed," Lawler said. "Come over here."

I walked over and stood beside the piano. Now I could see the girl only by looking over my shoulder. Instead, I looked down at Lawler. His face was clean shaven and square. He was neither tall nor fat, but he must have weighed two hundred. His hands rested quietly on the piano keys. They looked like chunks of stone.

"Here I am," I said. "Why?"

"I want to be able to reach you in case you haven't got a good reason for busting in here."

"I've got a reason. You tell me if it's good."

"I'll let you know. One way or another."

"I want to talk about a couple people you know. Or knew. Your brother and Constance Markley." He didn't budge. His face stayed still, his body stayed still, the hands on the keys stayed still as stone. "It's lousy. I'd be bored to death."

"Is that so? I'm beginning to get real interested in them."

"That's your mistake. While we're on mistakes, I'll point out another. He isn't my brother. Not even step-brother. Foster brother."

"That makes it less intimate, I admit. Not quite impersonal, though. Wouldn't you like to know where he is? How he is? Or maybe you already know."

"I don't. I don't want to."

"Well, I never heard the like. A man's wife disappears. He doesn't care. A man's foster brother disappears. He doesn't care. The indifference fascinates me."

"Let me figure this." His right hand suddenly struck a bass chord and dropped off the keys into his lap. The sound waves lingered, faded, died. "I've got a sluggish mind, and I think slow. Regis and Constance ran away. You're a private detective. Could it be you're trying to make yourself a case?"

"I'm not making any case. The case is made. I'm just working on it."

"Take my advice. Don't. Drop it. Forget it. It isn't worth your time."

"My time's worth twenty-five dollars a day and expenses. That's what I'm getting paid."

"Who's paying?"

"Sorry. I'm not at liberty to say."

"It's not enough."

"I get by on it."

"Not enough to pay a hospital bill, I mean. Or the price of a funeral, even."

The girl stood up suddenly and stretched. She made a soft mewing sound, like a cat. I turned my head and watched her over my shoulder. Her breasts thrust out against her dress, her spread thighs strained against her tight skirt.

"I think I'll go away somewhere," she said. "I abhor violence."

"You do that, honey," Silas Lawler said.

She walked across to the door, and she walked pretty well. She had nice legs that moved nicely. You could follow the lines of her behind in the tight skirt. I'd have been more impressed if I hadn't seen Faith Salem lying in the sun. At the door, before going out, she paused and looked back at me and grinned.

"You couldn't hurt his face much," she said. "You could change it, but you couldn't hurt it."

She was gone, and I said, "Lovely thing. Is it yours?"

"Now and then." He shrugged. "If you're interested, I won't be offended."

"I'm not. Besides, I'm too ugly. Were you threatening me a moment ago?"

"About the hospital, yes. About the funeral, no. It wouldn't be necessary."

"You never can tell. I get tired of living sometimes."

"You'd get tireder of being dead."

"That could be. The way I hear it explained, it sounds pretty dull."

"You're a pretty sharp guy, Hand. You've got a nose for what's phony. I'm surprised a guy like you wouldn't smell a phony case."

"I won't say I haven't. I'm open to conviction."

"All right. Regis and Constance had a real fire going. It didn't develop, it was just there in both of them at first sight. First sight was right here. Downstairs in the lounge. Don't ask me to explain it, because I can't. Regis was there, and Constance was there, and to hell with everyone else. Everyone and everything. They got in bed, and whatever they had survived. They ran away together, that's all. Why don't you leave it alone?"

"You make it sound so simple. I can't help thinking, though, that running away's one thing, disappearing's another. You see the difference? There is one you know."

"I see. It wouldn't seem so strange if you'd known the woman. Constance, I mean. She'd had a bad time. She was sad, lost, looking for a way to somewhere. You get me? She was a real lady, but she had queer ideas. When she left, she wanted to leave it all, including herself. It's pathetic when you stop to think about it."

"I get the same picture everywhere. The same idea. I'm beginning to believe it. I'm skeptical about Regis, though. He doesn't seem the type."

"He wasn't. Not before he met Constance. Before he met her, he was a charming, no-good bastard, but then he met her, and he changed. Queer. You wouldn't have thought she'd have appealed to him, but she did. He'd have done anything she wanted. Very queer."

"Yeah. Queer and corny."

"I don't blame you for thinking so. You'd have to see it to believe it."

"Did Regis have an interest in this restaurant?"

"Regis didn't have a pot. Just what I gave him. Spending money."

"What did they use for cash when they left? What are they using now? And don't feed me any more corn. You don't live on love. Some people get a job and live in a cottage, but not Regis and Constance. Everything they were and did is against it."

The fingers of his left hand moved up the keys. It was remarkable how lightly that chunk of rock moved. The thin sounds of the short scale lasted no longer than a few seconds. The left hand joined the right in his lap.

"I'll tell you something," he said. "I don't know why. What I ought to do is throw you out of here. Anyhow, Regis had cash. Enough for a lifetime in the right place. See that picture over there? It's a copy of a Rembrandt. Behind it there's a safe. Regis knew the combination. The night he went away, I had seventy-five grand in it. Regis took it."

"That's a lot of cash to have in a safe behind a picture."

"I had it for a purpose. Never mind what."

"You let him get away with it? You didn't try to recover it?"

"No. To tell the truth, I was relieved. I always felt an obligation toward him because of the woman whose lousy kid he was. Now the obligation is wiped out. We're quits." He lifted both hands and replaced them gently on the keys of the piano. There was not the slightest sound from the wires inside. "Besides, I figured it was partly for her. For Constance. I liked her. I hope she's happier than she ever was."

I started to refer again to corn, but I thought better of it. Then I thought that it would probably be a good time to leave, and I turned and went as far as the door. "Hand," he said.

"Yes," I said.

"Forget it. Drop it. You hear me?"

"I hear you," I said.

I opened the door and went out. After three steps in the hall, I heard the piano. What I heard from it was something else by Chopin.

CHAPTER 5.

On the way in, no one had spoken to me. On the way out, someone did. The lower hall was the place, and Robin Robbins was the person. She was standing in the entrance to the cocktail lounge, at the edge of the shallow step, and although she was standing erect, like a lady, she somehow gave the impression of leaning indolently against an immaterial lamppost. Her voice was lazy, threaded with a kind of insolent amusement. "Buy me a drink?" she said.

"I'm too poor," I said.

"Tough. Let me buy you one."

"I'm too proud."

"Poor and proud. My God, it sounds like something by Horatio Alger."

"Junior."

"What?"

"Horatio Alger, Junior. You forgot the junior."

"I'm sorry I didn't forget him altogether. What do you say we start trying?"

"I'm surprised you know anything about him to start trying to forget. He was a long time ago, honey. Were kids still reading him when you were a kid?"

"I wouldn't know. I was never a kid. I was born old and just got older."

"Like me. That gives us something in common, I guess. Maybe we ought to have that drink together after all. I'll buy."

"No. I've got a better idea for a poor, proud man. In my apartment there's a bottle of scotch left over from another time. Someone gave it to me. We could go there and drink out of it for free."

"I don't care for scotch. It tastes like medicine."

"There's a bottle of bourbon there too. In case you don't care for bourbon, there's rye."

"No brandy? No champagne?"

"Anything you want."

"That's quite a selection to be left over from other times. Was it all given to you?"

"Why not? People are always giving me something. They seem to enjoy it."

"Thanks for offering to share the wealth. However, I don't think so. Some other time, maybe,"

She opened a small purse she was holding in her hands and extracted a cigarette. I went closer and supplied a light. She inhaled and exhaled and stared into the smoke with her smoky eyes. Her breath coming out with the smoke made a soft, sighing sound.

"Suit yourself," she said. "It's just that I've got something I thought you might be interested in."

"You've got plenty I might be interested in, honey."

She dragged again and sighed again. The smoke thinned and hung in a pale blue haze between us. In her eyes was a suggestion of something new. Something less than insolence, a little more than amusement. Her lush little mouth curved amiably.

"That's not quite what I meant, but it's something to consider. What I meant was something I can tell you."

"Information? Is it free like the scotch and the bourbon and the rye? Don't forget I'm a guy who wears ready-made suits."

"I remember. Poor and proud and probably honest. Right out of H. Alger, Junior. Don't worry about it, though. It's free like the scotch and the bourbon and the rye."

"Everything free. No price on anything. I hope you won't be offended, honey, but somehow I got an idea it's out of character."

"All right. Forget it. You were asking questions about a couple of people, and I thought you were, interested. My mistake, Horatio." Her mouth curved now in the opposite direction from amiability. What had been in her eyes was gone, and what replaced it was contempt. I thought in the instant before she turned away that she was going to spit on the floor. Before she could descend the step and walk away nicely on her nice legs with the neat movement of her neat behind, I took a step and put a hand on her arm, and we stood posed that way for a second or two or longer, she arrested and I arresting, and then she turned her head and looked at me over her shoulder.

"Yes?" she said.

"Make mine bourbon," I said.

We went the rest of the way down the hall together and down the two steps and outside. Beside the building was a paved parking lot reserved for patrons, and I had left my car there, although I was not properly a patron. We walked around and got into the car and drove in it to her apartment, which was in a nice building on a good street. It was on the fifth floor, which we reached by elevator, and it didn't have any terrace that got the sun in the afternoon, or any terrace at all, or any of many features that the apartment of Faith Salem had, including several acres, but it was a nice enough apartment just the same, a far better apartment than any I had ever lived in or probably ever would. Besides, it was certainly something that someone had just wanted to give her. For a consideration, of course. An exchange, in a way, of commodities.

"Fix a bourbon for yourself," she said. "For me too, in water. I'll be back in a minute."

She went out of the room and was gone about five times as long as the minute. In the meanwhile, I found ingredients and mixed two bourbon highballs and had them ready when she returned. She looked just the same as she'd looked when she'd gone, which was good enough to be disturbing.

"I lose," I said.

"Some people always do," she said. "Lose what, exactly?"

"A bet. With myself. I bet you'd gone to get into something more comfortable."

"Why should I? What I'm wearing is comfortable enough. There's practically nothing to it."

I was facing her with a full glass in each hand. She approached me casually, as if she were going to ask for a light or brush a crumb off my tie. She kept right on walking, right into me, and put her arms around my neck and her mouth on my mouth, and I stood there with my arms projecting beyond her on both sides, the damn glasses in my hands, and we remained static and breathless in this position for quite a long time. Finally she stepped back and helped herself to the glass in one of my hands. She took a drink and tilted her head and subjected me and my effect to a smoldering appraisal.

"I've always wanted to kiss a man as ugly as you," she said. "It wasn't bad."

"Thanks," I said. "I've had worse myself, but under better conditions."

"I'm wondering if it's good enough to develop. I think it might be."

"You go on wondering about it and let me know."

"I'll do that."

She moved over to a chair and lowered herself onto her neat behind and crossed her nice legs. From where I found a chair and sat, across from her, I could see quite a lot of the legs. She didn't mind, and neither did I.

"If you decide to develop it," I said, "won't Silas Lawler object?"

She swallowed some more of her highball and looked into what was left. Her soft and succulent little mouth assumed lax and ugly lines.

"To hell with Silas Lawler," she said.

"Don't kid me," I said. "I know he pays the bills."

"So he pays the bills. There's one bill he may owe that he hasn't paid. If he owes it, I want him to pay in full."

"For what?"

"For the murder of Regis Lawler."

She continued to look into her glass. From her expression, she must have seen something offensive on the bottom. I looked into mine and saw nothing but good whisky and pure water. I drained it.

"Maybe you don't know what you said," I said.

"I know what I said. I said he *may* owe it. I'd like to know."

"And I'd like to know what makes you think he may."

"Start with that fairy tale about Regis and Constance Markley running off together. Just disappearing completely so they could have a beautiful new life together. Do you believe it?"

"I don't believe it. I don't disbelieve it. I've got an open mind."

"Brother, if you'd known Regis Lawler as well as I did, you'd know the whole idea is phony. He just wasn't the type."

"I've heard that. I've also heard that he was in love with Constance. It's been suggested that he might have done for her what he wouldn't have done for anyone else."

"That's another phony bit. His being in love with Constance, I mean. He wasn't."

"No? This is a new angle. Convince me."

"Maybe I can't. I don't have any letters or tapes or photographs. Neither does anyone else, thank God. I could give you some interesting clinical descriptions, but I won't. Basically I'm a modest girl. I like my privacy."

"I think I get you, but I'm not sure. Are you telling me more or less delicately that Regis had love enough for two?"

"Two? Is that all the higher you can count? Anyhow, what's love? All I know is, we went through the motions of what passes for love in my crowd, and he seemed to enjoy it. Whatever you call it, he felt more of it for me than he felt for anyone else, including Constance, and I guess you couldn't have expected more than that from Regis." Her little mouth had for a moment a bitter twist. The bitterness tainted the sound of her words. She did not have the look and sound of a woman who had been rejected. She had the look and sound of a woman who had been accepted with qualifications and used without them. Most of all, a woman who had understood the qualifications from the beginning and had accepted them and submitted to them.

"Excuse me," I said. "I always have trouble understanding anything when it gets the least complicated. You were having Regis on the side of Silas, and Regis was having you on the side of Constance. Not that I want to make you sound like a chaser or a dish of buttered peas. Is that right?"

"Damn it, that's what I said."

"And Silas killed Regis in anger because he found out about it. Is that what you mean?"

"It's a solid thought. I like it better than the fairy tale."

"I'm not sure that I share your preference. I don't want to hurt you, honey, but I doubt like hell that Silas considers you worth killing for. He just gave me permission to try my luck if the notion struck me, but maybe he didn't really mean it. Anyhow, you'll have to admit that it doesn't sound like a case of homicidal jealousy."

"Who mentioned jealousy?" She shrugged angrily, a small gesture of dismissal. "He's proud. He's vain and sensitive. He's made a hell of a lot out of nothing at all, but he can't forget that he only went to the fourth grade and got where he is by doing things proper people don't do. He still feels secretly inferior and insecure, and he always will. The one thing he can't stand is the slightest suggestion of contempt. He'd kill anyone for that. Can you think of anything more contemptuous than taking another man's wife or mistress?"

I thought of seventy-five grand. It seemed to me that helping yourself to that much lettuce was a contemptuous act too, and I thought about discussing it as a motive for murder, but I couldn't see that it would get me anywhere in present circumstances, and so I decided against it.

"So he killed Regis," I said. "That was a couple of years ago. And ever since he's gone on with you as if nothing at all had happened. After murder, business as usual at the same old stand. Is that it?"

"Sure. Why not? Laughing like hell all the time. Feeling all the time the same kind of contempt for Regis and me that he imagines we felt for him. Silas would get a lot of satisfaction out of something like that." She looked down into her glass, swirling what was left of her drink around and around the inner circumference. Bitterness increased the distortion of her mouth. "He'll throw me out after a while," she said.

"You're quite a psychologist," I said. "All that stuff about inferiority and insecurity and implied contempt. I wish I had as much brains as you."

"All right, you bastard. So I'm the kind who ought to stick to the little words. So I only went to the eighth grade myself. Go ahead and ridicule me."

"You're wrong. I wasn't ridiculing you. I never ridicule anyone. The trouble your theory has is the same trouble that the other theory has, and the trouble with both is that they leave loose ends all over the place. I can mention a few, if you'd care to hear them."

"Mention whatever you please."

"All right. Where's the body?"

"I don't know. You're the detective. Work on it"

"Where's Constance? Did he kill both of them? If so, why? He had no reason to hate her. As a matter of fact, they should have been on the same team. You, not Constance, would have been the logical second victim."

"I know. Don't you think I've thought of that a thousand times? Maybe she knew he killed Regis. Maybe she learned about it somehow or even actually witnessed it. Damn it, I've told you something you didn't know. I've told you about Regis and me. I've told you he was not really in love with Constance and would never have run away with her for any longer than a weekend. I've told you this, and it's the truth, and all you do is keep wanting me to be the detective. You're the detective, brother. I've told you that too."

"Sure you have. I'm the detective and all I've got to do is explain how someone killed a man and a woman and completely disposed of their bodies. That would be a tough chore, honey. Practically impossible."

"Silas Lawler's been doing the practically impossible for quite a few years. He's a very competent guy."

"He is. I know it, and I'm not forgetting it. However, I can think of a third theory that excludes him. It's simpler and it ties up an end or two. You said Regis didn't love Constance. He just had an affair with her. Suppose he tried to end the affair and got himself killed for his trouble? She was a strange female, I'm told. Almost psychotic, someone said. Do you think she was capable?"

Robin Robbins stood up abruptly. She carried her glass over to the ingredients and stood quietly with her back to me. Apparently she was only considering whether she should mix herself another or not. She decided not. Depositing her glass, she helped herself to a cigarette from a box and lit it with a lighter. Trailing smoke, she returned to her chair.

"Oh, Constance was capable, all right," she said. "She was much too good to do a lot of things I've done and will probably do again and again if the price is right, but there's one thing she could have done that I couldn't, and that's murder. And if you think that sounds like more eighth grade psychology, you can forget it and get the hell out of here."

"I don't know about the psychology," I said, "but I'm pretty sure that you don't really think she killed Regis. If you did, you'd be happy to say so."

"That's right." She nodded in amiable agreement. "I wouldn't mind at all doing Constance a bad turn, but she didn't kill Regis. That's obvious."

"I'm inclined to agree. In the first place, she couldn't have got rid of the body. In the second place, if she could and did, why run away afterward? It wouldn't be sensible."

"Well, it's your problem, brother. I guess it's time you went somewhere else and began to think about it."

"Yeah. I'm the detective. You've told me and told me. You haven't told me much else, though. Not anything very convincing. You got an idea that Silas killed Regis because you and Regis made a kind of illicit cuckold of him, and you lure me here with free bourbon and tell me so, and I'm supposed to be converted by this evangelical message. It's pretty thin, if you don't mind my saying it. Excuse me for being skeptical."

"That's all right. I didn't expect much from you anyhow. I just thought I'd try."

"Try harder."

"I've got nothing more to tell you."

"Really? That's hard to believe. You're not exactly inexpensive, honey, and I'll bet you have to earn your keep. What I mean is, you and Silas surely get convivial on occasions. Even intimate. Men are likely to become indiscreet under such circumstances. They say things they wouldn't ordinarily say. If Silas killed Regis because of you, I'd think he'd even have an urge to gloat. By innuendo, at least."

She moved her head against the back of her chair in a lazy negative. "I'm a girl who knows the side of her bread the butter is on, and I earn my keep. You're right there. But you're wrong if you think Silas Lawler is the kind who gets confidential or careless. He's a very reserved guy, and he protects his position. He tends to his own business, and most of his business nowadays is on the three floors of the building we just left. To be honest, he's pretty damn dull. He works. He eats and sleeps and plays that damn piano, and once in a while he makes love. Once a month, for a few days, he goes to some place called Amity."

"Amity? Why does he go there?"

"I wouldn't know. I guess he has interests."

"Do you ever go with him?"

"No."

"Why not?"

"I'm never invited, thank God. Who wants to go to Amity?"

I took a deep breath and held it till it hurt and then released it.

"That's right," I said. "Who does? Incidentally there's something else that nags me. It seems to me that you're trying to ruin a good thing for yourself, and I don't understand it. What happens to you and all this if Silas turns out to be a murderer?"

"Whatever it is, I'll try to bear it. I may even celebrate. In the meanwhile, on the chance that I'm wrong about him, I may be as well be comfortable."

I stood up and looked down, and she stayed down and looked up, and because she was a shrewd and tough wench with looks and brains and queer attachments and flexible morals, I though it would be pleasant and acceptable to kiss her once in return for the time she'd kissed me once, and that's what I did, and it was. It was pleasant and acceptable. It even started being exciting. Just as her hands were reaching for me, I straightened and turned and walked to the door, and she came out of the chair after me. She put her arms around my waist from behind.

"It's worth developing," she said. "I've been thinking about it, and I've decided."

"Sorry," I said. "My own mind isn't made up yet. I'll let you know."

I loosened her hands and held them in mine against my belly. After a few seconds, I dropped them and opened the door and started out.

"You ugly bastard," she said.

"Don't call me," I said. "I'll call you."

"Go to hell," she said.

I got on out and closed the door softly and began wishing immediately that I hadn't.

CHAPTER 6.

The next morning I checked a couple of morgues. The newspaper variety. I turned the brittle bones of old dailies and disturbed the rest of dead stories, but I learned nothing of significance regarding Constance Markley. She was there, all right, briefly and quietly interred in ink. No one had got excited. No one had smelled anything, apparently, that couldn't eventually be fumigated in divorce court. I left the second morgue about noon and stopped for a steak sandwich and a beer on the way to my office. In the office, sitting, I elevated my feet and began to think.

Maybe thinking is an exaggeration. I didn't really have an idea.

All I had was an itch, a tiny burr of coincidence that had caught in a wrinkle of my cortex. It didn't amount to much, but I thought I might as well worry it a while, having nothing else on hand or in mind, and what I thought I would do specifically was go back and see Faith Salem again, and I would go, if I could arrange it, when Faith and the sun were on the terrace. She had said to call ahead of time, and so I lowered my feet and reached for the phone, and that's when I saw the gorilla.

He was a handsome gorilla in a Brooks Brothers suit, but a gorilla just the same. There's something about the breed that you can't miss. They smell all right, and they look all right, and there's nothing you can isolate ordinarily as a unique physical characteristic that identifies one of them definitely as a gorilla rather than as a broker or a rich plumber, but they seem to have a chronic quality of deadliness that a broker or a plumber would have only infrequently, in special circumstances, if ever. This one was standing in the doorway watching me, and he had got there without a sound. He smiled. He was plainly prepared to treat me with all the courtesy I was prepared to make possible.

"Mr. Hand?' he said.

"That's right," I said.

"I have a message from Mr. Silas Lawler. He would appreciate it very much if you could come to see him as soon as possible."

"I just went to see him yesterday."

"Mr. Lawler knows that. He regrets that he must inconvenience you again so soon. Apparently something important has come up."

"Something else important came up first. I was just getting ready to go out and take care of it."

"Mr. Lawler is certain that you'll prefer to give his business priority."

"Well, I'll tell you what to do. You go back to Mr. Lawler and tell him I'll be around this evening or first thing tomorrow."

"Mr. Lawler is most urgent that you come immediately. I have instructions to drive you there and bring you back. For your convenience, of course."

"Of course. Mr. Lawler is notoriously considerate. Suppose I don't want to go."

"Mr. Lawler hopes you will want to accommodate him."

"Let's suppose I refuse."

"Mr. Lawler didn't anticipate that contingency, I'm afraid. He said to bring you."

"Even if I resist?"

"As I understood my orders, Mr. Lawler made no qualifications."

"Do you think you're man enough to execute them without qualifications?"

"I think so."

"In that case," I said, "we'd better go."

I got my hat and put it over the place where the lumps would have been if I hadn't. Together, like cronies, we went downstairs and got into his car, which was a Caddy, and drove in it to Silas Lawler's restaurant plus. In the hall outside Silas Lawler's private room, we stood and listened to the piano, which was being played. What was being played on it this time was not something by Chopin, and I couldn't identify who it was by certainly, but I thought it was probably Mozart.

The music was airy and intricate. It sounded as if it had been written by a man who felt very good and wanted everyone else to feel as good as he did.

"Mr. Lawler doesn't like to be interrupted when he's playing," the Brooks Brothers gorilla said.

"You can't be too careful with artists," I said. "They're touchy."

"Mr. Lawler's a virtuoso," he said.

He didn't even blink when he said it. It was obviously a word he was used to and not something special for effect. I wondered if they were granting degrees to gorillas these days, but I didn't think it would be wise to ask. There wouldn't have been time for an answer, anyhow, for the virtuoso stopped playing the music by Mozart, or at least not Chopin, and the gorilla knocked twice on the door and opened it, and I walked into the room ahead of him.

Silas Lawler got off the bench and walked around the curve of the grand and stopped in the spot where the canary usually perches in nightclubs. He didn't perch, however. He merely leaned. From the same chair in which she had sat yesterday, Robin Robbins looked across at me with a poker face, and I could see at once, in spite of shadows and cosmetics, that somebody had hung one on her. A plum-colored bruise spread down from her left eye across the bone of her cheek. There was still some swelling of the flesh too, although it had certainly been reduced from what it surely had been. She looked rather cute, to tell the truth. The shiner somehow made her look like the kid she said she never was.

"How are you, Hand?" Lawler said. "It was kind of you to come."

"Your messenger was persuasive," I said. "I couldn't resist him."

"Darcy, you mean. I can always depend on Darcy to do a job like a gentleman. He dislikes violence almost as much as I do. I'm sure you didn't find him abusive."

"Not at all. I've never been threatened half so courteously before." I turned my head and looked down at Robin Robbins. "Apparently you weren't so lucky, honey. You must have run into an interior gorilla somewhere."

"I fell over my lip," she said.

Lawler laughed, and I could have sworn that there was a note of tenderness in it. "Robin's impetuous. She's always doing something she later regrets, and I'm always prepared to forgive her eventually, although I sometimes lose my temper in the meanwhile. Isn't that so, Robin?"

"Oh, sure," she said. "We love each other in spite of everything."

"I won't deny that Robin's been punished," Lawler said, "but I'm afraid I must charge you with being partially responsible, Hand. You ought to be ashamed of yourself for taking advantage of her innocence."

"I am," I said, "I truly am."

"Well," he said, "I don't think we need to be too critical. Robin, I realize, is even harder to resist than Darcy. For different reasons, of course. She's told me what the two of you talked about yesterday after leaving here together, and she understands now how foolish she was. Don't you, Robin?"

"Sure," she said. "I was foolish."

"She wants me to ask you to forget all about it, don't you, Robin?"

"Sure," she said. "Forget it."

"You see?" Lawler shrugged and shifted his weight against the piano. "Robin and I are really very compatible. We are never able to keep secrets from one another for very long."

"That's sweet," I said. "I'm touched."

He was looking directly at Robin for the first time now. "Wouldn't you like to apologize to Mr. Hand for causing him so much trouble, Robin?"

"I apologize, Mr. Hand, from the bottom of my heart," she said.

"I liked it better when you told me to go to hell," I said.

Lawler stood erect and stopped looking at Robin in order to look at me. "That wasn't a very gracious response, Hand. However, let it pass. I also want to apologize to you."

"What for?"

"I'm afraid I was a little unreasonable yesterday. I understand now that you were hired to investigate the matter we discussed, and you're naturally concerned about your fee. I have no right to ask you to sacrifice that, of course. What do you think it will amount to?"

"That depends on how long the job lasts. I get twenty-five dollars a day and expenses."

"Very reasonable. I'll pay you five thousand dollars to drop the case. That should be adequate."

"Bribery?"

"Don't be offensive. Compensation for the loss of your fee."

"It's not enough."

"Really? I figure that it comes to two-hundred days' work. What do you think would be fair?"

"Make it a million, and I'll take it."

"Your joke isn't very funny, Hand. It's bad taste to joke about a serious matter."

"I'm not joking. You see, I've got to be compensated for more than the loss of a fee. I've got to be compensated for the loss of my integrity, such as it is. I don't figure a million's too much for that."

"Nonsense. You're wasting your time, anyhow. I assured you of that. Is it ethical to go on accepting a fee under false pretenses?"

"I explained to my client that it might not come to anything. Probably wouldn't, as a matter of fact. We're both satisfied."

"Perhaps I could persuade your client that he is making a mistake. Would you care to give me his name?"

"No, I wouldn't. The truth is, I don't particularly care for your methods of persuasion."

"No matter. If I really want to learn the identity of your client, I can do it easily enough. Now, however, I don't propose to discuss this matter with you any longer. I believe I've made you a fair proposition. Do you still refuse to accept it?"

"Sorry. I'm holding out for the million."

If there was the slightest sign between him and Darcy behind me, the lifting of a brow or the twitch of a tick, I never saw it. It could be, I guess, that they'd developed a kind of extra-sensory communication that functioned automatically when the time was precisely right. Anyhow, sign or not, Darcy grabbed me abruptly above the elbows from behind and wrenched my arms and shoulders back so violently that I thought for a moment I'd split down the middle like a spring fryer. At the same instant, Lawler made a fist and stepped forward within range.

"I regret this, Hand," he said. "I really do."

"I know," I said. "You dislike violence. You and Darcy both."

"It's your own fault, of course. You're behaving like a recalcitrant boy, and it's necessary to teach you a lesson."

"Don't you think you ought to teach me somewhere else? You wouldn't want to get blood on this expensive carpet."

"It's acrilan. Haven't you heard of it? One of these new miracle fabrics. Blood wipes right off."

"Is that a fact? Better living through chemistry. I'm impressed." He was tired now of the whole business. I could see in his face that he was tired, and I believe that he actually did regret what he considered the necessity of having to do what he was going to do. It was only that he knew no other way to fight, in spite of Chopin and Mozart and the veneer of respectability, than the way of violence. He wanted to get it over with, and he did. He drove the fist into my face, and it was like getting hit with a jagged boulder. Flesh split on bone, and bone cracked, and darkness welled up internally.

I sagged, I guess, and hung by my arms from the hands of Darcy, and after a while, I guess, I straightened and lifted my head and was hit again in the face. When I opened my eyes after that, I was lying on the carpet, and there was blood on it. In my mouth there was more blood, and a thin and bitter fluid risen from my stomach. I was sick and in pain, but mostly I was ashamed. I got up slowly, in sections, and looked at Lawler through a pink mist.

"Your carpet's a mess," I said. "I hope you're right about acrilan."

"Don't worry about it," he said. "You're a tough guy, Hand, and I like you. If you think I get any kicks out of pushing you around, you're wrong. There's a lavatory in there. Through that door. Why don't you go in and wash your face?"

"I think I will," I said.

I went in and turned on the cold tap and caught double handfuls of water and buried my face in them. The water burned like acid, but it revived me and dispelled the pink fog. In the mirror above the lavatory, I saw that a cut on my cheekbone needed a stitch or two. I found some adhesive tape in the medicine cabinet and pulled the cut together and went back out into the other room.

Lawler was seated at the grand again. Darcy was leaning against the wall behind him. Robin Robbins, in her chair, was still wearing her poker face. I thought I saw in her eyes a guarded gleam of something appealing. Compassion? Camaraderie based on mutual beatings? A raincheck? Who could be sure with

Robin? I kept right on walking toward the door, and I was almost there when Lawler spoke to me.

"Hand," he said.

I stopped but didn't turn. I didn't answer either. It hurt to talk, and I saw no sense in it.

"One thing more," he said. "I made a reasonable offer, and you'd be wise to accept it. This is just a suggestion of what you'll get if you don't. I'll put a check for five thousand in the mail today. You'll get it tomorrow."

"Thanks very much," I said.

I started again and kept going and got on out of there.

CHAPTER 7.

In a sidewalk telephone booth I dialed Faith Salem's number and got Maria.

"Miss Salem's apartment," she said.

"This is Percy Hand," I said. "Let me speak with Miss Salem."

"One moment, please," she said.

I waited a while. The open wire hummed in my ear. My head felt three times its normal size, and the hum was like a siren. I held the receiver a few inches away until Faith Salem's voice came on.

"Hello, Mr. Hand," she said.

"You said to call before I came," I said. "I'm calling."

"Is it something urgent?"

"I don't know how urgent it is. I know I just turned down five grand in a chunk for twenty-five dollars and expenses a day. Under the circumstances, I feel like being humored."

She was silent for ten seconds. The siren shattered my monstrous head.

"You sound angry," she said finally.

"Not at all," I said. "I'm an amiable boob who will take almost anything for anybody, and my heart holds nothing but love and tenderness for all of God's creatures."

Silence again. The siren again. Her voice again in due time.

"You'd better come up," she said. "I'll be expecting you."

"Fifteen minutes," I said.

When I got there, the sun was off the terrace, and so was she. She was waiting for me in the living room, and she was wearing a black silk jersey pullover blouse and black ballerina-type slippers and cream-colored Capri pants. On her they looked very good, or she looked very good in them, whichever way you saw it. She was lying on her side, propped up on one elbow on a sofa about nine feet long, and she got up and came to meet me between the sofa and the door. I thought I heard her breath catch and hold for a second in her throat.

"Your face," she said.

"It must be a mess," I said.

"There's a stain on the front of your shirt," she said.

"Blood," I said. "Mine."

She reached up and touched gently with her fingertips the piece of adhesive that was holding together the lips of the cut that needed a stitch or two. The fingers moved slowly down over swollen flesh and seemed to draw away the pain by a kind of delicate anesthetization. It was much better than codeine or a handful of aspirin. "Come and sit down," she said. I did, and she did. We sat together on the nine-foot sofa, and my right knee touched her left knee, and this might have been by accident or design, but in either event it was a pleasant situation that no one made any move to alter, certainly not I.

"I'm so sorry," she said.

"So am I," I said. "I'm sorrier than anyone."

"Would you like to tell me about it?"

"It's hardly worth while. I took a job, and this turned out to be part of it."

"It's all my fault."

"Sure it is."

"But I don't understand. Why should anyone do this to you?"

"Someone wanted me to give up the job, and I didn't want to. We had a difference of opinion."

"Does that mean you've decided to go ahead with it?"

"That's what it means. At least for a while longer. When anyone wants so hard for me to quit doing something I'm doing, it makes me stubborn. I'm a contrary fellow by nature."

"You must be careful," she said.

She sounded as if it would really make a difference if I wasn't. She was sitting facing me, her left leg resting along the edge of the sofa and her right leg not touching the sofa at all, and she lifted her hand again and touched the battered side of my face as if she were reminding herself and me of the consequences of carelessness, and it seemed a natural completion of the gesture for her hand to slip on around my neck. Her arm followed, and her body came over against mine, and I was suddenly holding her and kissing her with bruised lips, and we got out of balance and toppled over gently and lay for maybe a minute in each other's arms with our mouths together. Then she drew and released a deep breath that quivered her toes. She sat up, stood up, looked down at me with a kind of incredulity in her eyes.

"I think I need a drink," she said. "You too."

"No gin and tonic, thanks," I said. "Straight bourbon."

"Agreed," she said.

She walked over to a cabinet to get it. I watched her go and watched her come. Her legs in the tight Capri pants were long and lovely and worth watching. This was something she knew as well as I, and we were both happy about it. She handed me my bourbon in a little frosted glass with the ounces marked on the outside in the frost, and the bourbon came up to the third mark. I drank it down a mark, leaving two to go, and she sat down beside me and drank a little less of hers.

"I liked kissing you, and I'm glad I did," she said, "but I won't do it again."

"All right," I said.

"Are you offended?"

"No."

"There's nothing personal in it, you understand."

"I understand."

"There are obvious reasons why I can't afford to."

"I know the reasons. What I'd like to do now, if you don't mind, is to quit talking about it. I came here to talk about something else, and it would probably be a good idea if we got started."

"What did you come to talk about?"

"About you and Constance Markley. When I was here before, you said you knew her in college. You said you shared an apartment that she paid the rent on. I neglected to ask you what college it was."

"Amity College."

"That's at Amity, of course."

"Yes. Of course."

"What was your name then?"

"The same as now. Faith Salem."

"You told me you'd been married a couple of times. I've been wondering about the Miss. Did you get your maiden name restored both times?"

"Not legally. When I'm compelled to be legal, I use another name. Would you believe that I'm a countess?"

"I'd believe it if you said it."

"Well, I don't say it often, because I'm not particularly proud of it. The count was attractive and quite entertaining for a while, but he turned out to be a mistake. I was in Europe with my first husband when I met him. You remember the publisher's son I married in college? That one. We were in Europe, and he'd turned out to be rather a mistake too, although not so bad a one as the count turned out later. Anyhow, I met the count and did things with him while my husband was doing things with someone else, and he was a very charming and convincing liar, and I decided it would probably be a smart move to make a change. It wasn't."

"Wasn't it profitable?"

"No. The amount of his income was one of the things the count lied about most convincingly. Are you being rather nasty about it, incidentally? I hope not. Being nasty doesn't suit you somehow."

"Excuse me. You'll have to remember that I've had a hard day. The publisher's son and the count are none of my business. At your request, Constance Markley is. I'd like to know exactly the nature of the relationship that caused you to share an apartment at college."

"It was normal, if that's what you mean."

"It isn't." I lowered the bourbon to the first mark. My mouth was cut on the inside, and the bourbon burned in the cut. "I don't know just what I do mean. I don't even know exactly why I asked the question or what I'm trying to learn. Just tell me what you can about Constance."

She was silent, considering. Her consideration lasted about half a minute, and after it was finished, she took time before speaking to lower the level of her own bourbon, which required about half as long.

"It's rather embarrassing," she said.

"Come on," I said. "Embarrass yourself."

"Oh, well." She shrugged. "I liked Constance. I told you I did. But I wasn't utterly devoted to her. She was rather an uncomfortable girl to be around, to tell the truth. Very intense. Inclined to be possessive and jealous. She often resented the attention and time I gave to other people. At such times, she would be very difficult and demanding, then withdrawn and sullen, and finally almost pathetically repentant and eager to make everything right again. It was a kind of cycle that she repeated many times. Her expressions and gestures of affection made me feel uncomfortable. Not that there was the least sign of perversion in them, you understand. It was only that they were so exorbitant."

"Would you say that she admired you?"

"I guess so. I guess that's what it was."

"Well, I. understand it isn't so unusual to find that kind of thing among school girls. Boys either, for that matter. Do you have anything left over from that time? Any snapshots or letters or anything like that?"

"It happens that I do. After you left the other day, I got to thinking about Constance, the time we were together, and I looked in an old case of odds and ends I'd picked up different times and places, the kind of stuff you accumulate and keep without any good reason, and there were this snapshot and a card among all the other things. They don't amount to much. Just a snapshot of the two of us together, a card she sent me during the Christmas holiday of that year. Would you like to see them?"

I said I would, and she went to get them. Why I wanted to see them was something I didn't know precisely. Why I was interested at all in this period of ancient history was something else I didn't know. It had some basis, I think, in the feeling that the thing that could make a person leave an established life without a trace was surely something that had existed and had been growing for a long time, not something that had started yesterday or last week or even last year. Then there was, of course, the coincidence. Silas Lawler wanted this sleeping dog left lying, and once a month he went to the town where Constance Markley had once lived with Faith Salem, who wanted the dog wakened. It was that thin, that near to nothing, but it was all there was of anything at all.

Faith Salem returned with the snapshot and the Christmas card. I took them from her and finished my bourbon and looked first at the picture. I don't know if I would have seen in it what I did if I hadn't already heard about Constance Markley what I had. It's impossible to know how much of what we see, or think we see, is the result of suggestion. Constance and Faith were standing side by side. Constance was shorter, slighter of build, less striking in effect. Faith was looking directly into the camera, but Constance was looking around and up at the face of Faith. It seemed to me that her expression was one of adoration. This was what might have been no more than the result of suggestion. I don't know.

I took the Christmas card out of its envelope. It had clearly been expensive, as cards go, and had probably been selected with particular care. On the back, Constance Markley had written a note. It said how miserable and lonely she was at home, how the days were interminable, how she longed for the time to come when she could return to Amity and Faith. Christmas vacation, I thought, must have lasted all of two weeks. I read the note with ambivalence. I felt pity, and I felt irritation.

Faith Salem had finished her bourbon and was looking at me over the empty glass. Her eyes were clouded, and she shook her head slowly from side to side.

"I guess you've got an idea," she said.

"That's an exaggeration," I said.

"Why are you interested in all this? I don't understand."

"Maybe it's just that I'm naturally suspicious of a coincidence. Every time I come across one, I get curious."

"What coincidence?"

"Never mind. If I put it in words, I'd probably decide it sounded too weak to bother with. I'm driving to Amity tomorrow. The trip'll hike expenses. You'd better give me a hundred bucks."

"All right. I'll get it for you." She got up and went out of the room again. I watched her out and stood up to watch her in. From both angles and both sides she still looked good. She handed me the hundred bucks, and I took it and shoved it in a pocket and put my arms around her and kissed her.

She had meant what she had said. She said she wouldn't kiss me again, and she didn't. She only stood quietly and let me kiss her, which was different and not half so pleasant. I took my arms away and stepped back.

"I'm sorry," I said.

"So am I," she said.

Then we said good-bye, and I left. Going, I met Graham Markley in the hall, coming. We spoke politely, and he asked me how the investigation was getting along. I said it was getting along all right. He didn't even seem curious about the condition of my face.

CHAPTER 8.

I didn't get out of town the next day until ten o'clock. It was three hundred fifty miles by highway to Amity. In my old clunker, allowing time for a couple of stops, I did well to average forty miles an hour. Figure it for yourself. It was almost exactly eight and a half hours later when I got there. About six-thirty. I was tired and hungry, and I went to a hotel and registered and went up to my room. I washed and went back down to the coffee shop and got a steak and ate it and went back to the room. By then it was eight. I lit a cigarette and lay down on the bed and began to wonder seriously why I was here and what the hell I was going to do, now that I was.

I thought about a lot of things. I thought about Robin Robbins looking like a tough and lovely kid with her beautiful shiner. I thought about Faith Salem lying in the sun. I thought about Silas Lawler and Graham Markley and Regis Lawler and Constance Markley. The last pair were shadows. I couldn't see them, and I couldn't entirely believe in them, and I wished suddenly that I had never heard of them. I did this thinking about these people, but it didn't get me anywhere. I lay there on the bed in the hotel room for what seemed like an hour, and I was surprised, when I looked at my watch, to learn that less than half that time had passed. The room was oppressive, and I didn't want to stay there any longer. Getting up, I went downstairs and walked around the block and came back to the hotel and bought a newspaper at the tobacco counter and sat down to read it. I read some of the front page and some of the sports page and all the comics and started on the classified ads.

Classified ads interest me. I always read them in the newspapers and in the backs of magazines that publish them. They are filled with the gains and losses and inferred intimacies of classified lives. If you are inclined to be a romantic, you can, by a kind of imaginative interpolation, read a lot of pathos and human interest into them. Someone in Amity, for instance, had lost a dog, and someone wanted to sell a bicycle that was probably once the heart of the life of some kid, and someone named Martha promised to forgive someone named Walter if he would come back from wherever he'd gone. *Someone named Faith Salem wanted to teach you to play the piano for two dollars an hour.*

There it was, and that's the way it sometimes happens. You follow an impulse over three hundred miles because of a thin coincidence, and right away, because of a mild idiosyncrasy, you run into another coincidence that's just a little too much of one to be one, and the first one, although you don't know why, no longer seems like one either.

I closed my eyes and tried to see Faith Salem lying again in the sun, but I couldn't. I couldn't see her lying in the sun because she was in another town teaching piano lessons for two dollars an hour. It said so in the town's newspaper. I opened my eyes and looked again, just to be certain, and it did. Piano lessons, it said. 1828 Canterbury Street, call LO 3314, it said. Faith Salem, it said.

I stood up and folded the newspaper and stuck it in my coat pocket and looked at my watch. The watch said nine. I walked outside and started across the street to the parking lot where I'd left my car, but then, because it was getting late and I didn't know the streets of the town, I turned and came back to the curb in front of the hotel and caught a taxi. I gave the driver the address, 1828 Canterbury Street, and sat back in the seat. The driver repeated the address after me and then concentrated silently on his driving. I didn't try to think or make any guesses. I sat and listened to the ticking of the meter that seemed to be measuring the diminishing time and distance between me and something.

We hit Canterbury Street at 6th and went down it twelve blocks. It was an ordinary residential street, paved with asphalt, with the ordinary variations in quality, you will find on most streets in most towns. It started bad and got better and then started getting worse, but it never got really good or as bad in the end as it had started. 1828 was a small white frame house with a fairly deep front lawn and vacant lots between it and the houses on both sides, which were also small and white and frame with fairly deep front lawns. On the corner at the end of the block was a neighborhood drug store with a vertical neon sign above the entrance. It would be a place to call another taxi in case of necessity, and so I paid off the one I had and let it go. I got out and went up a brick walk and across a porch. There was a light showing at a window, but I heard no sound and saw no shadow on the blind. After listening and watching for perhaps a minute, I knocked and waited for perhaps half another.

Without any prelude of sound whatever, the door opened and a woman stood looking out at me. The light behind her left her face in shadow. She was rather short and very slim, almost fragile, and her voice, when she spoke, had an odd quality of detached airiness, as if it had no corporeal source. "Yes?" she said.

"I'm looking for Miss Faith Salem," I said.

"I'm Faith Salem. What is it you want?"

"Please excuse me for calling so late, but I was unable to get here earlier. My name is Percival Hand. You were referred to me as an excellent teacher."

"Thank you. Are you studying piano, Mr. Hand?"

"No." I laughed. "My daughter is the student. We're new in town, and she needs a teacher. As I said, you were recommended. May I come in and discuss it with you?"

"Yes, of course. Please come in." I stepped past her into a small living room that was softly lighted by a table lamp and a floor lamp. On the floor was a rose-colored rug with an embossed pattern. The furniture was covered with bright chintz or polished cotton, and the windows were framed on three sides by panels and valences of the same color and kind of material. At the far end of the room, which was no farther than a few steps, a baby grand occupied all the space of a corner. Behind me, the woman who called herself Faith Salem closed the door. She came past me into the room and sat down in a chair beside the step-table on which the table lamp was standing. It was apparently the chair in which she had been sitting when I knocked, for a cigarette was burning in a tray on the table and an open book was lying face down beside the tray. The light from the lamp seemed to gather in her face and in the hands she folded in the lap. The hands were quiet, holding each other. The face was thin and pretty and perfectly reposed. I have never seen a more serene face than the face of Constance Markley at that moment.

"Sit down, Mr. Hand," she said. I did. I sat in a chair opposite her and held my hat on my knees and had the strange and inappropriate feeling of a visiting minister. I felt, anyhow, the way the minister always appeared to be feeling when he called on my mother a hundred years ago when I was home.

"What a charming room," I said.

"Thank you." She smiled and nodded. "I like bright colors. They make a place so cheerful. Did you say you are new in Amity, Mr. Hand?"

"Yes. We just arrived recently."

"I see. Do you plan to make your home here permanently?"

"I don't know. It depends on how things work out, Miss Salem. Is that correct? I seem to remember that you're single."

"That's quite correct. I've never married," she said, and nodded.

"I'm surprised that such a lovely woman has escaped so long. Do you live here alone?"

In her face for a moment was an amused expression that did not disturb the basic serenity, and I wondered if it was prompted by the trite compliment or the impertinent question. At any rate, she ignored the first and answered the second simply.

"Yes. I'm quite alone here. I like living alone."

"Have you lived in Amity long?"

"Many years. I came here as a student in the college and never left. I wouldn't want to live anywhere else."

"Forgive my asking, but don't you find it difficult to live by giving private music lessons?"

"I'm certain that I should if I tried it. I give private lessons only in my off hours. Evenings and weekends. I'm also an instructor in the Amity Conservatory. A private school." She hesitated, looking at me levelly across the short space between us, and I thought that she was now slightly disturbed, for the first time, by my irrelevant questions. "I understand that you should want to make inquiries of a teacher you are considering for your child, Mr. Hand, but yours don't seem very pertinent. Would you like to know something about my training and qualifications?"

"No, thanks. I'm sure you're very competent, Miss Salem. I'm sorry if my questions seemed out of line. The truth is, I know so little about music myself that I hardly know what to talk about."

"Do you mind telling me who sent you to me, Mr. Hand?"

"As a matter of fact, it was the Conservatory. They recommended you highly, but they didn't mention that you were an instructor there."

"I see. Many students are directed to me that way. The ones who are unable to attend the Conservatory itself, that is."

I looked down at my hat, turning it slowly in my hands, and I didn't like the way I was beginning to feel. No one could accuse me fairly of being a particularly sensitive guy, and ordinarily I am conscious of no corruption in the dubious practices of my trade, dubious practices being by no means restricted to the trade I happen to follow. By now I was beginning to feel somehow unclean, and every little lie was assuming in my mind the character of a monstrous deception. I was suddenly sick of it and wanted to be finished with it, the whole phony case. I had been hired for twenty-five and expenses to find a woman who had disappeared two years ago, and here she was in a town called Amity, living quietly under the name of Faith Salem, which was the name of the woman who had hired me to find her, and it had all been so fantastically quick and easy, a coincidence and an itch and a classified ad, and now there seemed to be nothing more to be done that I had been hired to do.

But where was Regis Lawler? Here was Constance, but where was Regis? Well, I had not been hired to find Regis. I had been hired to find Constance, and I had found her, and that was all of it. Almost all of it, anyhow. All that was left to do for my money to get up and get away quietly with my unclean feeling after my necessary deceptions. Tomorrow I would drive back where I had come from, and I would report what I had learned to the woman who was paying me, and then she would know as much as I did, and what she wanted to do with it was her business and not mine.

There were still, however, so many loose ends. So many mental itches I couldn't scratch. I did not know why Constance had come to Amity. Nor why she had assumed the name of Faith Salem. Nor certainly why, for that matter, the real Faith Salem wanted her found. Nor why Silas Lawler did not. Nor where in the world was Regis Lawler. Nor if, in fact, he was. In the world, that is.

Suddenly I looked up and said, "*Mrs. Markley, where is Regis Lawler?*"

Her expression was queer. It was an expression I remembered for a long time afterward and sometimes saw in the black shag end of the kind of night when a man is vulnerable and cannot sleep. She stared at me for a minute with wide eyes in which there was a creeping dumb pain, and then, in an instant, there was a counter expression which seemed to be a denial of the pain and the pain's cause. Her lids dropped slowly, as if she were all at once very tired. Sitting there with her hands folded in her lap, she looked as if she were praying, and when she opened her eyes again, the expressions of pain and its denial were gone, and there was nothing where they had been but puzzlement.

"What did you call me?" she said.

"Mrs. Markley. Constance Markley."

"If this is a joke, Mr. Hand, it's in very bad taste."

"It's no joke. Your name is Constance Markley, and I asked you where Regis Lawler is."

"I don't know Constance Markley. Nor Regis Lawler." She unfolded her hands and stood up, and she was not angry and apparently no longer puzzled. She had withdrawn behind an impenetrable defense of serenity. "I don't know you either, Mr. Hand. Whoever you are and whatever you came here for, you are obviously not what you represented yourself to be, and you didn't come for the purpose you claimed."

"True. I'm not, and I didn't."

"In that case, we have nothing more to discuss. If you will leave quietly, I'll be happy to forget that you ever came."

I did as she suggested. I left quietly. She had said that I was in bad taste, and I guess I was, for the taste was in my mouth, and it was bad.

I turned left at the street toward the drug store on the corner, and I had walked about fifty feet in that direction when a man got out of a parked car and crossed the parking to intercept me, and the car was a Caddy I had ridden in before, and the man was Silas Lawler.

"Surprised?" he said amiably.

"Not especially," I said. "I heard you've been coming out here pretty regularly the last couple years."

"I was afraid that might have been one of the things you heard. Robin has a bad habit of knowing things she's not supposed to. Not that it matters much.

You've just made me make an extra trip, that's all. Darcy's really annoyed, though. He's the one who's had to tail you since you got into this business, and Darcy doesn't like that kind of work. He figures it's degrading."

"Poor Darcy. I'll have to apologize the next time I see him."

"That could be right now. Just turn your head a little. He's sitting over there behind the wheel of the Caddy."

"I'll have to do it some other time. Right now I'm on my way to the corner to call a cab."

"Forget it. Darcy and I wouldn't think of letting you go to all that trouble. We've been waiting all this time just to give you a lift."

"I hope you won't be offended if I decline."

"I'm afraid I would. I'm sensitive that way. I always take it personally if my hospitality's refused. You wouldn't want to hurt my feelings, would you?"

"I wouldn't mind."

"That's not very gracious of you. Hand. I offer you a lift, the least you can do is be courteous about it. What I mean is, get in the Caddy."

"No, thanks. The last time we got together, you didn't behave very well. I don't think I want to associate with you any more."

"It won't be for long."

He took a gun out of his pocket and pointed it at me casually in such a way that it would, if it fired, shoot me casually through the head. I could see, in a glimmer of light, the ugly projection of a silencer.

"Now who's not being gracious?"

I said. "It seems to me a guy with any pride wouldn't want to force an invitation on someone."

"Oh, I won't force it. You don't want a lift, have it your own way. I'd just as soon kill you here."

"Wouldn't that be rather risky?"

"I don't think so. Odds are no one will hear anything. You probably wouldn't even be found for a while. Anyhow, I'm not here. I'm in my room at the restaurant. So's Darcy. If it got to be necessary, which it probably wouldn't, we could find a half dozen guests who are with us."

I thought about it and decided that he could. Maybe even a full dozen. And so, after thinking, I conceded.

"I believe you could," I said, "and I've decided to accept the lift after all."

"Thanks," he said. "I appreciate it."

I crossed the parking to the Caddy, and while I was crossing, Darcy reached back from the front seat and unlatched the door, which swung open, and I got in like a paying passenger, with no effort, and Silas Lawler got in after me and closed the door behind him.

"Good evening, Mr. Hand," Darcy said.

"I'm beginning to doubt it," I said.

He laughed softly and politely and slid under the wheel of the Caddy and started the engine and occupied himself with driving. He drove at a moderate rate of speed, with careful consideration of traffic regulations, and where he drove was out of town on a highway and off the highway onto a country road. I admired the erect and reliable look of the back of his head. He looked from the rear exactly like a man whose vocabulary included virtuoso.

"You're a very stubborn guy, Hand," Silas Lawler said. "You simply won't take advice."

"It's a fault," I said. "All my life I've been getting into trouble because of it."

"You're through with that," he said. "This is the last trouble you'll ever get into."

This was not merely something he was saying. It was something he meant. I began trying to think of some way to change his mind, but I couldn't, and so I began trying then to think of some way to get out of the Caddy and off in some dark field with a sporting chance, but I couldn't think of that either. In the meanwhile, Darcy drove most of another mile and down a slope and across a culvert, and it was pitch dark down there in the little hollow where the culvert was. Silas Lawler leaned forward slightly and told him to stop the Caddy and turn off its lights, and Darcy did. The window beside Darcy was down, and I could hear clearly the infinite variety of little night sounds in the hollow and fields and all around.

"It's a nice night to die." I said. Lawler sighed. He really did. A long soft sibilant sound with weariness in it.

"I'm sorry, Hand. I rather like you, as I've said before, and I wish you hadn't made this necessary."

"I fail to see the necessity," I said.

"That's because you don't know enough about something you know too much about."

"Is that supposed to make sense?"

"It is, and it does."

"Excuse me for being obtuse. I don't know much of anything about anything that I can see. I know that Constance Markley is alive, and to teach piano lessons, in Amity at two bucks per. I know she's calling herself Faith Salem. So what? She's got a right to be alive and teaching piano lessons and what she calls herself is her business. I was hired to find her, and I found her. That's a capital offense?"

"Murder is. Murder's capital almost everywhere."

"You've got the wrong guy. I haven't committed any murder."

"I know you haven't," he said. "But Constance has."

I sat and listened to the sounds of the night from the hollow and fields and all around. For a few moments they were thunderously amplified and gathered in my head, and then they faded in an instant to their proper dimensions and places.

So that's where Regis is, I thought. *Regis is where I almost am.*

And I said, "I don't know anything about that. I haven't got a shred of evidence."

"Sorry." He shook his head and took his gun out of his pocket again. "You know where Constance is, and that's enough. You'll tell the client who hired you, and your client will tell others, and the cops will know. Everyone thinks she and

Regis ran away together, and when they learn that Regis isn't with her and hasn't ever been, they'll wonder where he is, and he's dead. It wouldn't take them long to find that out. She couldn't hold out against them for an hour. So you see? So you know too much to be trusted. So you've got to die. I'm glad for your sake that it's a nice night for it."

I didn't try to convince him that I'd swap silence for life. The risk in a deal like that would have been all his, and he was too good a gambler to consider it. I sat and listened some more to the sounds in the nice night to die, and I was thinking pretty clearly and understanding a number of things, but there were some other things I wanted to understand and didn't, and they were things that Silas Lawler could explain. Moreover, the longer we talked, the longer I lived, and this was important to me, if not to him.

"All right," I said. "Constance killed Regis, and for some reason you want her to get away with it. Why? After all, Regis was your brother."

"Foster brother."

"Okay. Foster brother. It's still in the family."

"Regis was no damn good. Dying was the best thing he ever did, and he had to have help to do that. He wasn't fit to touch Constance, let alone sleep with her, and why she ever loved him is something I'll never understand. But she did. She loved him, and she killed him."

"It sounds paradoxical, but it's possible. It wouldn't make her the first woman to kill a man she loved. Anyhow, I'm beginning to get a picture. You're on her side, maybe because you both play the piano, and you helped her get away after she killed Regis. I'm guessing that you disposed of the body too, and that poses a puzzle I've been trying to figure. No body, no murder. Why should Constance run? And why, since she did, only to Amity? With your collusion, which she had, why not to Shangri-La or somewhere?"

He stared past me out the window into the audible night, and he seemed to be considering carefully the questions I'd asked, and after a while he sighed again, the sibilant weariness with the job he had to do, or thought he had to do. Either way, unless I could prevent it, it would come to the same end for me.

"I guess it won't hurt to tell you," he said. "It'll take a little time, but I've got plenty, and you've got practically none, and maybe it won't hurt to allow you a little more."

"Thanks," I said. "That's generous of you."

"Don't mention it. And you'd better listen close because I'm only going over it once lightly. The night it happened, I went up to Regis's apartment to see him about something personal. I punched the bell a couple times, but no one answered, so I tried the door, and it wasn't locked. I went in, and there they were. Regis on the floor and Constance in a chair. Regis was dead, and she was gone. What I mean, she was in a state of shock. She was paying no more attention to Regis than if he'd just lain down for a nap. She hardly seemed aware that I'd come into the room. I checked Regis and saw that he'd been shot neatly between the eyes. She just sat there and watched me without moving or saying a word, her eyes as big and bright and dry as the eyes of an owl. I asked her what had happened, but she only shook her head and said she didn't understand. She said she was confused and couldn't seem to get things clear in her mind. I wanted to help her, and I held her hands and kept talking to her, trying to get her to remember, but even a dumb guy like me could see pretty soon that it wasn't any use. She was gone, not home, and it wasn't any act. She kept insisting she didn't understand. She didn't understand where she was, or why, or who Regis was, or I was, or a damn thing about anything. She said her name was Faith Salem. She said she lived in Amity. She said she just wanted to go home.

"That's the way it was. Whatever I did to help her, I had to do blind. So it was a big chance. So I was an accessory after the act. To hell with all that. What I finally did, I took her to my room at the restaurant and made her promise to stay there, and then I got Darcy and went back for Regis. Darcy's a guy I trust. Maybe the only guy. We got the body out of the building the back way between us. I've got a place in the country I sometimes go to, and we took Regis there, and Darcy put him in a good deep hole in the ground with a lot of quick lime, and I went back to the restaurant, and that was all for Regis. It was good enough. I haven't lost any sleep because of Regis."

He said all this quietly and easily, without the slightest trace of anger or excitement. He said it in exactly the same manner in which he would kill me in a little while, in his own time when he was good and ready, and I sat and waited for him to finish the story, whatever was left of it, and I had a strange and strong sense of revelation, a kind of gathering of loose ends in an obscure pattern.

"She wasn't there," he said. "She had simply walked out of the restaurant and was gone. I went looking for her. I beat the whole damn city, but I never found her. It was two weeks later before I saw her again. I remembered what she'd called herself: Faith Salem. I remembered where she'd said she lived: Amity. I went to Amity and tried to find her, but she wasn't there, and so I waited and kept looking, and finally she came. About two weeks later. I don't know where she'd been in the meanwhile, or how she got there, but she was dressed differently, in a plain suit, and she seemed to be in perfectly good condition. She'd had money in her purse the night she left. I know because I checked. Almost seven hundred dollars. Anyhow, I let her alone and kept watching after her, the same as I've done ever since, waiting to see what she'd do. What she did was rent that little house she lives in and start giving piano lessons.

"She advertised. She called herself Faith Salem. She got along all right, and finally she started teaching at a private conservatory. The point is, she wasn't acting or consciously hiding. *She really thought she was someone named Faith Salem.* I'm pretty ignorant about such things, but I did some reading and fished a little information out of a medico who had a debt in the game rooms, and finally I got an understanding of it. She was in a kind of condition that's called a fugue. Same name as a kind of musical composition. Unless something happened to shock her out of it, she might go on in this condition for years. Maybe the rest of her life. I figured it was safer for her to leave her as she was. As long as she was in the fugue state, she'd act perfectly normal in the identity she'd assumed and would never give herself away.

"There were obvious dangers, of course. The thing I worried most about was that she'd come out of the fugue. She wouldn't remember anything since the murder, because the fugue period is entirely forgotten after recovery, but the murder was before the fugue, and she'd remember it as the last thing that happened to her, and if I wasn't around to help her then, she'd be done for. God knows what she'd do. So I've been keeping watch over her the best I can, and everything's been all right, except now you've come along and made like a God-damn detective, and I've got to kill you, and now's the time for it."

That was Darcy's cue. He got out of the front seat and opened the door to the back seat on my side, and I was supposed to get out quietly into the road to save the cushions, but I didn't want to do it. What I wanted to do was live, and in the growing sense of revelation and gathering ends, I thought I could see a faint chance.

"You're making a mistake," I said, "and if you go ahead and finish making it, it won't be your first, but it may very well be your last and worst."

Darcy stood erect by the open door and waited patiently and politely. Silas Lawler made an abrupt gesture with his gun and then became utterly still and silent for the longest several seconds there have ever been. Finally he sighed, and the tension went out of him.

"All right," he said. "Another minute or two. What mistake?"

"Assuming that Constance Markley killed Regis Lawler," I said.

"She was in the room with him. He was dead."

"Conceded. But you said you checked her purse and saw seven hundred dollars. Did you see a gun?"

"No. No gun."

"Was it in the room? Anywhere in the apartment?"

"No."

"You think maybe she shot him with her finger?"

"I've wondered about that. You explain it."

"I already have. She didn't shoot him."

"You're just guessing."

"Maybe so. But I've got better reasons for my guess than you've got for yours. You think she went off the deep end and killed him because he was getting tired of her. Is that it?"

"She'd had troubles. Things had piled up. Regis was more than a lover. He was a kind of salvation."

"I'll tell you something I've learned. The night Regis died, Constance Markley's maid helped her dress. According to this maid, she was eager. She wasn't angry or depressed or particularly disturbed in any way. She was only eager to see her lover. Does that sound like a woman betrayed and ready to kill? It sounds to me more like a woman who was still ignorant of whatever defections her lover was committing."

"Say she was ignorant. She learned after she got there."

"Sure. And shot him with her finger."

Again, for the time it took to draw and release a long breath, Silas Lawler was silent. At the open door, Darcy shifted his weight with a grating of gravel.

"You got anything else to say?" Lawler said.

"Only what you're already thinking," I said. "Constance Markley didn't kill Regis. Neither did you. But *someone did*. Pretend for a minute that it *was* you. You murdered a man, and the night of the murder the man's mistress vanishes. No one knows where she went. No one knows why. In your mind these two things, the murder and the disappearance, are inevitably associated. It's too big a coincidence. There must be a connection. But what is it? Does she know something that may be placing you in jeopardy every second of your life? Or every second of hers? You must learn this at any cost, and you must learn it before anyone else. You may pretend indifference, but in your mind are the constant uncertainty, the constant fear. They're there for two long years. Then a garden variety private detective stumbles onto something. Maybe. He makes a trip to a town named Amity where the vanished mistress once lived with the same woman who has hired the detective to find her. Several people, in one way or another, learn of this trip. Including you, the murderer. What do these people do? They stay at home and mind their own business. Except you, the murderer. You don't stay home and mind your own business, because your business is in Amity."

That was all I had. It wasn't much, but it was all, and I had a strong conviction that it was true. Silas Lawler was still, and so was Darcy. In the stillness, like a living and measurable organism, was a growing sense of compelling urgency. I could hear it at last in Lawler's voice when he spoke again.

"Darcy," he said, "let's go back."

Darcy got under the wheel, and we turned and went. We went as fast as the Caddy's horses could run on the road and highway and streets they had to follow. On Canterbury Street, in front of the small frame house in which Constance Markley lived, Silas Lawler and I got out on the parking and looked up across the lawn to the house, and the light was still on the blind behind the window, and everything was quiet. Then, after a terrible interval in which urgency was slowly becoming farce, there was a shadow on the blind that was not a woman's, a scream in the house that was.

The scream was not loud, not long, and there was no shadow and no sound by the time Lawler and I reached the porch. I was faster than he, running on longer legs, and he was a step behind me when I threw open the door to see Constance Markley hanging by the neck from the hands of her husband.

Interrupted in murder, he turned his face toward us in the precise instant that Lawler fired, and in another instant he was dead.

Constance Markley began to scream again.

She screamed and screamed and screamed.

I had a notion that the screams were two years old.

CHAPTER 9.

I took a week to get things cleared up. I stayed in Amity that week, and then I went home, and the day after I went home, I went up to the apartment of Faith

Salem. I made a point of going when the sun was on the terrace. Maria let me in, and I crossed the acres of pile and tile and went out where Faith was. She was lying on her back on the bright soft pad with one forearm across her eyes to shade them from the light. She didn't move the arm when I came out.

"Good afternoon, Mr. Hand," she said.

"Good afternoon," I said.

"Excuse me for not getting up. Will you please sit down?"

"It's all right," I said. "Thanks."

I sat down in a wicker chair. It was very warm on the terrace in the sun, but the warmth was pleasant, and after a while I began to feel it in my bones. Faith Salem's lean brown body remained motionless, except for the barely perceptible rise and fall of her breasts in breathing, and I suspected that her eyes were closed under her arm.

"So it was Graham after all," she said.

"That's what you suspected, wasn't it?"

"In a way. I had a feeling, but it was a feeling that he had done something to Constance. I can't understand why he killed this man."

"Not because of the affair. He didn't care about that."

"Why, then?"

"Regis Lawler tried to blackmail him. It went back to something that happened several years ago. Graham Markley and Constance were driving back from the country. They'd been on a party, and Graham was drunk. He hit a woman on the highway and killed her and kept right on driving. It was a nasty business. Constance isn't a strong person, nor even a very pleasant person, and she agreed with Graham that it was better to keep quiet about the incident. It's easy for some people to rationalize that kind of attitude. Then, in due time, after the death of her child, she met Regis Lawler, and she wanted to do with Regis just what everyone actually assumed she had done. She wanted to run away from everything—her marriage, her guilt, everything associated with her child's death, all the unhappiness that people like her seem doomed to accumulate.

"Apparently Regis let her believe that he might be willing to go along with this, but he had no money. Silas Lawler told me that Regis stole seventy-five grand from a wall safe at the restaurant, but it wasn't so. It was only a lie Silas used to make their running away plausible. What really happened was that Constance told Regis about the woman's death on the highway, and Regis tried the blackmail, although he actually had no intention, it seems, of going anywhere at all with Constance. The blackmail didn't work. Graham Markley wasn't the kind of weak character to submit. He went to Lawler's apartment and killed him. When Constance went there later the same night and found his body, she knew immediately what had surely happened. Her own burden of guilt was too heavy to bear in addition to everything else, and so she escaped it by becoming someone else to whom none of this had ever happened. It was something that could only have happened under certain conditions to a certain kind of person. She became the one woman she had known that she completely admired and envied, and she went back to the place where she had, for a while, been happier than she had ever been before or since. She became you, and she went back to Amity. With a break or two and a couple of hunches, I got the idea that she might be there, and I went there to see if I could find her, and Graham Markley learned from you where I was going. He was terribly afraid of what Constance might know to tell if she was found, and it was imperative, as he saw it, to get rid of her for good and all. And so he followed me and found her and tried to kill her, but it didn't turn out that way."

"I'm sorry I told him," she said. "It was a mistake."

"Not for me," I said. "It made me a smart guy instead of a corpse."

"What do you mean?"

"Nothing," I said. "It's not important."

The sun in the sky was nearing the tooled ridge of stone. I wished for a drink, but nobody brought one. Faith Salem's breasts rose and fell, rose and fell. Her long brown legs stirred slightly in the sun.

"Did Constance tell all this?" she said.

"The part about the murder. Not the rest."

"How strange it is. How strange simply to forget everything and become someone else."

"Strange enough, but not incredible. It's happened before. People have gone half around the world and lived undetected in new identities tor years."

"Is she all right now?"

"She remembers who she is and everything that happened until she found the body of Regis Lawler in his apartment. She doesn't remember anything that happened in the time of the fugue. That's a long way from all right, I guess, but it's as good as she can hope for."

"Why become me? Why me of all people?"

There was honest wonderment in her voice. Looking at her, the lean brown length of her, I could have told her why, but I didn't. I had a feeling that it was time to be going, and I stood up.

"I think I'd better leave now," I said.

"Yes," she said. "I think so."

"I'll send you a bill."

"Of course. I'll be here as long as the rent's paid. That's about three months."

"Are you going to look at me before I leave?"

"No. I don't think so. Do you mind letting yourself out?"

"I don't mind."

"Good-bye, then, Mr. Hand. I wish you had a lot of money. It's a shame you're so poor."

"Yes, it is," I said. "It's a crying shame."

She never moved or looked at me, and I went away. The next day I sent her a bill, and two days after that I got a check. I saw her twice again, but not to speak to. Once she was coming out of a shop alone, and once she was going into a theater on the arm of a man. I learned later that she married a very rich brewer and went to live in Milwaukee.

✗